W0013597

*To the mom's who gave up everything to raise their family,*
*this one is for us.*

# Playlist

Whats Left of You- Chord Overstreet
Surrender (Kina Remix)- Natalie Taylor
Freefall (Runn)- Illenium
You- Chase Rice
Litost- X Ambassadors
Dirt- Florida Georgia Line
What Now- Rhianna
Your Bones- Chelsea Cutler
How Long Will I Love You- Ellie Goulding
If I Didn't Love You- Jason Aldean &
Carrie Underwood

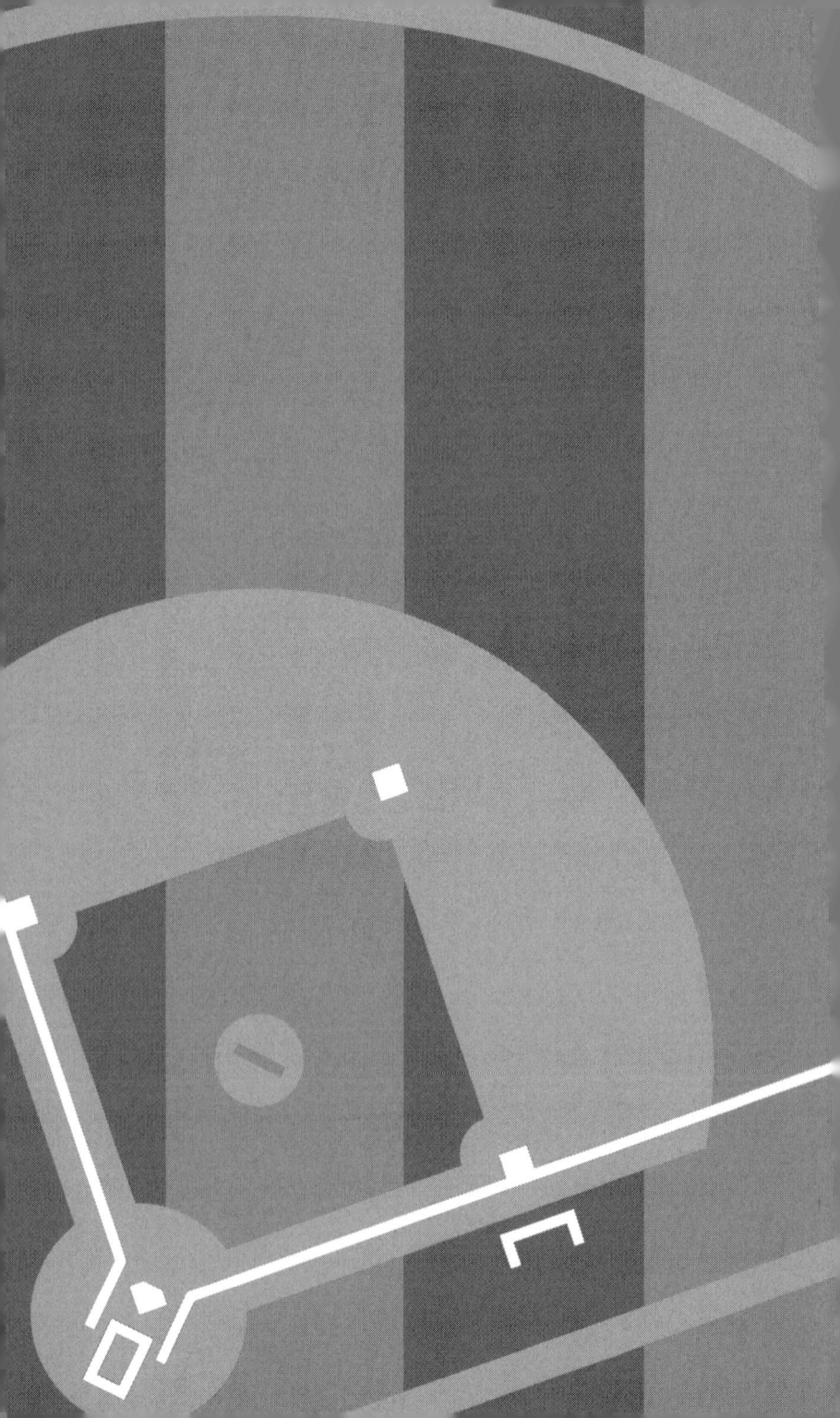

# CHAPTER 1

## Kessler

*THUMP,* THE SOUND OF THE BALL HITTING THE BACKSTOP echoes through the cage.

"Shit," I mutter under my breath.

I wait for the pitching machine to load up another ball. I set up my stance and take another swing as the ball leaves the machine. Another *thump* sounds as I swing and miss... again. The pulling in my shoulder is getting worse with each pitch. I hit the button to turn off the machine, probably harder than necessary, and roll my shoulder a few times trying to loosen the tightness that is setting in.

Two surgeries and the most intense physical therapy I've ever endured and I still can't bat worth shit. I take off my batting gloves, grab my bat, and head out of the cage. Up ahead I spot the batting coach talking to one of the other players and make a beeline for the locker rooms. Any other day I would be happy to talk to him about my swing and what to work on, but today I just don't want to hear it.

This was going to be the make-it-or-break-it year. I'm 36, not old by any means, even though my knees say otherwise most mornings, but in the world of baseball that is getting up there. I'm not ready to hang it up yet, but if I don't figure shit out, I might not have a choice. I toss my bat and gloves in my locker and grab my phone. Unlocking it with my fingerprint I scroll through the texts that came in while I was in the cage.

> **MOM**
>
> Don't forget Judy and her Daughter Claire are coming to the next Sunday dinner.

I roll my eyes. She mentioned it at family dinner yesterday. I don't need a reminder this early. I don't need a reminder at all actually. I told her yesterday I didn't have the time to get involved with anyone, but my mother has been on a mission since my injury to get me married off. *I'm not getting any younger, I want grandchildren and to know my boys are taken care of when I'm gone.* She's 56 and doesn't look or act her age.

> **ME**
>
> I already told you last night at dinner I don't have the time.

> **MOM**
>
> You're never going to have time, unless you make time Kessler. What's going to happen when you do have to retire, and finally have time and have no family to spend it with?

> **ME**
>
> Then I'll have the time to date. Plus I'll have you and Dad and Judd

> **MOM**
>
> No ones going to want to date you. You'll be too grouchy about not being able to play baseball anymore, then you'll become a recluse and live in the mountains and have pet squirrels.

Ok, that makes me laugh. My mom can be a little overly dramatic, and the longer these rants go, the weirder they get. I better cut it off while I'm ahead.

> **ME**
>
> I'll think about it ok. I have to go and stretch out my shoulder.

> **MOM**
>
> That's all I ask. Good luck at your game honey.

Satisfied I delayed the crazy mom train, I click over to my brother's text.

> **ME**
>
> You know she'd be pissed and probably double down her efforts at the next family meal.

My brother Judd is younger than me by four years. He plays for the Junction City Jackals a few cities away from here as their starting pitcher. He knows he'll be in Mom's matchmaking crosshairs soon. She means well. We know she does, but it's a part of our life we don't need her meddling in.

> **JUDD**
>
> Wanna ditch Sunday? Moms already texted me 3 times.

> **JUDD**
>
> How was batting?

ME

Don't ask.

JUDD

That good huh? Still tight?

ME

Yep

JUDD

OK Mr. Grumpy Gills

ME

Grumpy gills? What the fuck is this, Finding Nemo?

JUDD

*sends GIF of Dory* Just keep swimming

I smirk and send him a middle-finger emoji. Leave it to my brother to bring up my spirits. Pocketing my phone, I head over to the medical room to have my shoulder stretched and taped before tonight's game.

"Hey Paul," I say, hopping up onto one of the tables.

"Kessler, how's the shoulder?"

"Tight. Hit some balls a bit ago and it tightened right up," I tell him rolling my shoulder around. I've never been worked on so much in my whole career as I have in the few months since my injury. Having an injury to this extent, at this age, well let's just say I'm lucky I can use it at all. I took a dirty hit during the playoffs last year, fracturing my clavicle and tearing and stretching my tendons. Recovery has been an uphill battle since day one.

Paul grabs my left arm, puts one hand on my shoulder and uses the other to slowly lift my arm. "Let me know when it starts to pull."

He gets my arm almost above my head when I let him know that it's pulling.

"Any pain?" he asks, lowering my shoulder back down.

"No, not pain really, just tight."

"That's good. Not the tightness, but that you don't have pain with it. I'll go get the heating pad and put that on you for 20 minutes before we stretch you out and tape you up."

"Thanks, man." We bump fists as he leaves to grab the heating pad.

NINETY MINUTES LATER, I'm stretched, taped, and heading to the lounge we have in the clubhouse. Everyone has different rituals before a game. Some guys watch tapes of the opposing team. Some do light workouts. Others zone out and listen to music. Most of the time I watch TikToks and send the hilarious ones to my brother. I see Reese Hayes, our shortstop and one of my best friends, sitting over on a couch. I walk over and plop down at the opposite end.

"'Sup man," I say, digging my phone out of my pocket.

"Not much man, how's the shoulder?" Hayes asks, nodding to my left shoulder.

"Eh, you know. It's getting there. I'm ready to be back on the field." I'm a catcher for the Salem Silverbacks and today is my first official game back. I'm ready to get back behind the plate.

"No doubt man. We've missed you. Dawson's great, but the kid is getting a big head. Time to check that ego." Miles Dawson was called up from the minors for a few months before my injury. The kid is good, but he has an ego on him like the Empire State Building.

"That's the plan," I say, opening an email that pops up on my screen. I read the email and look at Reese.

"Are you going to the meet and greet for that little league team after the game?"

"Hell yeah. I love those things. Sign a few things, talk with the kids. It's always a good time. Are you?"

I nod my head. "Dale suggested I go. Not that I need the suggestion. I'd go without it. I think it's important to show the kids we're just regular people." I mean, I see myself as a regular person, I just have an irregular job, that happens to make me somewhat famous.

Brent Attwood makes his appearance just then, slapping my feet off the couch and plopping down next to me. "You're anything but regular, but sure, we'll go with that."

I roll my eyes. "Coming from the man who doesn't get laid because he thinks it, and I quote '*helps his game*'."

"Bite me, Davis. Don't knock it till you try it."

"I don't have to try it. You know I haven't been with anyone in a while, and my swing is shit," I grumble

He nods to my shoulder. "Still giving you trouble?"

I shrug. "Off and on. It'll work out."

Brent claps me on the shoulder. "Yeah man, it will."

*It has to. I'm not ready for the big R.* I don't say it out loud, but it hangs there, unsaid. This is not what I should have my mind on before a game. As if reading my thoughts, Reese leans over Brent and shows me a TikTok on his phone. We all stare at the screen, it's one about voice overs with dogs, and it's exactly what I needed. We all burst out laughing, and the thought of retirement moves to the back of my head.

# CHAPTER 2

## Lucy

"Hudson! We gotta leave for the stadium in 20 minutes!" I call to my 11-year-old son from the kitchen.

"OK! I'm almost done with my math. Are we wearing our jerseys?"

"Yep," I reply. "Hats too."

A few minutes later he appears in the living room in his baseball jersey and hat, excitement all over his face. "This is so awesome. I wonder what players we're going to meet!

I shrug. "I guess we'll find out after the game. Come on bud let's get goin'. Aunt Kara and Kade are riding with us."

I grab my purse and keys, lock up the house, and make my way to my car. Kara, Kade, and Hudson are already in the car when I get there. Kara is my best friend, backyard neighbor, and the assistant coach for my son's little league team. We met when I moved in nine years ago and have been inseparable ever since.

I climb in and start the car, backing out of my driveway, and head downtown to Silverbacks stadium. Our team has been invited to the game tonight, as part of a community outreach program. The boys get to meet some of the players afterward and ask them questions, have them sign stuff, and take pictures. Hudson has been talking about it since I received the phone call last week from the team's PR rep.

"I hope Kessler Davis is at the thing afterward" Hudson says to Kade, his best friend and Kara's ten-year-old. Hudson is also a catcher for our team and has looked up to Davis since he started playing that position a couple of years ago. Meeting his idol would be the icing on the cake for him tonight.

"Just don't get your hopes up bud. He might not even play tonight, remember he's coming back from a pretty serious injury." I hope he does get to meet him, but I don't want him to be too bummed if it doesn't work out.

"I know, but it'd be really cool if he does," he says, bouncing in his seat a little.

I look over at Kara and cross my fingers. She does the same. The last thing we both want is our boys being disappointed.

We pull into the stadium a few minutes later and meet up with my team out front. A representative for the team greets us and takes us to our seats behind home plate. All 12 boys are front and center, parents sitting behind them in the next row. The palpable excitement the boys are feeling has them dancing in their seats.

I get up and go down in front of my team. I'm their head coach and have been for the last six years. "Ok boys, real quick." I wait for them all to settle and focus on me. A pretty hard feat for 12 excited 10 and 11-year-olds. When they're mostly settled and quiet I proceed, "I know this is a really exciting and cool opportunity we've been given. I want you guys to have fun and enjoy the game. I also want you to watch the players in your position and see how they play. Pick one thing they do well, and try to apply that next practice. But most of all have fun guys." I give them all high fives and return to my seat.

"Nice speech Coach," Kara says, giving me a fist bump when I get back to my seat.

"Now let's see if they actually listen."

Kara shrugs her shoulders giving me the who knows look. The players come out onto the field and start warming up. Some of the boys stand up to see who's playing.

"Mom!" Hudson screeches, pointing at the field. " Kessler Davis is playing!" I look to see where he's pointing and see Davis turn around and give him a wave with his glove. "MOM! Did you see that? He waved at me!"

"Very cool bud, that's awesome." I give him a thumbs up and he turns back to watch Kessler warm up.

"Oh, I am not going to mind this view for the game," Kara whispers to me.

"He's ok," I say back to her

"Just OK? Girl, do you need glasses?" she lowers her voice so the other parents and kids don't hear her. "Have you *seen* that ass? God built that one right."

I chuckle. "I don't think God had much to do with it. More like the insane amount of squatting being a catcher requires. Plus, you know how I feel about ball players."

She rolls her eyes. "Ok, but you can't hold what happened with Captain Dickhead against them all."

"I'm not, I just have no desire to date anyone, *especially* a ball player." I shift in my seat, leaning closer to her. "I don't even know why we're talking about this. What MLB player would be interested in a single mom?"

"Have you heard of the term MILF?"

"Ok, now it's my turn to roll my eyes," I say, doing just that.

"Whatever, girl. You know I'm right."

"Mmhmm ok," I reply, ending the discussion.

The announcer starts announcing the lineup, indicating the beginning of the game. *Saved by the bell.* As players for the Silverbacks are announced the crowd cheers. Some players get more noise than others. Kessler Davis is announced and all the boys along with the crowd go nuts. I even find myself clapping a little harder for him. Kara gives me a look and I ignore her. It's not that I'm interested in him. He came back from a pretty serious injury that could have been career ending, and as a Physical Therapist, I respect the work he did to make it back to the game.

BY THE BOTTOM of the eighth inning, the Silverbacks are ahead by two with two outs. It's been a good battle from both teams. The only reason the Silverbacks got those two runs is because of an error made by the San Diego Suns first baseman in the bottom of the third. The Silverbacks have two outs and Kessler Davis is up to bat. Hudson stands and goes to the fence like he has each time his idol has been up. Normally Davis is a force to be reckoned with, today he's struggling. He's been missing easy strikes and pulling up short in his swing when he does take a swing at a pitch. I find myself worrying away at my thumbnail as he takes his stance. The pitcher checks his runner at first, steps forward and throws his pitch. Kessler takes a swing and misses.

"Strike one!"

Kessler steps out of the batter's box and takes a few half swings. If I were a betting woman, I'd put money on the fact that his shoulder is tight and causing him to pull up early on his swings. Tendons are tricky bastards and take a long time to properly heal. Even then, they may not fully heal correctly and cause issues, like what Kessler seems to be dealing with now. Kessler looks to the third base coach, who gives him a sign and steps back into the box. The pitcher winds up again and sends a perfect fastball right down the center. The ball makes a *Thump* sound as it hits the catcher's mitt.

"Strike two!"

Hudson looks back at me, sadness in his eyes. I give him a reassuring smile and cross my fingers. We look back at Kessler and I can see the tendon in his jaw working overtime. Kessler steps into the box and sets up his stance one last time.

Before I know what I'm doing I jog down to the fence and yell "BUNT!"

The pitcher winds up and sends another pitch right down the middle. Just before Kessler takes a swing, he chokes up on his bat and bunts, shocking everyone. The ball bounces off his bat and slowly rolls towards the pitcher's mound.

"YES!" I yell, jumping up and down. "RUUUUNNN!" I scream. Kessler takes off like his pants are on fire and is a quarter of the way to first before anyone realizes what happened. "Go go go go go," I'm chanting, clinging to the fence. All the boys are out of their seats, jumping up and down and yelling for Kessler to run. The catcher snags the ball and lobs it to first, but overthrows it and makes the first baseman run after it, allowing Kessler to safely make it to the bag.

"YEAH!" Hudson yells, giving Kade a high five. "Mom, I think he heard you!" Hudson says as we head back to our seats.

"It was the next logical step bud, his third base coach probably gave him the signal."

I sit back in my seat and Kara gives me a look.

"What's that look for?"

"What was that?" she asks, one eyebrow raised at me.

"What? I got into the moment."

"Mmhmm."

The next batter, Carson Jones, hits the ball into far center, sending Brent Attwood home and Kessler to third. Jones makes it to second before the ball is thrown back. Duke Keller comes up to the plate and the crowd gets loud. The boys get on their feet and go back to the fence line. Duke is a power hitter and is bound to send our boys home. The pitcher is in a full-on sweat now, wiping his brow with his sleeve. He winds up at lobs one toward the plate. Keller swings and connects. The *crack* of the bat seems to echo throughout the stadium.

Everyone jumps to their feet as they watch the ball make its way through the outfield and over the wall. The stadium is in an uproar over the home run. The boys are all jumping up and down screaming. Kessler and Carson wait for Duke to cross the home plate and each give him a high five. The next batter strikes out and brings us to the top of the ninth. All they have to do is hold off three batters and they win the game.

"WHAT A GAME!" Hudson says for the third time since the game ended. "I hope Kessler Davis is here." He's mentioned that a few times as well.

We're sitting in a room they set up for this meet and greet. There are snacks and drinks for us to enjoy while we wait for the players to join us.

Kara leans over and whispers "Me too" into my ear just loud enough for me to hear. I roll my eyes and give her arm a little tap with the back of my hand.

"Behave." I warn her with a smirk.

She sighs. "You know I will. I can enjoy looking though."

*You won't be the only one.*

I keep that thought to myself. I don't need to hear it from

Kara. I love her to death, but she will never let me live it down if I admit that I do in fact find Kessler Davis attractive. I mean, I'm not dead. Anyone with a pulse can see how damn fine he is. With his beautiful forest green eyes, and eyelashes that should be illegal for a man to have. I bet he can wink the underwear right off a woman. Not to mention I am a complete sucker for a man with a beard. Not too long and burly of course, but a nice trimmed scruff. The kind that'll leave a beard burn in all the right places. Don't even get me started on the man's arms. Whew, watching those forearm muscles twist and ripple when he's catching. It's enough to give me a lady boner.

"Earth to Lucy." I hear Kara say as she waves her hand in front of my face.

*Shit.*

I blink my eyes a few times and turn my head towards her. "I'm sorry, what were you saying?"

"Where were you?" she asks with an amused look on her face

"Oh, uh, just.... Thinking about my schedule for the week," I say, praying she doesn't push further.

"Mmhmm, right." She eyeballs me like she doesn't believe me. She opens her mouth to say something else, but the doors open and some of the players start trickling in, putting a stop to her questioning.

*Thank you, Jesus.*

All the boys grow quiet and their eyes widen at being in such close vicinity to the players. The PR rep introduces the players that are here to the boys. I quickly look to see if Kessler is among them, but don't see him. Probably for the best. I don't need to be caught ogling him by Kara or Hudson.

After a few minutes of awkwardness from the boys, they start to open up and chat with the players. Among the guys who showed up are Reese Hayes, Brent Attwood, and Duke Keller. I sit back and enjoy watching Hudson get to interact with the players. A little seed of resentment hits me in the stomach, but I push it away. Now is not the time for that. A few minutes later, Hudson walks over to me showing me the ball in his hand that has all the players' names on it.

"Mom look," he says, handing me the ball. "Can we get one of those plastic cases for it?" he asks with a hopeful look.

"Absolutely bud, I'll order one tonight."

The door to the event space opens again, when I look up to see who it is, my breath catches in my chest. Kessler Davis.

*Holy hell.*

He's one hundred percent sexier in person. Our eyes lock for a brief second as he scans the space, and I feel a zap of energy hit me in the stomach.

*Nope.*

Shut that shit down girlfriend.

"MOM," Hudson whisper-yells as he tugs on my arm. "It's Kessler Davis!"

I give myself a mental shake and turn to Hudson. "I see that. Go talk to him."

Hudson gives me the deer-in-headlights look and shakes his head. "I can't," he whispers, suddenly growing shy.

The other boys don't waste any time and rush up to Kessler. He chuckles and starts signing what the boys shove in his face, answering their questions and laughing a sexy laugh that makes my insides do weird things. Hudson still hangs back fidgeting and scuffing the toe of his shoe on the floor.

"Come on," I say, placing my hand on his back and gently guiding him over to Kessler. Hudson hesitates for a second, then gives into the pressure of my hand. We get in line behind the last of the boys and wait. When it's our turn, Hudson just stands there and stares.

"Hey bud, got something for me to sign?"

Hudson silently hands Kessler his ball. Kessler signs it and hands it back. "What position do you play?"

"I, I'm the catcher," Hudson squeaks out.

"Alright, a catcher," Kessler says, holding up his fist for a bump. Hudson bumps his fist, and the spell is broken.

"You were so awesome today, Mr.Davis."

"Please call me Kessler." He looks at me and gives me a smile that could melt the panties off a woman. "Who's this?" he asks Hudson.

"This is my mom, did you hear her yell at you to bunt? Is that why you did it? She said your coach probably gave you the sign, but I told her I think you heard her. Did you?" Hudson asks, talking a mile a minute.

I put my hand on his shoulder. "Woah Hud, take a breath. Give Mr.Davis a chance to answer." I hold out my other hand for a shake and Kessler takes it, his warm hand engulfing mine. "I'm Lucy. Sorry, he's just really excited to meet one of his idols."

"No need to apologize, and please call me Kessler." He holds my hand a few seconds longer, then releases it, leaving my hand tingling.

"That was your mom?" he asks Hudson, who shakes his head up and down vigorously.

"Actually I did hear you, and no, my coach did not signal me to bunt. I actually got my aa... butt chewed for it, But I owe you a thanks. No one expected it." His eyes stare into mine and I feel my heart speed up. " I'm not much of a bunter, but it worked out. I've uh," He pulls on the back of his neck and looks down. "I've been in a little rut with batting, that helped knock some of the rust off." He looks back up at me, an almost shy smile on his lips.

"See, Mom! I told you he heard you!" Hudson practically screams.

I try to ignore the butterflies taking flight in my stomach and chuckle. "Ok, calm down. We should get going, we don't want to take up any more of Mr. Davis' time."

Kessler starts to say something when the PR rep steps forward. "Actually, can we get a few pictures of the guys with your team, Coach?" Kessler raises his eyebrows at me when he hears me being called coach.

Oh yeah, I completely forgot about that. I turn to Charlie. I think that's her name, and smile. "Sure. Where do you want us?"

"I think a picture out on the home plate would be good."

"Whatever you want," I say, turning towards my players. I clap my hands a couple of times to get their attention. "Picture time boys, please follow this lovely lady out onto the field." I pause and look at the boys giving them my stern coach face. "No running around until *after* they have the pictures they need please."

"Yes, Coach," they all mumble in unison as they follow their parents out behind Charlie.

I turn Hudson to follow the crowd.

"Coach huh?" Kessler asks, falling in step beside us.

"Yeah. Mom's been my coach since I was in T-ball. Her and Aunt Kara," Hudson answers for me.

Kessler raises his eyebrows. "Wow, that's impressive."

I must make a face because he adds, "Not impressive as in, women don't know anything about baseball, impressive as in, women coaches aren't common in baseball, especially two female coaches."

I give him a shrug. "Yeah, well, no one stepped up to coach when Hudson and Kade were starting T-Ball. So I figured 'why not?' It's just one season and I didn't want the kids missing out just because no one wanted to coach. Kara, my best friend and

Kade's mom said she'd help me out. Fast forward six years, and we're still here."

We reach the rest of the group and Charlie instructs us on where she wants us, ending our conversation. Kara and I are on opposite ends of our team and the players are mixed in with the boys. Kessler stands on my left side. He places his hand at the small of my back and sends shivers up my spine, making goosebumps break out all over my body.

*Jesus.*

Has it really been that long that a single touch makes my body want to combust? I quickly run my hands down my arms to rid them of goosebumps and place my hands on Hudson's shoulders.

Kessler leans down and whispers "Cold?" into my ear, sending a new round of goosebumps coursing through my body.

*Sweet Jesus, what is happening?*

I give my head a slight shake. "No, I'm fine," I whisper back.

The photographer prompts us to smile and snaps a bunch of pictures and lets Charlie know that they have plenty to work with. Some of the players say their goodbyes and head off. A few stay, still talking to some of the boys and their parents. Kessler removes his hand from my back but stays beside me.

"The boys can run around if they want," Charlie says, walking up to me.

"Are you sure?"

"Absolutely, turn 'em loose."

I turn to the boys and tell them they can check out the field, if it's ok with their adults. Cheers erupt and 12 boys take off. Some running the bases, others seeing who can reach the outfield wall first.

"Hudson seems like a great kid," Kessler says, watching the boys run off their excess energy.

I sigh. "He's the best. I hit the jackpot with that one."

Kara makes her way over to us, giving me a knowing smirk. I'll definitely be hearing about this later.

Kessler clears his throat and turns to me. "So I wanted to thank you again, for the bunting suggestion. I may have gotten my ass chewed for it, but it really helped in the confidence area."

I can feel my face heat up, I wave my hand like I'm brushing away the compliment, which I am. "Fans yell things all the time. I was just another fan yelling."

"No, you weren't. After you've played for as many years as I have, you learn to tune out the crowd, or at least what they're yelling. Your voice came through." He gives me a look I can't quite read. "I'd really like to thank you properly, with dinner, or something." He looks down at my left hand and back up to my eyes. "If that's appropriate?"

I'm about to tell him *no*, that I'm flattered but not interested–when my loud mouth *ex*-best friend butts in.

"Totally appropriate and she accepts." Kara smirks at me. "I'll leave you two to discuss the details, I'm going to go talk to the parents." She twiddles her fingers at Kessler and moves off.

I'm going to kill her and it will be worth the jail time, I think while glaring after her retreating backside.

"Why do I have the feeling you don't accept," he asks, seeing my annoyance.

I sigh and glance at him. "It's not you, I promise. I just... don't date." I debate on whether or not to add especially ball players, and decide against it.

He lifts his eyebrows in surprise. "Like ever?"

I shake my head. "Nope." Popping the P.

"What if I wasn't asking you out on a date? Just a... Thank you?"

I feel my face heat. Of course he doesn't want to date me.

What the hell is my problem? He's just trying to be nice. "No, of course, I, uh nevermind. Um, you don't have to thank me. Today was enough. Seeing Hudson happy was enough." I move to go collect Hudson and maim my best friend. Kessler puts his hand on my arm, stopping me.

"Wait, I–"

I cut him off and pull my arm away, giving him a polite smile. "We don't want to take up any more of your time. Thank you for everything Mr. Davis." I turn and walk away, but not before seeing the resignation in his face. I call the boys in and tell them it's time to leave. I need to get out of here before I make a bigger fool of myself.

# CHAPTER 3

## Kessler

I WAKE UP THE NEXT MORNING TO A TEXT WITH THE information I asked Charlie for before I left the field yesterday. I feel like I fucked up with that little league coach yesterday and I need to fix it. Why? I'm not sure, but the feeling is there. She intrigued me, and that hasn't happened in a while.

I get out of bed and stretch, my body screaming at me from my various injuries throughout the years. After a quick shower, I make my way into the kitchen to make breakfast. Turning the TV on *SportsCenter*, I scramble up some eggs for an omelet. I add green onions, mushrooms, and cheese to the bowl and pour it all into the pan. While my eggs cook, I shoot off a quick text putting my plan in motion. I flip my omelet and my phone pings, indicating a text.

KARA

How do I know this is really Kessler Davis?

Valid question. I snap a quick picture and send it also.

KARA

How do I know this isn't just a photo off the internet? Oh hold on, I can reverse search.

Jesus this woman. I mean, I get it. I would be hesitant too if I was randomly texted by a number claiming to be me.

KARA

Ok nothing came up, so it's not a stock photo. But just to make sure, take a picture in a mirror with you holding up 3 fingers.

ME

That's oddly specific.

KARA

Exactly 😊

I do as she asks, send the picture over. While waiting for her reply, I put my omelet on a plate and sit at the breakfast bar to eat. I'm halfway through my eggs when my phone pings.

KARA

I mean you could have put a shirt on, but I'm not one to complain. OK I believe you. Now, what did you have in mind?

I chuckle and send my reply.

ME

I was thinking of flowers? And something for the team, which is where you come in. What does the team need that I can provide?

KARA

mmmm flowers are good... But coffee, coffee will get you somewhere. A large hazelnut cold brew from LatteDaze.

ME

Oh, I've been there. Think I should send one of their muffin tops too?

KARA

Oh damn, speaking her language already. Up the ante and send over a dozen Muffin Tops for her office, I'll send you the address.

ME

And for the team?

KARA

*thinking face emoji* The only thing I can think of that would be beneficial to the boys is more practice lol.

ME

Would Lucy be mad if I offered to help?

KARA

Absolutely 😂 but if it's for the boys, she won't complain. She would do anything for those boys.

ME

Send me your practice schedule and I'll look at my schedule and see what I can do.

KARA

Before I do, Why are you doing this? Not that I don't approve, because I do.

I pause before answering. Why am I doing this?

*Because you can't get her out of your head.*

True, but it's not just that. I felt something between us yesterday. Call it a spark, energy, whatever. I've never in my 36 years felt a pull to someone, like I felt with Lucy, and I want to explore that feeling. But I'm not about to disclose that, not yet anyway.

ME

I want to show Lucy my appreciation... for the batting thing. This is how I'm showing my thanks.

KARA

I'll accept that answer... for now....

KARA

*picture of practice schedule*

I can't help but chuckle at Kara's response as I look over the schedule and compare it to mine. It just so happens I have an available day this week for one of their practices.

ME

I'm available Wednesday. I'll talk to some of the guys and we'll come out to practice.

KARA

You're serious?

ME

Yes, don't say anything to anyone though. If the media got a hold of this, it would be impossible to practice.

KARA

Aye Aye captain.

Finished with breakfast, I rinse my plate off and place it in the dishwasher. I check the time on my phone, grab my wallet and keys, switch off the TV, and head out the door. I'll talk to Reese and Brent at conditioning today to see if they're down for helping me out.

I'm SITTING in the parking lot of the field where Lucy's team practices. I sent Kara a text earlier letting her know I was still on for today. She sent me the address and told me Lucy usually shows up about 15 minutes early to set things up. I decided I should come early to talk to her before everyone got there. I have a feeling she's not going to like this.

Reese and Brent were on board of course, but not before giving me a bunch of shit about it.

I see an SUV pull up with music bumping. Looking over I see Lucy and Hudson singing at the top of their lungs and dancing in their seats. Laughing, I get out of my truck and walk over to her window. I rap on the driver's side window with my knuckles and Lucy jumps in her seat and screams. Laughing, she rolls down her window. Her smile drops and her laugh disappears once she sees it's me.

"What the hell are you doing here?" she asks, almost shouting.

I can tell she's shocked and trying to compose herself. Lucy clears her throat and holds up her finger to me. Rolling her window up, she turns off her car. She says something to Hudson, but I can't make out what she says. Stepping out of her car, she closes the door and leans against it, crossing her arms in front of her.

"Mr. Davis, what can I do for you?" Lucy asks not quite looking me in the eye, but over my shoulder .

I clear my throat and stick my hands in my front pockets, wondering if this is a good idea. "First of all, call me Kessler, Please. Secondly, I said I wanted to thank you for helping me the other day. I was able to get Kara's number." I put one of my hands up, halting her from saying anything. "Don't be mad, she just wants to help." Lucy clamps her mouth shut and gives me the proceed motion with one of her hands, still not looking at me. "Anyway, I wanted to say 'Thank You' and Kara suggested I come help out at a practice. She mentioned the catchers needing some help with reaction times." I look at my watch, then back at her. "Plus, I asked a couple of the guys to meet me here to help with the rest. That way everyone is included."

She stands there in silence and I can see the wheels turning in her head. Before she has a chance to say no I add, "Kara said to tell you it's for the kids. She said you'd do anything for these boys. So let me do this, for them." I tilt my head and finally get her to make eye contact with me. "Besides, when will they ever get another chance to have coaching from MLB players?"

A look passes in her eye, but it's gone as quickly as it appears. She takes a deep breath and lets it out. " OK" she says reluctantly. "Anything for the boys." Pushing off her car, she walks away from me to the back of her car. She pushes a button for her hatch to open. I hear her say, "Ok Hud, you can come out and help me."

I go around to the back to join them. "Here, I can help," I say, grabbing a bucket I assume is filled with balls. Lucy nods but doesn't say anything. Hudson on the other hand is ecstatic.

"Mr. Davis, what are you doing here?" he asks, barely containing his excitement.

I chuckle at his enthusiasm. "Again, call me Kessler. And I'm here to help you guys out for practice. Coach Kara let me know you guys were having some issues with your catching and fielding. So I figured a good way to say thank you to your mom was to help you guys out. I happen to know a thing or two about catching."

Hudson's eyes widen, and he looks from his mom, back to me. "You're going to help us practice?"

"Yep, if that's ok with you?" I ask him.

"Holy shi-"

"Hudson James," Lucy interrupts

Hudson stops himself mid-sentence. "Sorry," he mumbles to

his mom. "The guys are going to freak out," he says to me, grabbing gear and heading towards the field.

"At least someone is excited to see me here," I comment, waiting for her to hand me something else.

Lucy lets out a heavy sigh, turning to me. "I appreciate you taking the time out of your schedule for this. It absolutely was not necessary for you to do this, but I know the boys will love this. So thank you."

"But you don't love this idea," I state

"It's not personal Mr. Davis."

"Kessler."

She shakes her head and reaches up to press the button on the hatch. "Fine. It's not personal, *Kessler*." She doesn't offer any further explanation of her displeasure.

I bend down and pick up the gear bag by her feet before she can grab it. She lets out another little huff but doesn't say anything. She walks towards the field and I fall in step beside her.

I glance at her out of the side of my eye, taking her in. She has her dirty blonde hair pulled back and shoved into a baseball hat. She's at least six inches shorter than me, so I can't see her eyes from this angle, but I can take a guess that they would be shooting flames if they could.

The weird feeling in my chest is back. The same feeling I had when I saw her at the field the other day. Her back is ramrod straight and I actually have to walk at a good pace to keep up. We get to the field and she deposits the gear she was carrying onto the ground. I do the same. We both turn at the sound of cars approaching and I see that it's Reese and Brent arriving. They park and get out of their cars. I lift my hand to them and they head in our direction.

"Oh wow, Reese Hayes and Brent Attwood are here too! Kade's gonna freak," Hudson says, seeing the guys.

"Speak of the Devil," Lucy mutters as another car pulls up.

Kara and her son Kade get out and make their way over to us too.

When Reese and Brent get to us, Lucy shakes their hands and thanks them for taking the time out of their schedules for this. She sounds a lot more sincere to them than she did to me.

Kara and Kade get to the growing group next. Lucy cocks her eyebrow at Kara and gives her a pointed stare. Kara smirks at her and winks at her. A whole conversation is happening between them, with no words being said. I clear my throat and everyone looks at me.

"So I was thinking after the boys warm up, we would split off into three groups. Each of us will take four boys, we'll rotate every 20 minutes, then for the last 30 minutes we'll put our work into play and see what the boys retained." I look at Lucy for confirmation of my plan. She nods but says nothing further, arms firmly crossed in front of her. Brent and Reese look at me with questioning looks but also don't say anything.

Over the next 10 minutes, kids and parents start to show up, both parties riddled with excitement over me and the guys being here. Once everyone has arrived. Lucy tells everyone we're here to work with them today. More excitement ensues. Lucy asks parents to proceed as normal, so as not to distract us and the kids. She splits the boys into three groups, then heads to the dugout throwing a "Let me know if you need help" over her shoulder. I give her a nod and we get to work.

# CHAPTER 4

## Lucy

FOR THE NEXT HOUR, I WATCH THE BOYS RUN DRILLS with the guys. I make notes on what I can incorporate into future practices. I try to focus on all the groups, but I find my eyes constantly wandering to Kessler. He has his hat turned backwards on his head, and it's doing things to my lady bits that I'd rather not have happen. Especially at practice... in front of children.

Kara is over with Reese helping him with a drill, so I don't have to worry about her commenting on where my eyes are. Plus I'm still a little salty about her sneakiness on this whole thing. I know she means well, but right now I'm choosing to be cranky about it. Plus, seeing Hudson practice with Kessler does something weird to my heart and stomach and I'm not sure how to deal with those feelings. So naturally, I shove them deep down to deal with later.

Kessler claps his hands together and gets everyone's attention. I leave my safe space in the dugout and head over to the group.

"Everyone ready to apply what we've learned?" Kessler asks the boys.

A chorus of yeses goes up and he sends everyone to their positions. The boys not out on the field are up to bat first. He sends Reese to stand at third and Brent to first for coaches, then comes and stands where Kara and I are. He crosses his arms over his chest and leans up against the dugout. I take a moment to run my eyes up his body, starting at his muscular calves, and working my way up his cargo shorts. They don't give away much, but I do notice how his hips and catcher's ass fill out the normally boring shorts. His fitted T-shirt hangs loose around his abdomen but quickly tightens around his chest and shoulders. The short sleeves stretched within an inch of their life, threatening to rip at any moment. He catches me staring, even through my sunglasses, so I avert my eyes and look out to the field like I'm checking on the boys.

Out of the corner of my eye, I see him smirk before clearing his throat. "These boys have some great skills, we really didn't have to tweak much to get them honed in." He looks at Kara, then at me. "You've both done a great job." I feel my cheeks redden at the compliment. I know we've done a great job with these boys and I don't know why I'm embarrassed. I dip my head and offer a small smile, but don't comment further. Kara however feels the need to elaborate.

*Shocking.*

"Well most of the credit goes to my girl here," she says, hitching her thumb my way. "I'm just the extra body. Lucy eats, sleeps, and breathes baseball. Always has. Even after... Ooof!" she belts out, rubbing the spot where my elbow met her side. I give her a pointed look and she widens her eyes and shuts her mouth. "Uh anyways, most of the credit goes to Luce. Let's get this going, shall we? Parents will be here to pick kids up soon," Kara spews out in one breath.

Kessler raises his eyebrows but doesn't comment further. He claps his hands and moves off getting the mini-game started, leaving me and Kara alone.

"Jesus Kara, what the hell was that?" I whisper.

"Sorry! I'm sorry, you know how I am. I just talk and don't think about what's coming out of my mouth."

I pinch the bridge of my nose, take a deep breath, then blow it out.

"I know! I swear, it won't happen again!"

I nod my head knowing she didn't mean to say anything. "Let's just get through the rest of practice. The boys look excited to put their skills to the test."

Kara nods in agreement and we both take a seat in the dugout. The boys cycle through, each taking a turn batting, every one showing off the new skills they've learned in the field and at bat. I'm impressed by how much quicker everyone is in their plays. We get to the last group of batters and everyone makes it on base. With no batters left and parents starting to show up, I stand and walk out of the dugout to dismiss practice.

"OK boys, great practice. Let's thank Mr. Davis, Mr. Attwood, and Mr. Hayes for their time." The boys groan, not ready to be done.

"Hold up," says Kessler, giving me a cocky smirk. "Why don't we make this interesting."

I cock an eyebrow at him. "How?" I ask, not sure if I'm liking where this is going.

"You come up and bat. The boys get you out, I buy everyone ice cream." Cheers erupt amongst the boys. "Hold on, I'm not done," he says, quieting down the boys. "Like I said, the boys get you out, I buy everyone ice cream. You get on base, and the boys owe you laps." All the boys groan. "Then I buy everyone ice cream." Everyone erupts in cheers.

I let out a laugh. "So either way, the boys get ice cream?"

Kessler shrugs and gives me a wink, making my heart stutter quickly. "Seems like a win-win situation to me. So what do you say, Coach? You game?"

I look at the boy's hopeful faces, then back at Kessler, who has the same look as the boys.

"Game on, Davis."

All the boys cheer. I grab a bat and make my way to the plate. Hudson smirks at me from behind his catcher's mask. I give him a wink and tap the plate with my bat. I take my position and wait for my pitch. Joey, one of our top pitchers, winds up and sends a pitch my way. I take a swing and hear it hit Hudson's glove.

"Strike one," calls Kessler, acting as the umpire.

I get back into position and Joey winds up again, sending another pitch over the plate. This time I don't swing, not liking the pitch sent my way.

"Strike two," Kessler bellows. I step back and look at him.

"That was NOT a strike," I argue

"Outside corner," is all he says.

I roll my eyes but don't argue. I take my position again.

"Hold up." I hear Kessler say and I back out of the box.

"How do we feel about me giving Coach Lucy a few pointers? It's only fair since you guys got some today."

I hear the boys all murmur in agreement.

"I'm fine," I argue.

"It's just a couple of small adjustments," Kessler says, stepping out from behind Hudson. "Take your position."

I look at him for a second before doing as he asks. He comes up behind me, placing his arms over mine. I suck in a breath and his scent fills my nose. It's a mixture of leather and spice.

"Rotate this hand like this," he says into my ear, rotating my left hand inward. "You're also lifting your right shoulder a bit before you swing. Make sure you keep it level as you swing through." He places a hand on my shoulder and gently pushes it down. He softly traces his fingertips from my shoulder to my elbow, giving me goosebumps. "Cold?" he asks with amusement in his voice.

I clear my throat. "Nope, I'm good. Let's do this." I step away from him and back into the batter's box. I hear him chuckle as he walks back behind Hudson. I set up my stance and make the minor adjustments Kessler gave me. Joey launches a pitch at me and I take a swing.

*Crack.*

I launch the ball into center field. Dropping the bat, I take off towards first, making it in plenty of time before the ball reaches my first baseman.

"Wooo," I yell, jumping up, "looks like you boys owe me some laps!" Groans ensue, so I add, "Not today though. Maybe next practice." Walking over to Hudson, I hold my fist up for a bump.

"Nice job today bud." He returns my bump and gives me a big grin.

"Today was awesome," he says and starts to take his catcher's gear off. Seeing him this happy makes me happy. That's all I've ever wanted for him, and thanks to Kessler, he's had a day he will never forget.

I look at Kessler and hold my hand out for a shake. "Thank you for doing this. The boys... this is a day they will remember forever." He takes my hand and gives it a slight shake. I notice again how warm and comforting it is, like a hug. A slight roughness to it from years of use.

"I enjoyed today. It reminded me why I fell in love with the game in the first place." He stares into my sunglasses like he can see my eyes. I stare back, still holding onto his hand. The air between us crackling. Neither of us pulls our hands away. In the distance, I hear the distinct music of an ice cream truck. Something clicks in my brain, breaking the trance. Pulling my hand away, I look over my shoulder at the increasing sound of the music. An ice cream truck is entering the parking lot. I look back at Kessler.

"Did—did you have an ice cream truck come to us?" I ask in disbelief.

His smirk turns into a big grin. "I know a guy."

"You know an Ice Cream guy?" Not believing him because from what I've seen of this man's body, he does not eat ice cream. Period. End of story.

He nods his head. "My best friend growing up opened up an ice cream shop a few years ago after he retired from the military. I gave him the start-up money. He recently expanded by adding a truck. It was a smart investment. Who doesn't love ice cream?"

"Lactose intolerant people?" I answer.

That gets a chuckle out of Kessler. "I guarantee they still love it, it just doesn't love them back. Plus Garrett has a variety of lactose-free options, so they're included too."

"Inclusion at its finest," I say, getting another chuckle out of Kessler. I find myself liking the sound of the deep rumble in his chest. Which raises the alarms in my brain that I need to get away from this man before I develop... feelings.

"I uh, need to talk to the parents about the truck," I say pointing to the truck behind me and backing away. I'm not looking where I'm going of course, because I'm too busy trying to get away from the man currently doing things to my body that I don't want. My foot lands on something round. Kessler moves forward just as I feel my foot roll out from under me, making me land square on my ass.

"Ooof," I say as the breath rushes out of me.

Kessler rushes forward and kneels down next to me. "Are you ok?" Concern on his face.

"Mom!" Hudson yells running up to me and landing on his knees next to me. "Are you ok?"

I hold up my hands. "I'm fine." I pick up the damn ball I tripped over and hand it to Hudson. "I just wasn't watching where I was going." I get to my feet and I feel Kessler's hand land on the small of my back, lighting my skin on fire.

"Are you sure you're ok?" His green eyes bore into me.

"I'm good. Just a bruised ego." I joke, brushing myself off and walking over to the group of parents that have formed at the bleachers. I explain the bet with Kessler and ask if it's okay if we treat their kids to ice cream. Everyone agrees, kids line up at the truck and ice cream is distributed.

Kara walks up to me, an amused look on her face. "You good?"

"Peachy." I deadpan her. "Of course that would happen to me."

She laughs and grabs me by the elbow dragging me to the back on the line with our boys "Come on, Ice cream fixes everything."

All the kids have gotten their ice cream and left by the time Kara and I have gotten up to the window with our boys. Kessler is at the window talking with his ice cream man friend.

The boys are ahead of us ordering their ice creams. Kara turns to me, eyes wide, mouthing the letters O M G. I side-eye her with raised eyebrows.

I mouth back to her "I know." This man was not the ice cream man we had when we were kids. It was like Zeus and Fabio had a baby and gave him the gift of creating creamy, sweet treats. His chiseled jaw was lightly dusted with a five o'clock shadow, I don't even mind the dirty blond man bun sitting atop his head, and I'm usually not attracted to long hair. It gives his face a more defined, viking look. Tattoos are everywhere you look, down his neck, over his knuckles, up his arms. Instead of taking away from his looks, they only enhance them. He looks at us after giving our kids their chosen sugar rush and flashes us what I will forever refer to as a 'fuck me' smile. "Oh holy Jesus," I whisper, glacier blue eyes piercing my retinas.

"Ladies," the Greek God greets us.

We both stare longer than what is probably socially acceptable before greeting him with matching "hi's". His chest rumbles with a low chuckle and he leans out the window. "Garrett," he says, holding out his hand. Kara takes it and gives it a shake introducing herself. He looks at me and I give his hand a shake also, noticing that while he's absolutely stunning, I don't feel the spark I do when I touch Kessler.

"What can I get you two lovely creatures?"

"Do you come in an ice cream flavor?" I hear the words leave my mouth before I can stop them. My eyes widen and my cheeks grow hot. I see Kara look at me from the corner of my eye. Her eyes wide and an amused look on her face. I hear Kessler clear his throat and when I make eye contact with him he has a scowl across his face.

*Interesting.*

"I mean, what do you recommend? There's just so many to choose from."

"Nice save," Kara whispers out of the corner of her mouth.

Garrett stares at each of us for a few seconds and holds up his finger, disappearing back into the truck. Kara and I give each other questioning looks. I look at Kessler, who just rolls his eyes.

Garrett comes back to the window with mystery cones. He holds out a pink and blue swirled ice cream cone to Kara. She takes it and takes a lick. Her eyes widen. "Oh my Jesus," she says, taking another lick. "That is delicious. What, what flavor is this?"

He gives her a sexy smirk. "I call it Unicorn Delight. It's a mixture of strawberry and cotton candy ice cream. It's my new flavor."

"It's fucking delicious," Kara says, practically making out with her cone now.

"And for you," Garrett says, handing me my waffle cone. I thank him and take a lick.

"Holy... how. How did you know?" I question taking another lick.

He shrugs his shoulders. "It's a gift." He looks at Kara and gives her a wink. "One of many." Kara giggles. Freaking giggles and I see a blush form on her cheeks.

*Interesting.*

I take another lick of my almond chocolate mocha cone and look over at Kessler. His arms are still crossed but his left hand is slightly pinching his lower lip and he's watching me intently. I clear my throat and his eyes jump back up to mine. He gives me a smirk not caring at all he was caught red-handed.

*Oh boy.*

I need to get away from this man before I want things I haven't wanted in a long time.

"Hudson!" I yell turning around to find him and Kade sitting in the bleachers finishing up their cones. "Let's grab the gear and head out bud. It's a school night." I take off towards them, putting distance between me and Mr. Sex Appeal. I shift my cone to my left hand and grab the gear Hudson couldn't with my right. We make it back to my car and I see Kessler leaning up against the hatch. Looking sexy and shit.

*Fuck.*

I take a deep breath and close the distance to my car. Kessler reaches over and pushes the button on my hatch to open it. He grabs the bags from me and he and Hudson load up the car. For the second time today, I feel a breath catch in my throat watching them. The warning bell goes off in my head telling me I need to get out of here.

"So, thank you again for today. It really meant a lot to the boys," I say, looking everywhere but at him.

"Just the boys?" he questions, eyes boring into me.

Hudson decides to be a savior, *bless him*. "Yeah, Mr. Davis! That was awesome! I wish every practice could be like that."

"Hey! I make practice fun," I object.

"Yeah, I know. But Mom, it's Kessler Davis." He shrugs his shoulders and toes the ground. "You can't beat that."

"Well, at least I know where I rate," I say, elbowing Hudson in the side playfully. "Shake Mr. Davis's hand and tell him thank you, so we can let him get on with his night."

Hudson holds out his hand and Kessler takes it. "Thanks again Mr. Davis."

"It's Kessler, and anytime kid," Kessler says, giving Hudson a firm shake.

I put my hands on Hudson's shoulders. "Come on kid, let's go get some dinner."

"You guys haven't had dinner yet?"

I pause before answering him, feeling like that's a loaded question. However, Hudson answers for me.

"No, we're going to go get pizza from Tony's. Have you ever had their pizza? Mom says everyone else doesn't rate."

This kid, I swear.

Kessler chuckles. "I have been to Tony's." He pauses and gives me a look. "And your mom's right, no one else rates."

Why do I feel like he means something else?

"You should come with us," Hudson suggests enthusiastically.

*Shit.*

"Oh bud, I'm sure Mr. Davis…"

"Kessler," Kessler says, interrupting me.

I give a small huff. "I'm sure *Kessler* has other things to do." I raise both my eyebrows, suggesting he agree with me.

Kessler smiles like the Cheshire cat from *Alice in Wonderland*. "Actually, I was just going to go home and have boring rice and steamed vegetables, but Tony's sounds like a much better option. That is, if your mom doesn't mind me tagging along?"

Hudson turns to me with puppy dog eyes. "You don't mind, right Mom?"

Well hell, how can I say no to that face.

I sigh looking from Hudson to Kessler. "How can I deny anyone Tony's?"

# CHAPTER 5

## Kessler

SHE'S ANNOYED. I CAN SEE IT ALL OVER HER FACE, BUT she won't say anything in front of Hudson. We pull into the parking lot for Tony's. After we get out of our cars, I jog ahead to open the door for them. Lucy gives me a tight smile as she walks through. I follow them in and inhale the aroma that is Tony's. The scent of pizza dough and various spicy meats smack me in the face, making my mouth water. So much better than steamed veggies and rice. We make our way over to the counter and Tony himself pops out of the back.

"Kessler!" He shouts in greeting with his mild Italian accent. He immigrated here when he was 10 with his parents and four siblings. His accent has softened through the 50 years he's lived here. "My Lucy and Little Hud too? What a special day. Come, come sit. I will get you the usuals, yes?"

*His Lucy?*

Lucy and I look at each other then nod our heads at Tony. We take our seats in one of the booths while Tony rushes off to the back. It's busy, as usual, but we've missed the big dinner rush. No one seems to notice me, thankfully. I want to have dinner with Lucy and Hudson with no distractions. Get to know them more, maybe convince Lucy to go out with me again.

"So how did you discover Tony's?" I ask, starting the conversation.

She sets her water down after taking a sip and fidgets with the glass, spinning it in its place. "I actually waited tables here in college." *Well, that explains why Tony called her* his *Lucy.* She pulls her top lip into her mouth, biting it before speaking again. "Tony's oldest daughter, Izzie, babysat Hudson for me off and on while I was going to school and working." She gives Hudson a smile and ruffles his hair. "They're like our extended family."

Hudson pipes up, "Yeah, even though it's just me and Mom, we still have a big family. Mom says family doesn't always have to be blood. Right, Mom?" He looks at her and she gives him a warm smile.

"That's exactly right, bud. Family is what you make it."

Watching Lucy with her son makes me think back to the conversation I had with my mom earlier in the week. My mom's right.

*Damnit.*

I want someone, or someone's to call my family. I mean, yeah I have my parents and brother, but I don't have someone to share my life with. I feel my heartbeat increase as I realize that weird feeling I've been having, that ache in my chest, is loneliness... I want a family. That shouldn't surprise me, it's not like I've always been one to sleep around with multiple women. I've just never found anyone that holds my interest for more than a few months, or who I've been interested in enough to want more than a surface relationship with. Most women just want me for my bank account or status.

I look at the woman sitting in front of me. She doesn't want anything from me, and yet I have the urge to give her everything. Which is crazy because I know virtually nothing about her. Yet, that feeling, that urge, is there.

Hudson suddenly gets up from the booth. "Be right back, I need to go to the bathroom!" he yells over his shoulder jogging to where the bathrooms are.

Lucy smirks and shakes her head as she watches him head towards the back. Without Hudson, an awkward silence falls over the table. Lucy's looking at everything but me. I clear my throat and ask a question I feel she won't answer, but ask anyway.

"So Hudson's father, is he..." I start, but she interrupts before I can finish my sentence.

"He's not in the picture and never has been," she says with an edge to her voice. She looks to the bathrooms, then at me, looking me in the eye for the first time since we sat down. "We don't talk about him. End of story." She holds my gaze for a few more seconds giving me what I can only think of as a fierce mama bear stare, then looks back over my shoulder. Her face softens and a few seconds later Hudson sits back in his seat.

I know that's not the end of that story, but I respect her wishes and don't push any further. It's none of my business, and she definitely doesn't want to talk about it, especially in front of Hudson.

I talk with Hudson about baseball while we're waiting for our food. He reminds me a lot of myself when I was a kid.

"So Lucy," I say, turning my attention towards her. "I don't think I caught what it is you do, besides coach Hudsons team."

"Oh. I'm a physical therapist," she says, as if it's nothing.

"Really?" I say, trying not to sound surprised, but apparently fail.

"Yes, really. You don't think women can be PTs?" she challenges sitting forward in her seat.

I hold up my hands. "No, that's not what I'm saying at all. What I meant was that it's impressive. Especially being a single mom."

She visibly relaxes, sitting back in her seat. "Thank you. I'm sorry. I didn't mean to get defensive." She gives me a small smile.

A few minutes later Tony comes to our table and sets down two identical pizzas.

"Two Loaded Luces," Tony announces.

"You like the loaded Luce?" Lucy says, eyebrows raised in surprise.

I grab two huge slices and plop them down on my plate. "It's the best pizza here. Nothing else comes close. I dare anyone to fight me on that opinion too." The pizza is perfection. A delectably thin, yet sturdy crust, topped with salami, pepperoni, bacon, olives, mushrooms, and spinach. All held down with three different types of cheese. The finishing touch is the fresh avocado on top after it's baked. Chef's Kiss. "Tony, you broke the mold when you created this masterpiece."

Tony chuckles. "Well Mr.Kessler, I did not create it. You are sitting across from the creator."

I pause mid bite and look over at Lucy. Her cheeks flush red as she hands Hudson his plate and dishes herself up. "You created this pizza?"

"Uh well, technically Hudson created it. I had a craving when I was pregnant with him." She shrugs her shoulders.

An image of a pregnant Lucy pops into my head and makes my stomach do a weird flip. What the?

*Slow down.*

I just met her.

Tony laughs. "Craving? My Lucy was obsessed. I made this

pizza every shift you worked for a month straight. People saw it and asked what it was, and it just grew from there. It's one of our most popular pizzas."

Lucy smiles warmly at Tony. "Glad my pregnancy cravings came in handy."

Tony lets out another laugh. "I will let you enjoy your meal."

Tony heads back to the kitchen and we eat in silence for a few minutes.

"So how do you know Tony?" Lucy asks after inhaling her first slice. She's not one of those women who pretend they don't eat. She has two more slices on her plate.

"My apartment is a couple blocks from here. I was jogging past one day shortly after moving here and the most amazing smell hit my nose. My stomach grumbled and I came in. Ordered the Loaded Luce." I give her a smirk. "And the rest is history. I come here for my cheat days."

She makes a hmm noise and finishes what's in her mouth before she speaks. "I wonder if we ever crossed paths and I just didn't recognize you?"

I stare into her eyes. "I would have noticed you."

She blushes and casts her eyes back down to her plate. "I doubt that."

"I don't."

Her eyes shoot back to mine and I hold her gaze. We stare at each other for a few seconds before a loud belch interrupts our silent thoughts.

"Hudson!" Lucy laughs. "Manners, please. I did raise you with manners."

"Sorry. Excuse me," Hudson says, a yawn following his apology.

Lucy looks at her watch. "Oh man, it's later than I realized. Hud, go grab some boxes from Tony please."

Hudson does as he's asked, leaving us alone at the table.

Lucy busies herself with stacking plates and gathering the napkins littering the table. I lay my hand on hers, stopping her. She stills and stares at our hands.

"I'd really like to see you again. Maybe take you out on a date?"

"Why?" She breathes out.

I exhale a laugh. "Well that's what people do when they're interested in someone."

"But, you don't. You don't even know me."

"That's kinda the point of a date."

She shakes her head. "I, I don't know."

I squeeze her hand. "You don't have to decide now." I let go of her hand and turn mine over. "Here, give me your phone."

"Wh, why?"

"So I can put my number in it," I say as if it's obvious.

She digs her phone out of her purse and places it in my palm. I type my number in and save the contact. I take a selfie and put it as my contact picture. I hand it back to her and she looks at the screen. She raises her eyebrows and gives me a smirk. "World's Sexiest Catcher?"

"I didn't want you to get me confused with anyone else."

She chuckles. "Yes, because I have so many other Kesslers in my phone, especially ones with your picture. Do, do you want me to put my number in yours?"

"I would love nothing more than to have your number. But, I'm going to let you contact me. I don't want to rush you, and if I had your number, I'd be calling you and texting you every possible second of the day."

Her cheeks flush red again, but Hudson comes back then, so nothing more is said. We place our leftovers in the boxes and head to the front to pay. Marie greets us when we get to the front.

"Kessler, Lucy, Hudson! It's so nice to see you guys!" she

says. Marie is one of Tony's four daughters and around my age. She comes around the counter and gives us all a hug. "Dad said your pizzas are on the house tonight," she holds out her hand, "before you argue, you know it's not going to do you any good, so you might as well save your breath."

Lucy rolls her eyes but gives her a huge smile and another hug. "We need to have girls' night when our schedules align. It's just been way too long."

"Absolutely sign me up. I'm in need of wine and gossip," Marie says, looking from Lucy to me and back to Lucy. "Apparently there's lots to catch up on."

Lucy blushes and looks at me, then back at Marie. "There might be."

We say our goodbyes and head out the door. When we get to the cars, I open Lucy's door for her. She gives me a shy smile and climbs in. I shut the door and she rolls down her window. "Thank you again, Kessler."

"Bye, Mr. Davis!" Hudson yells from the passenger seat.

I give him a wave, then look back at Lucy. "I look forward to hearing from you." I give her car a few taps, then head back towards my truck.

# CHAPTER 6

## Lucy

I'M SITTING IN MY OFFICE FRIDAY MORNING PREPPING for my patients for the day when Rhonda, our receptionist, comes in with a familiar peach-colored box and a large cold brew coffee.

"Ooo, what is this?" I ask excitedly, hoping they're for me. I could definitely use the caffeine this morning. I haven't had a decent night's sleep since everything that transpired. The Silverbacks flew out yesterday for their away games, so at least I don't have to worry about Kessler popping up somewhere unexpectedly. I still haven't contacted him about a date, and I'm not sure I'm going to. Kara keeps telling me not to let my past dictate my future. It's not like I'm not over what happened 11 years ago.

I am.

I just don't date. My life is good the way it is, I don't need someone coming in and messing everything up.

"These were just delivered, for you," she says, setting the box and coffee on my desk.

"Delivered? Was there a note with it? Are you sure it's for me?"

"The delivery guy said your name and handed me this too." She hands me a little white envelope with my name on the front. I raise one eyebrow and open the envelope.

Lucy,

A little bird told me this was your favorite coffee shop. I hope you enjoy the goodies (I ordered enough Muffin tops for the whole office), and think of me with every sip ;)
I look forward to hearing from you.

World's Sexiest Catcher

*Holy Shit!*

I LOOK UP AT RHONDA. "Can you put these in the break room? There's enough for everyone."

"Certainly. Who might they be from?" she asks curiously, tipping her head to see the note.

I fold the note back up and slip it into my purse. "Oh, just a friend."

She makes a hmm noise as she picks the box back up and

leaves my office. I take a drink of my coffee and hum my appreciation. Hazelnut, my favorite. I grab my phone and hover my thumb over the new message button. I look at the clock, my first client isn't due to arrive for another ten minutes. Clicking the button, I tap out a quick message.

ME

Thank you for the treats and coffee. The extra caffeine was much needed this morning. You didn't have to do that, but it is much appreciated.

I set down my phone and go back to my computer. My phone pings seconds later and I pick it up.

WORLD'S SEXIEST CATCHER

I just wanted to make your morning a little brighter, like you just made mine.

Well Damn. If he keeps talking like that, I'm going to have a hard time resisting him.

*No, Lucy. You don't need a man, especially a ball player who's gone half the year.*

WORLD'S SEXIEST CATCHER

Plus, I knew you wouldn't contact me willingly and I figured sending you goodies would at least get a text from you. So now I have your number.

Ok, he got me there.

ME

but I haven't done anything. And you got me. You're crafty, I'll give you points for that.

WORLD'S SEXIEST CATCHER

You didn't delete my number. That means you're thinking about it.

WORLD'S SEXIEST CATCHER

Or should I say me... 😊

Busted. That's all I've been thinking about. Thus the lack of sleep and need for coffee. But I don't need him to know that.

ME

No, I just forgot to hit the delete button. But now that you mention it...

WORLD'S SEXIEST CATCHER

You wound me, and after I provide you with caffeine and sugary treats?

ME

You're right. I'm sorry. I guess I'll keep your number... for now.

WORLD'S SEXIEST CATCHER

I'll take it.

I look at the clock and quickly type out one last text.

ME

I have to go, my first patient is here, but thank you again.

WORLD'S SEXIEST CATCHER

Anytime Coach. Have a good day.

I put my phone on silent and put it in my desk drawer. I push all thoughts of Kessler out of my brain and get to work.

It's 12:30 before I stop for lunch. The morning has been busy, as usual, but it makes the day go by quickly, so I don't mind. I take my phone out of my drawer and see my screen full of notifications. I click on the text thread from Kara.

KARA
Don't freak out.

KARA
Someone leaked a picture of Kessler at our practice.

KARA
and there's an article.

My heart jumps into my throat as I click on the link.

*Is Davis off the Market?*

*Kessler Davis, star catcher for the Silverbacks, was recently spotted at a little league practice on Wednesday, looking awfully comfy with their coach, Lucy Carver, 31. Carver and her team were recently seen at a Silverbacks game, where they met some of the players afterward for an outreach program the team runs. Did Davis and Carver hit it off there?*

I scroll down and see the team picture with the MLB players from Monday. The next picture is of me and Kessler at practice Wednesday. It was taken when he was helping me with my swing. From the picture, it looks like we're having an intimate moment, and was completely taken out of context.

*Fuck.*

This is why I don't do relationships, especially with ballplayers. There's no privacy and I don't need anyone digging into my life. I scroll down to finish the rest of the article.

*We reached out to Davis' agent who denied any relationship, saying it's just a part of Davis' mission of giving back to the community.*

It goes on to list past things Kessler has done over the years to give back to the community. I click out of the article, feeling like an idiot. Of course, Kessler doesn't want a relationship with me. I knew it and I allowed myself to get sucked in. This is probably just a fun game for him. Once he's bored, he'll toss me to the side.

*But his feelings felt real at dinner.*

No, that was just him turning on the charm, all athletes have it. Been there. Not interested in going back.

My phone buzzes again. I look down and see his contact across my screen. Against my better judgment, I open it.

WORLD'S SEXIEST CATCHER

> Lucy, there was an article published, someone leaked a picture of us at practice. Please don't read it.

I chew on the inside of my cheek, my finger hovering over the reply button.

*Fuck it.*

I hit reply.

ME

> Too late. But don't worry Kessler, I knew it wasn't real.

Ok, so for a minute a small part of me was hoping it was, but that bitch better sit down and shut up from now on.

WORLD'S SEXIEST CATCHER

No, Lucy, it is. I meant what I said the other night, and today. I asked my agent to publish that to throw the media off. I'm not ready to share you.

I read the text, then read it again.

*He wouldn't be trying so hard if he was lying.*

That small part of me pipes up. My phone buzzes again.

WORLD'S SEXIEST CATCHER

Please Lucy, trust me.

Trust him? I barely know him.

ME

I'm sorry Kessler, I just. I don't know.

WORLD'S SEXIEST CATCHER

Don't give up on me yet Lucy. I'll earn your trust.

I want to block his number and be done with this whole thing, but I can't bring myself to do it. He's done nothing wrong. Kara would tell me I'm just projecting from my past, and I know she's right. Why does this have to be so hard?

ME

Ok.

I put my phone back on silent and shove it into my desk. I look at my untouched lunch and put the lid back on it, having lost my appetite. I'm about to work on some patient notes when a knock sounds at my office door.

*What now?*

"Come in," I call out.

My door opens and a huge bouquet of flowers walks in. Rhonda peeks out behind it. "Delivery," she says in a sing-song voice. She sets the beautiful array of stargazer lilies with sprigs of baby's breath and lavender on my desk and plucks the card out, handing it over to me. I take the card from her and open it.

*These reminded me of you,*
*Kessler*

Five simple words and my stomach is doing things it's never done before. I've never had anyone give me flowers, and here I am getting flowers from someone I haven't even agreed to go out with.

*Yet.*

Rhonda clears her throat, startling me from my thoughts. "Muffin tops and coffee from your favorite place this morning, beautiful flowers this afternoon. Looks like someone has an admirer," she says, amusement in her voice.

I feel my cheeks heat.

"Don't be embarrassed hun." She sits in one of the chairs across from me. Rhonda is in her 60s and shows no signs of retiring. I only hope to be half as active as her when I'm her age. She's been the office mother hen since I was an intern. She and her husband, Frank, never had children of their own, so in a sense, I guess we're her children. "You deserve to be happy. I'm not saying you need a man to make you happy." She gives me a wink. "But it doesn't hurt if one does." She holds her hands out. "Or woman, I don't judge. Love is love." She shrugs. "Either way, you deserve someone who makes you happy."

I huff a laugh. "Thanks Rhonda." I pause worrying my lip. "But what if it doesn't work out? I, I just don't know if I can go through the heartbreak." I pick at the torn cuticle on my thumb. "And what about Hudson? It's not just me I have to think about." I let out a sigh and slouch into my chair.

Rhonda uncrosses her legs and sits forward. "Honey, how do you know it'll end, if you don't begin?" She stands and walks to the door. "Just something to think about." She closes the door behind her, leaving me to think the rest of my lunch.

I'M SITTING in bed later that night reading the latest Amelia Morgan book when my phone pings with a text. I look at my watch and see it's 9 pm. The only person who texts me this late is Kara. Grabbing my phone, I look at the screen and see it's Kessler. A swarm of butterflies take flight seeing his name on my screen. I didn't text him after receiving the flowers. After the article and my conversation with Rhonda, I was in a weird place and needed time to process my thoughts and feelings. Apparently, that time is up now. I unlock my phone and click on the waiting text.

WORLD'S SEXIEST CATCHER

Hey Beautiful. I'm sorry if I'm texting too late. I just got back to the hotel. I hope you had a good rest of your day.

Beautiful? He thinks I'm beautiful?

> **ME**
>
> Hi. Not too late. I'm just reading. I had an ok rest of my day. Thank you for the flowers by the way. I've never had anyone give me flowers before. They make my office smell amazing.

> **ME**
>
> Good game btw. That throwdown to second in the 5th was spot on.

**WORLD'S SEXIEST CATCHER**

I'm sorry, I think I misread that. You've never been given flowers before???

**WORLD'S SEXIEST CATCHER**

You watched my game huh? And thanks. At least my fielding is decent because my batting is still shit. The only good hit I had was the day I met you. Maybe you're my good luck charm *wink face emoji*

I snort. I'm no one's good luck charm.

> **ME**
>
> Uh no? I don't date, sooo there's no one to give me flowers.

> **ME**
>
> and we watched our favorite team's game. You just happen to play for them. As for the batting, you'll get there. Your injury was not minor and honestly it's just impressive you made it back at all.

**WORLD'S SEXIEST CATCHER**

Challenge accepted.

Challenge? What challenge? No, no one challenged anyone. I'm about to say as much when another text comes through.

> **WORLD'S SEXIEST CATCHER**
> So you're impressed by me? Good to know. And what are you reading?

> **ME**
> Such a healthy ego you have. And a book...

> **WORLD'S SEXIEST CATCHER**
> Comes with the territory. And thank you Captain Obvious. I didn't know that's what you were supposed to do with those. What book are you reading Lucy?

> **WORLD'S SEXIEST CATCHER**
> And don't say one with words. My brother, Judd, already used that one last time I asked him.

I laugh, damn it. That's what I was going to say.

> **ME**
> I should say the latest article on the benefits of redlight therapy, but that would be a lie.

It isn't a total lie. I did pick up the article earlier and start it, but I just wasn't in the mood to read it, so now it's lying on my nightstand.

> **WORLD'S SEXIEST CATCHER**
> So what's the truth?

> **ME**
> *sigh* smut. I'm reading one of the best smutty books I've ever read in my life.

> **WORLD'S SEXIEST CATCHER**
> *Gasp* Lucy... are you... are you a smut slut?

**ME**

Guilty as charged. I love smut and I cannot lie.

**WORLD'S SEXIEST CATCHER**

Who's your favorite author?

**ME**

Amelia Morgan, hands down.

**WORLD'S SEXIEST CATCHER**

Why?

**ME**

Her writing is just *chef kiss* She can rip my heart out and make me laugh within a few chapters. And the scenarios she comes up with. Her brain is an amazing place.

**WORLD'S SEXIEST CATCHER**

Sounds like you have a girl crush Lucy.

**ME**

I won't deny that lol

**WORLD'S SEXIEST CATCHER**

I might be a little jealous.

**ME**

You shouldn't be.

**WORLD'S SEXIEST CATCHER**

Oh yeah?

**ME**

Yeah, you couldn't compete with her.

**WORLD'S SEXIEST CATCHER**

Ouch

**ME**

**WORLD'S SEXIEST CATCHER**

So, what's this book about?

> **ME**
> A baseball player who fake dates his friend to help her out and ends up falling for her.

> **WORLD'S SEXIEST CATCHER**
> Why are they fake dating?

> **ME**
> Because her Ex is a dick.

> **WORLD'S SEXIEST CATCHER**
> 😉 tell me how you really feel

> **ME**
> Sorry, I just really get into these books.

IT'S my only chance at romance. Well, so I thought, But I don't say that.

> **WORLD'S SEXIEST CATCHER**
> I can tell, but don't be sorry. I like a woman with passion.

*Shit.*

I can see myself being passionate about his man. Talking with him is easy. Effortless. Like we've known each other for years instead of days. He's hilarious, and sweet, and he's so good with Hudson. Which is what matters most to me.

*But he's a baseball player and gone a lot, and the media...*

I just don't know if I can handle that. Needing to talk this out, I pick up my phone and send a text.

> **ME**
> SOS.

Not even five seconds later, my phone rings. Kara. I accept the call.

"Speak to me," Kara says, not even bothering with a hello.

"Well, hello to you too."

"Psh, we don't need to bother with formalities when you text me SOS. Now, what's up."

I pick at my blanket. "So, I was texting Kessler," I start

"Hold on a second." I hear her shifting her phone. "Say that again, I had to make sure I actually called the right person."

"Oh shut up. *Anyways*, like I said, I was texting Kessler." I pause trying to figure out how to get the words out.

"Aaaand?" Kara prompts impatiently.

"I-" I sigh. "Shit, I like him,Kar."

Kara snorts. "Ya think? You guys were practically eye fucking each other at practice the other night. You know, when you weren't avoiding him like the plague."

"I was not avoiding him, I was busy," I state matter of factly.

"Yeah, busy avoiding him."

"Whatever, anyways back to the problem."

"And what exactly is the problem?"

"The problem *is* Kara-" I start, trying not to shout since Hudson is just down that hall. "I don't *want* to like him. He's a baseball player, and he's gone for like what? Half the year?"

Kara interrupts me, "Not really, but we can figure that out later."

"Whatever," I say continuing my rant. "And then there's the media, I don't want them digging into my life. What if they." I stop and lower my voice. "What if they dig into my past? And not only that, but he's incredibly sweet and kind."

"And fucking hot," Kara adds.

I snort. "And fucking hot, I don't know what to do with that. He practically begged me to give him a chance and show me he's different. And as much as it goes against everything I've ever said, I want to. I want him to prove me wrong."

"Still not seeing the problem. Well, besides the media part, but we can figure that out," she says like it's no big deal.

"Kara, I'm just. I'm scared."

"Oh, honey," she says softly, all notes of teasing gone from her voice. "It's perfectly normal to feel like this. Especially since you've shut down any interest in the past."

"So why can't I shut this one down?" I pout.

Kara chuckles. "Because you actually feel the same. It's easy to shut someone down you don't feel the same about. But now, you have feelings too."

"It's really annoying that you're making sense."

"I know, It's a gift." She pauses, then asks, "So, what are you going to do?"

I sink down lower into my pillow. "I don't know. That's why I called you! Make a decision for me. I don't wanna."

Kara laughs. "You know what you need to do."

"Hide my feelings and deny everything?" I ask hopefully.

"No. Try again."

I groan. "Put on my big girl panties and own up to that shit," I mutter.

"That's right," Kara says.

My phone pings with a text and I pull it from my ear to look. "He just sent me another text."

"Ooo what's it say?" Kara screeches into my ear.

"Jesus Kar, that was my ear."

"Sorry, sorry," she apologizes, lowering her voice, "I'm just so excited. Hey, isn't it like two hours ahead there?"

"Yeah, he said he just got back to the hotel room when he first texted me."

"Aww, he's staying up late to talk to you," she croons. "How cute! Now what does the text say?"

"Just hold your horses lady," I say, switching over to the speaker and clicking on the text.

WORLD'S SEXIEST CATCHER

> You still there? Did I lose you to your author?

I read Kara the text.

"What does he mean by that?" she asks.

I read her the texts Kessler and I sent to each other.

"Girl, you didn't text him back?"

"Uh NO! I called you and had my freak out after I realized I freaking like this man."

"OK, you've had your freak out. Now text him back! Tell him how you feel even."

I huff. "I'll text him back, but I'm not ready to tell him just yet. I need some time for it to sink in."

"Mull it over, sleep on it. Whatever. But Luce, don't hide your feelings. You deserve to be happy."

"Why does everyone think I'm not happy? I'm freaking happy damn it."

Kara laughs. "Yeah, it totally sounds like it. And I didn't say you weren't happy. I just meant, you deserve to share your life with someone." She pauses and quietly adds, "You don't have to be alone."

I sigh. "Neither do you Kar, but I get what you're saying. Thank you, for always being here to talk me through my thoughts."

"Hey, what are chosen sisters for? Now, text that fine specimen of a man back."

I laugh. "Ok, ok. Night girly."

I hang up and pull up my text thread with Kessler.

ME

> Sorry. No, Kara called. We were just going over things for the tournament next weekend.

Lies, but he doesn't need to know that.

WORLD'S SEXIEST CATCHER

> A coach's job is never done. You'll have to let me know how they do. We don't get back until late Sunday.

ME

> I can definitely do that.

WORLD'S SEXIEST CATCHER

> Well I better get to bed. Good night Coach.

I smile at the nickname.

ME

> Goodnight Kessler.

# CHAPTER 7

## Kessler

### ONE WEEK LATER

I AM DRAGGING MY ASS THIS MORNING. I'VE BEEN staying up late all week to talk with Lucy and while it's been 100 percent worth it, it's catching up to me. I'm usually one of the first out of my hotel room and on the bus. I hop up the steps and look down the aisle, today it looks like I'm one of the last. I see Reese hold up his hand and I make my way to him. Plopping down in my seat, I pull out my phone. I see a text from my mom, reminding me about dinner again tomorrow. I let out a sigh.

"Rough night?" Rees asks, messing around with his own phone.

"Not rough, just…late," I say, texting my mom back.

> I actually forgot. Can you please 🙏 cancel with Judy.

Reese looks over at me with interest. "Late?"

Brent pops his head over the seat in front of us. "Why that late night Davis? Did you have a girl in your room?" he asks, wiggling his eyes up and down.

I roll my eyes. "No."

"You sure? I could have sworn I heard a woman's moans last night," he says.

"Pretty sure I would know if I had a moaning woman in my room jackass. It was probably coming from the rookie's room. He was on the other side of you."

Brent snaps his fingers and points at me. "He's always bringing women back to his room."

I nod but don't say anything further. I lay my head back against the seat and close my eyes. I can still feel their eyes on me, so I open one and look at them. "Can I help you?"

"You didn't answer the question," Reese pushes.

I yawn and scrub a hand over my face. "What question would that be?"

"Why the late night?" Reese and Brent ask in unison.

"Jesus," I whisper. "I was just on my phone too late."

"Porn site?" Brent questions.

"Jesus fuck Brent," I complain. "You being celibate is not worth it."

"The fuck it's not! I'm the only one in the lineup who has been consistent with their batting."

"That's skill and practice, not celibacy," Reese chimes in.

My phone vibrates with a text and I ignore Brent's response and open the text.

MOM

No, I will not cancel with them. I think you and Claire would be a lovely match.

I groan inwardly and type my response.

ME

Don't make a big deal out of it, but I've been talking to someone and I really like her.

My phone starts vibrating and I look down to see my mom calling.

*Fucking great.*

"Mom," I answer

"You're seeing someone and didn't bother to tell me?" she says, sounding confused and if I'm hearing correctly, hurt.

"Not really," I say, but she doesn't hear me over her talking.

"And why didn't you say anything last week when I brought it up at dinner?" she demands. "I wouldn't have mentioned dinner to Judy at all."

I rub my eyes with my pointer finger and thumb. "Because I-" But I don't get to finish because I'm cut off again.

"Are you bringing her with you Sunday?" she asks, sounding hopeful. "Because-"

This time I cut my mom off.

"Jesus, Mom just stop!" I shout, a little louder than I intended but I just need her to... stop. Talking. I look around and notice most of the guys staring at me. I get up and step off the bus, walking back towards the hotel a little bit.

I let out a sigh and apologize. "I'm sorry, I didn't mean to snap. I haven't been sleeping or playing very well and I'm just ready for this stretch of away games to be over, so I can be back home in my own bed."

She's quiet and I hope I didn't hurt her feelings. I hear her adjust the phone before she speaks. " I'm sorry too Kessler. I didn't mean to push, I'm just surprised to hear you're seeing someone."

Kicking at a rock in front of me,I watch it skip down the cement. "Well, I'm not exactly seeing her, yet."

"I don't understand?" Mom says, sounding confused.

"I met someone at my last home game."

"A fan?" she asks, concern in her voice.

"Well, yes, and no. She's a coach for the little league team we had at one of our outreach nights." I pause thinking back to when I saw her that first time and how drawn to her I was. Well, am.

"And?" my mom prompts, bringing me out of my thoughts.

"And I went to one of their practices to help out, and we ended up going to dinner at Tony's, who funny enough, we both know well. I asked her out that night, but then an article was printed with a picture of us at the practice, which freaked her out for reasons I'm not sure of yet and I've been on this stretch of away games so I haven't been able to take her out. We have been texting back and forth for a week though and," I let out a breath, "I really like her, Mom."

Mom's quiet for a minute, probably processing the word vomit I just let out. "Wow, Kessler, I feel like I've missed a lot," she says with a hint of sadness in her voice. "So, she has a child?"

"Yeah, Hudson. He's 11." I smile. "He's a really cool kid and a catcher, like me."

"Wow, how old is she?"

I think back to what the article said. "Uh 31, I think?"

"She had him so young. And the father? Is he in the picture?"

I see Coach Dixon and the rest of the coaching staff come

out of the hotel. He gives me the 'wrap it up' signal. I nod my understanding to him.

"I asked her about him and she just said he's not in the picture and never had been, but I have to go, Mom. Coach is getting on the bus. I'll call you later."

"Ok, good luck today and I will expect a call later, I have more questions. Like does she have a name?"

I laugh. " Her name is Lucy and I know you do, Mom. I promise I'll call you later. I love you"

"Love you too sweetie."

I disconnect the call and hop back on the bus, I take my seat next to Reese, who's staring at me, eyebrows raised. "Everything good?"

I nod. "Everything's good. Just Mom, being Mom."

He nods. He knows my mom well. She's pretty much adopted him as one of her own. I wouldn't be surprised if she texts him and asks him about Lucy. I tap on my text thread with Lucy and read over a few of our texts from last night as we make our way to the stadium. I'm itching to text her and see how the boys are playing in their first game.I look at the time, they should be close to being done with their first game. I click over to TikTok to kill some time. I'm watching one my brother sent me when a text pops up on my screen from Lucy.

LUCY

Boys won 4-3.

I see more dots appear then disappear. They bounce on my screen again, then disappear again. I catch myself bouncing my leg up and down in anticipation. Finally another message pops up.

LUCY

Hudson had a beautiful throw down to second
in the last inning and got the out. Kinda
reminded me of someone else I know.

Pride fills my chest, and a huge grin takes over my face.

ME

Hell yes! That's awesome. I wish I could have
seen it.

LUCY

Me too...

That aching feeling appears in my chest again. I rub at it, like it'll help ease the feeling, but it doesn't.

ME

Tell him I'm proud of him.

LUCY

I will.

"Good news?" Reese asks, nodding towards my phone.

I look at my screen, then back at him. "Remember that Little League team we worked with last week?"

A shit eating grin spreads across his face. "Oh, you mean the one with the hot coach you have a thing for?"

Brent's head pops over the seat.

*Great.*

"You're talking to the hot coach?" He's not exactly quiet and a few of my teammates look over at us with confused stares.

I look up at the ceiling and back at Brent. "Jesus Brent, say it louder. I don't think everyone heard you."

"Sorry, sorry. I just, Oh-" he stops mid sentence, giving me a shit eating grin of his own. "Is that who kept you up late last night?"

"I need to find new friends," I mutter under my breath.

"Sorry bud, but you're stuck with us." Reese tips his head at my phone. "Spill."

So I do. I spill everything. What happened after that practice. Our dinner at Tony's. The stuff I had sent to her office. The damn article and the texts we've been sending each other. Her sending me updates on the boy's games today. By the time I'm done spilling my guts like a high school girl, we're out on the field and going through warm-ups.

"So, you've been texting for a week and she hasn't given you an answer yet about a date?" Brent asks, tossing a ball to me.

I shake my head, catching the ball and throwing it back. "That article really upset her and I don't want to push her. But at the same time she might need a push? I don't know."

"You need to prove to her that you're worth taking a chance on," Reese says, catching a ball Duke Keller, our first baseman, throws to him.

I jump for a ball Brent overthrows and catch it in my mit. "I know, but how?"

Duke, who's usually the quiet one of the group, speaks up. "Show up." Two words, that's it.

"Care to elaborate?" I ask.

He sighs like I'm a moron. "Show up, any way possible. Be there for her, and her kid. You said the dad isn't in the picture. Maybe she's worried you won't stick around either."

*Well fuck.*

Duke coming in with the wisdom, as usual. We finish with our warm-up routine and head to the locker room to change. I'm not in the lineup today, but injuries happen. I'm mulling over how I can show her I'm serious about pursuing a relationship with her, when Reese plops down on the bench next to me.

"So I've been thinking," he starts

I raise my eyebrows at him. "Did it hurt?"

"Fuck off, you want help with Hot Coach or not?" He gives me a pointed stare

"She has a name," I growl back at him.

He gives me a smirk. "I know, I just like seeing you get worked up over a chick."

"You're an asshole."

He shrugs his shoulders. "Yeah, but an asshole who has a brilliant idea. Do you want to hear it, or keep insulting me?"

I let out a sigh. "Give it to me." Hoping it's actually a good idea, because I have nothing.

He cracks his knuckles, like he's getting to work. "They have a tournament this weekend right?"

"Yes, I just told you that," I bite out.

"Chill grouch. I have a point," he says, holding up a hand to me. "They'll play tomorrow no matter what, it just depends on how they do in their next game, that determines how many games they play tomorrow."

I give him the go ahead motion.

"We fly home tomorrow morning. What if you flew home tonight?" I stare at him, the pieces he's laying out clicking into place.

"And show up at the tournament tomorrow," I finish for him.

He gives me a finger gun. "Bingo."

I mull the details over in my head, grabbing my phone to look at flights. Reese interrupts me.

"I already looked at flights, there's one heading home two hours after the game, You're already booked for it."

"I take back what I said earlier."

"Oh, I'm not an asshole?"

I slap him on the back, laughing. "No, you're still an asshole. I just meant about you not being bright. You have your moments."

He flips me off but gives me a grin.

FIVE HOURS later and I'm boarding the plane. I was worried I wouldn't make it. We went into the 10th inning tied 2-2. Duke came in clutch and hit a walk-off homer, sealing our win. I get to my seat and check my messages. I was in a rush getting off the field, so I didn't get a chance to look earlier. I take my seat next to the window and see texts from Judd and Lucy. I open Lucy's first, eager to see how the boys did.

LUCY

> Boys pulled it off. 8-7. It was a battle. We don't play again until 3pm tomorrow for the Championship.

Perfect. That gives me plenty of time. I text her back telling her to congratulate Hudson for me and that I'll try to check in with him before his game tomorrow. I chuckle to myself, if they only knew what I have planned.

A figure appears at my side and I look up to see a woman staring at me. She's around my age, pretty, but I find myself thinking she's nothing compared to Lucy. I give her a small smile. She blinks a few times then snaps herself out of whatever trance she was in, stores her carry-on above and takes a seat next to me.

"I, sorry, I didn't mean to stare, it's just, you look familiar."

"Uh, yeah, I get that a lot. Must have one of those faces," I comment back politely. I try not to draw attention to myself. So if this lady can't place me, I sure as shit am not going to place myself.

I move on to Judd's message.

JUDD

SOOOOO Mom called....

I rub my eyes with my thumb and pointer finger. Great, Mom told Judd. I pull my fingers from my eyes and continue to read his texts.

JUDD

A single Mom huh?

JUDD

That's hot.

ME

You were adopted.

JUDD

🙄 Nice try. I'm not 9 years old, won't work this time.

ME

😏 worth a shot.

JUDD

You still didn't answer me.

ME

Was there a question?

JUDD

Who is she?

The flight attendant comes over the speaker preparing us for take-off and asks all devices be switched off for take-off.

ME

Looks like I'm taking off, talk later bro.

I switch my phone off and pull the book Lucy mentioned the other night out of my carry-on. I went out and bought it the next day and I have to admit, I like it more than I thought I would. I feel my aisle mate looking at me again. Ignoring it, I flip my book open to where my bookmark is. The engines start to gear up and I can feel us slowly start to taxi the runway. The woman next to me sucks in a breath, I turn my head slightly to look at her. She has her eyes closed and she's gone pale.

*Great.*

I close my book and clear my throat.

"Don't like flying?" I ask.

"Nnot particularly," she stutters out. The plane accelerates and her hand slams down onto my arm in a vice grip.

Her nails dig into my skin. I place my other hand over hers, trying to comfort her and ease her grip at the same time. "I used to hate flying too, but I have to do it a lot for my job, so I had to find a way to get over that quickly," I say, trying to make conversation with her and get her mind off take-off.

"How, what did you do to get over it?" she asks, her eyes are still closed, but her grip eases a little.

"Well," I say, holding up my book, "I read most of the time. If I can get into the story before the plane even starts taxiing, I don't even notice we're taking off. Music helps too."

She cracks her eyes open and looks at me, then at my book. "I wouldn't picture you as someone who reads those types of books."

"It's my first one actually. I normally read thrillers or mysteries," I admit.

"Well, it's a great first choice," she says, relaxing back into her seat more.

"You've read it?" I ask, surprised.

The plane finally reaches its speed and lifts off into the air. The woman sucks in a breath, but doesn't appear nearly as frightened as she was earlier. She releases her breath and turns to answer me.

"Yeah, I've read all of Amelia Morgan's books, she's the Queen," she states.

I chuckle. "So I've heard. My uh, friend said the same thing the other day, which is why I picked this up. I wanted to see what the fuss was about."

The plane levels out and everything settles. The woman lets go of my arm and tucks her hand back into her lap. The fastened seat belt light clicks off and the flight attendants start making their way down the aisle with refreshments.

She clears her throat and gives me a shy smile. "Well your friend has great taste. I'm Layla by the way." She holds her hand out.

I take her hand and give it a small shake. "Kessler. Nice to meet you."

"Likewise. Thank you by the way. For being so kind. I hope I didn't hurt your arm." She nods at my arm.

I wave her off. "No thanks necessary. You're good."

The flight attendant reaches our seats and we both get water and some snacks. We spend the rest of the flight chatting. I learn she's a marketing executive for the Toronto Turnips Hockey Team. I disclose to her that I play ball for the Silverbacks. She snaps her fingers.

"That's why you look so familiar."

I grimace. "Yeah, sorry. I try not to draw attention to myself."

She holds her hand up. "Please, don't apologize. I get it." She looks around the plane then back at me. "But why are you flying commercial? Doesn't the team have a charter plane? Didn't you guys have a game today?"

"Uh yeah. I had to fly back early for something."

Layla laughs. "Because that's not evasive at all."

"I helped out with a little league team and they have their championship game tomorrow. I don't want to miss it."

"Oh, that's adorable. You know that would make a really good PR article for you and your team."

I raise an eyebrow at her.

"Sorry. Just my marketing brain. You probably don't want the attention."

I nod my head. "Yeah. I'm not even telling anyone I'm going to be there. I'm hoping I can stay hidden until the end. Less distraction that way."

She nods her head in understanding.

The fasten seatbelt sign clicks on and the captain comes over the speaker letting us know we're preparing for the descent, halting our conversation. Layla looks much more relaxed this time and I sit back in my seat going over the plan in my head one more time for tomorrow.

I'M JUST WALKING into my apartment when my phone goes off. I look down at the Caller ID and see my mom's name. Well better face the music I guess. I set my bags down by my door and hit the answer button on my phone. "Hey, Mom."

"Hi sweetie, are you free to chat? I know you're probably with the guys, but I was hoping to finish our conversation from earlier."

I set my keys down on the counter and head straight to the fridge and grab a beer. I twist the top off and take a few swigs before answering.

"I'm free to chat, I'm actually back at my apartment." Heading into the living room, I plop down on my couch, relaxing back into the cushions.

"Oh, I thought you were scheduled to fly back tomorrow morning." Surprise laces her voice.

I take another swig of my beer, before sitting up and setting it on the table and grabbing the remote to switch on the TV. "The team is, but I caught a flight back early. Hudson and the boys play tomorrow at three and I didn't want to miss it."

Silence follows on the other end of the phone. I pull the phone away from my ear to see if we're still connected, we are. "Mom?"

"Sorry, I'm here, I'm here." She clears her throat and continues, " I guess you just caught me off guard with all of this."

I take a deep breath and let it out. I know I've been keeping more to myself after my injury, trying to get back on track, but I realize that's also included my mom. I've always been close with my parents. I guess I've been pushing them away this last year and now I've unintentionally hurt my mom.

"I know, I'm sorry." I pause and make the decision to tell her everything. "I know I've been pushing away this past year. Getting injured and not knowing if I would be able to come back to baseball has taken a toll on my mental health," I admit to her.

"Kessler, you know you can always come to your father and I about these things. We didn't want to push you, we knew you were sorting through things." She pauses and I know what she's going to say before she says it. "Like I've always told you, as much as we all love it, there is more to life than baseball."

I tell her what I've always told her in response to that. "But baseball is my life."

She lets out a soft laugh. "I know." There's a few beats of silence before she adds, " But, I think you're beginning to realize what I've always meant by that."

I nod even though she can't see me. "I am," I admit. "Baseball has always been my family, but after not having it in my life while I was recovering, I realized what I was missing. I thought I would shake the empty feeling once I got back to it, but there's still something missing." I pause knowing once I say this out loud, there's no going back.

"When I met Lucy, I felt something. I thought it was just an attraction, but once I started spending more time with her and Hudson and texting with her all week, I realized I wanted a family. I wanted them as a family. Lucy is amazing. She's smart, funny and absolutely beautiful, and she doesn't even know it. And Hudson." I laugh and shake my head. "He reminds me a lot of myself when I was his age. Completely obsessed with baseball. He's a funny kid and Lucy has done an incredible job with him."

"Sounds like you're completely smitten," Mom says, humor in her voice.

"I am," I admit "I really am. I missed them while I was gone, and I barely know them. Is that crazy?"

"No honey, it's not crazy. Sometimes our hearts know before our brains do." She pauses before adding, "I'm sorry for being pushy lately, you know with Judy and her daughter. I guess I just thought if you had someone to share your life with, you'd come back to us. I've missed you, Kessler. I've always just wanted what was best for you. For both my boys."

*Shit.*

I know I've been going through a lot this past year, but I never thought about what it was doing to my parents, my mom especially. She's been there for me through everything. I know it's killed her to not go through this big change in my life with me. Not because she didn't want to, but because I didn't let her.

"No, Mom, it's me who should be apologizing. While, yes, I was annoyed with you pushing women onto me."

"I was not pushing women onto you, Kessler," she interrupts.

"You were, but never mind that. What I was trying to say is, I'm sorry for pushing you away. Dealing with the fact that I might have had a career ending injury hit me hard. I needed time. But that's not an excuse for shutting you out."

"Thank you, Kessler. Now that we've gotten all that mushy stuff out of the way, tell me all about Lucy and Hudson. They are coming to dinner tomorrow right?"

I laugh and feel a huge weight lift from my chest that I didn't even know I was carrying around. I've missed good conversations with my mom.

"I'm hoping they do. They don't know I'm coming to the game. I don't want to distract the boys from playing their best. I'm going to ask them to dinner after the game."

I tell my mom my plan, which she is excited about. Then I tell her everything about Lucy and Hudson that I know. Which isn't a whole lot, but I'm hoping, if everything goes to plan, it will change.

# CHAPTER 8

## Lucy

IT'S A HALF HOUR BEFORE OUR CHAMPIONSHIP GAME and the boys are warming up by tossing the ball back and forth to each other. They're joking around and having a good time. Nerves nowhere in sight, at least for them. I'm nervous as hell for them. These boys battled this weekend and a win would be the icing on the cake. I check my phone for what seems like the hundredth time. No new notifications. Kessler texted me this morning telling me to tell the boys good luck for him and that he wishes he could be at the game, but there's been nothing since.

"Nothing?" Kara asks, looking at my phone and then at me.

I shake my head, slipping my phone into my back pocket. "No, but I know he's flying today, so he's probably at the airport, or even on the plane by now."

"Wouldn't it be something if he actually made it here to watch?"

It would be something, but unfortunately, that's not possible. "Yeah, but he's in Ohio, or was in Ohio, I don't know when they're scheduled to fly back today." I shrug my shoulders and lower my voice, so only Kara can hear. "Which is another reason why this would never work. He'd never be here. They play eight to nine months out of the year, which means he's out of state for at least half that time."

"Hey, what happened to giving him a chance?"

I sigh, letting my shoulders drop. "I was, but then when I got up this morning, I just kept thinking how I missed him, then he texted me and I thought, 'is this what it would be like?' Having a relationship through text and phone conversations?" I shake my head. "And what about Hudson, he's already grown up without a dad, I don't want someone to *kinda* be in his life. I want fully present, here for his games, for him, for us. It'll never work."

Kara turns to me and grabs my upper arms. "Lucy, I say this with all the love and support in the world, but shut up."

I raise my eyebrows and open my mouth to say something but she stops me.

"You won't know if it'll work until you try. I've known you for, what? Nine years now?" I nod my head and she continues, "You have *always* put Hudson first, in everything. And that's admirable. But don't you think it's time to put you first?"

I stare at her knowing she's right, but not wanting to admit it. "Plus, it's not like he's going to be playing baseball forever. Realistically he has what? Another Five years *maybe*?" She shrugs her shoulders. "Seems like a small price to pay for happiness."

I tip my head back and look at the sky like an answer is going to magically fall out of it.

"You're right," I mutter

Kara cups her hand around her ear. "I'm sorry, I didn't quite catch that."

I huff and raise my voice a bit. "I said you're right. Are you happy now?"

"Not until you accept that date," she says.

"Let's just win this game and we can talk about it after."

I put my fingers to my lips and let out a whistle, letting the boys know I need them in the dugout. There are a lot of people here for this game from both teams and the others who didn't make the championship game. I look out and am drawn to someone wearing a hat and sunglasses in the sea of people. It's sunny out, so it's not like it's abnormal attire. An influx of people come in and I lose the person I was staring at. If I didn't know any better I would have thought it was Kessler, but that's impossible. I mentally give myself a shake, I need to focus and get my head in the game.

"Ok boys, listen up." I wait until they're all quiet and eyes are on me. "I know this is a huge crowd, bigger than we've ever played in front of before." The boys nod in agreement.

"But don't let that distract you. We're here to do what we do best, and that's play baseball. You guys have worked too hard to get here to let something like a few extra people get in the way. Focus on one play at a time, talk to each other, and trust each other. No matter what, you guys should be proud of making it this far." I look out over the 12 pairs of eyes staring at me and hold my hand out in the middle.

"Raptors on three." Kara and the boys all put their hands on top of mine. "One, two, three. RAPTORS!" we all yell in unison.

We're playing as the home team, so the other team is up to bat first. I give the boys their positions and they hustle out to their designated spots. Hudson is still putting on his pads, so I run out and help Joey, our starting pitcher, warm up. He gets a handful of throws in by the time Hudson is done getting on his gear and replacing me. I'm heading back to the dugout when I feel the sense of being watched, which is odd because I know there are a bunch of people here right now watching, but I feel like *I'm* specifically being watched. I turn to look out, but no one stands out of the crowd.

"You good, Coach?" Kara asks.

I nod. "All good." I give her a big grin. "Let's do this."

## KESSLER

I get to the field in plenty of time to find a spot to watch the game, yet hide in the crowd. I have a plain black hat and sunglasses on, hoping no one will realize it's me. I see Lucy talking to the boys in the dugout before the game. It's taking everything I have not to rush over there and wrap my arms around her, but I know that would be the ultimate distraction for the boys. I see the boys break and head out to their positions. Lucy heads to home plate to warm up the pitcher and I stare at her ass as she squats down in the catching position. I can't help but imagine what it would feel like to grip it in both my hands while she's riding me. I give myself a mental shake.

*Get it together Kessler, getting a hard on during a little league game would not be good.*

Lucy stands to head back to the dugout as Hudson comes to claim his position but turns around and stares directly at me.

*Shit.*

A group of people walk in front of me and I move with them, not wanting her to know I'm here. I decide to head to the outfield where there are less people and more places for me to hide. I'm not as close to the action as I would like, but that also means Lucy won't spot me either. My phone pings with a text and I pull it out of my pocket to see who it is.

JUDD
Thanks Dickhead.

ME
Woah Woah Woah. WTF did I do.

JUDD
Now that you've decided you're in love, Moms set her sights on me.

Love? Wait, no one said anything about being in love.

ME
Hold the fuck up. No one said anything about love. All I told Mom was that I was interested in someone.

JUDD
Better tell that to Mom then, because she specifically said the word love.

I scratch my head and think back to my conversation with my mom. I know for a fact I didn't say I was in love with Lucy. Because that would be crazy, right? We haven't even had a date yet.

ME
Mom's getting old.

JUDD
I'll tell her you said that.

ME
Go ahead, I'm not scared.

Lies. I'm completely scared, but if I bluff, Judd might buy it and not say anything.

JUDD

Great, because I just texted her 🐱

ME

Fucking Dick.

JUDD

👆 🐱

I'm in the middle of replying to Judd when my phone rings.

*MOM*

Fucking Judd. I release a huff and slide to answer.

"Hi, Mom."

"Kessler Howard Davis, did you call me *old*?"

I look up at the sky and sigh. "Technically? Yes, but I'm sure Judd made it sound worse than it is," I say, trying to get myself out of the hole.

"Mmmhmm ok, so tell me your version."

I'm half listening to my mom, half watching the game. Joey, the starting pitcher struck his first batter out and I fist pump.

"Kessler?"

"Oh, sorry. I was watching the game. Well, Judd was texting me. He was mad at me because it seems you've set your sights on his love life now that I'm interested in someone. Which by the way, I applaud. He mentioned I was in love, and I told him I never said I was in love. To which he said you told him I was. So actually, *Mother,* now that I think about it, don't you have some explaining to do?" I ask her, hoping putting this back on her gets me out of trouble. It doesn't.

"Oh please, you know for a fact you're in love, and there's

nothing wrong with it. So, just because you didn't say it out loud, doesn't mean it's not true and that you get to call me old," she says matter of factly.

The second batter hits a line drive to the shortstop, who catches it no problem. Two down.

I let out a resigned sigh. "Ok, Mom, I'm sorry I called you old. You're not. I just don't want everyone freaking out over something that hasn't happened yet. I haven't even got her to agree to go out on a date with me, so can we keep the 'L' word to a minimum, or you know non-existent, until I've actually gone out with her?"

"Yes, I'm sorry. I shouldn't have said anything to your brother. So you're at the game?" she asks, changing the subject.

"Yeah, the game just started a few minutes ago. We have one more out, then we're up to bat."

I hear my mom chuckle

"What?"I ask

"You say 'we', like they're your team. It's cute, and I'm happy for you, Kess."

I chuckle. "Thanks, Mom. I'm happy too. Now, get back to bugging Judd and let me focus on the game."

She laughs. "You got it. Just text me later and let me know how many to expect for dinner."

"I will Mom."

I disconnect the call and watch as Joey strikes out the third batter.

"Yeah, Raptors. Let's go!" I yell, clapping my hands a few times.

The other team takes the field and starts warming up. I haven't been this nervous for a baseball game since my rookie year in the majors. My mom's right. I'm completely invested. I see Lucy standing at third base and Kara at first. Our first batter takes steps up and takes his position. I squint to see who it is but can't quite make out the face. He lets two pitches go by him, one ball and one high strike. On the third pitch, he winds back and cracks it right in between shortstop and second, making it to first easily. The next batter I have no problem making out.

Hudson.

My nerves crank up and catch myself rocking back and forth onto my heels. The pitcher winds up and sends a ball just outside of the plate for ball one. He winds up again and sends a perfect strike right down the middle. Hudson watches it but doesn't swing. Strike one. I sway back and forth.

*Come on buddy, watch the ball.*

Another pitch sails over to the plate. This time Hudson swings, but misses. Strike two. I push out a breath and take off my hat running my hand through my hair. I replace the hat and watch as Hudson sets himself back up, determination in his stance. The pitcher nods his head and releases another pitch. This time Hudson is on it and makes contact.

*Crack.*

The ball sails between second and first and into the upper outfield.

"YES!" I yell, jumping up and down. Hudson makes it to first, and the first batter, who is freaking fast, makes it to third. He gives Lucy a fist bump and she taps his helmet.

"Is that your kid?" a guy standing next to me asks.

*Shit.*

"Eh, kind of. I'm a family friend," I answer, hoping that suffices.

The guy nods but doesn't say anything further.

The third and fourth batters end up striking out. The next batter comes up and I recognize Joey. He's got quite the swing on him from what I remember during our practice and if he can make contact he can at least get the kid on third base home. The pitcher winds up and lets one loose toward home. Joey doesn't even hesitate, swinging hard at the pitch. He makes contact and it sails into the outfield.

"Yes!" I yell, "that a boy!" The kid on third makes it home and Hudson makes it to third. Joey easily makes it to second before the ball is thrown in. I see Lucy also give Hudson a fist bump and tap his helmet. He says something to her and she cracks up. What I wouldn't give to be over there with them. Kade is up to bat next, he lets two high strikes go by him. The third pitch is a lower strike. He takes a swing and misses, ending the first inning.

## LUCY

It's the top of the 7th inning and we're up by one. All the boys have to do is hold them off and they've done it. There's one out and a runner on second. Hayden is pitching and I can tell he's getting tired, but I think he's got enough in him to win this thing. He lobs a pitch over the plate and gets a strike making it a full count.

"All right Hayden, you've got this. Work your plate buddy," I yell from the dugout, hoping my voice reaches him over the other voices in the crowd.

"I think this is our most nerve-wracking game to date," Kara says, chewing on her thumbnail, or what's left of it.

I nod my head in agreement, but don't take my eyes off the field. Hayden makes his next pitch. It sails beautifully into the bottom outside corner of the strike zone. I'm expecting the umpire to call a strike and am flabbergasted when I hear, "Ball four, runner take your base."

"Are you serious, Ump? That was a strike?!" I yell. Normally I don't argue with the umpires and take the bad calls in stride. I want to set an example for the boys. I guess, today is not one of those days where I'm able to let it go. The umpire gives me a warning look. I whip my sunglasses off and stare right back at him. Kara steps in between us.

"She's fine, she's good," she tells the ump and turns to me, looking me in the face. "Hey, cool it. Hayden needs you. If you get ejected. I am not the one to nurse him through this last batter."

I break eye contact with the ump and look at her and nod. Turning back to the field, I look at Hayden.

"Time out!" I yell to the ump and make a 'T' with my hands.

"Time," he calls and I jog out onto the mound.

"Are you going to pull me?" Hayden asks reluctantly.

I hold my hand out for the ball and roll it around in my hands. "Nope, you've got this. I just wanted to come out and ask you if you think the ump forgot his glasses today. My grandmother could make better calls than that."

Hayden laughs and I laugh with him. I don't usually allow bad mouthing of the officials. I know what they do is hard, and I am grateful that we have them, because without them, we wouldn't be playing, but apparently I have a bee in my bonnet today.

I tip my head towards home plate. "Give 'em all you got. You've got this buddy, and no matter what, know you've pitched a really good last half of the game." I hand him back the ball and head back to the dugout. The batter takes his position in the batter's box. Hayden set's up and fires a nice fastball straight down the center. The batter swings, but he's behind the pitch and misses.

"Strike One."

"Yes! Just like that, Hay," I yell, encouraging him.

Hayden takes a breath and lets it out. He checks his runner at second, a skill we've been working on this season. He sends another fastball over the plate. This time the batter tips it and it goes foul. I let out a breath.

"Oh shit," Kara whispers.

"Oh shit," I agree. Everyone's on their feet clapping and hooting and hollering. Hayden looks over at me and I lift my hands up as I take a deep breath in. I see his shoulders lift as he takes his own breath. I lower my hands, letting my breath out. Hayden releases his breath. I nod my head, and he nods back at me. He winds up and throws the ball. I see the batter follow the ball and take a swing.

The ball pings off the metal bat and sails straight to Hayden. He realizes what's happening and catches the ball. Shock crosses his face.

"Second! Throw it to second!" I scream. The runner took off to third, not tagging up. Hayden realizes this and whips the ball to second. Kade catches the ball and tags the runner just as he's coming back to tag.

"OUT!" yells the infield umpire.

Kara and I turn and grab each other and start jumping up and down as the remaining boys run out of the dugout and to their teammates on the field. They've all dog piled on Hayden.

"They did it!" Kara screams, still jumping up and down.

"They did it!" I yell back, jumping with her.

We stop jumping and give each other a hug. Parents are coming out onto the field to hug and congratulate their kids. We join the chaos and find our boys.

"We did it," Hudson yells when he sees me. I wrap him in a hug, catcher gear and all.

"You guys did it!" I say back. I scrunch up my nose as the scent of a sweaty boy hits it. "Whew, you need a shower," I joke. I untangle myself from him and look over at Kara, whose face looks similar to the one I just made a few seconds ago. I let out a laugh. I see the other team lining up, and get my team's attention.

"Hey! Let's line up and tell them what a great job they did, then we need to get pictures with your trophy!"

The boys, Kara and I line up and give high-fives to the other team. We shake the other coaches' hands and then set up for our pictures. The crowd has thinned out considerably and the only people who seem to be the only ones left are the parents of both teams. The photographer tells us he got what he needed. I'm about to release the boys when I start hearing gasps through the small crowd that's left. I look over at the mob of parents and see a man with a plain black baseball hat coming through the crowd. It's the same man I thought was staring at me earlier. He no longer has sunglasses on, and I recognize him now that he's closer.

I let out a surprised gasp.


*KESSLER.*

# CHAPTER 9

## Kessler

THEY DID IT.

They freaking won.

I make my way around the fence and into the field. I take my sunglasses off and make my way through the crowd. I know as soon as I start hearing gasps, people have recognized me, but I don't care. All that matters is getting to Lucy and Hudson. I can see them getting their picture taken. I'm almost through the pile of people when I make eye contact with Lucy. I hear her let out a surprised gasp and give her a big smile. She puts her hand up to her mouth. Hudson looks up at his mom, then in the direction she's staring.

"Kessler!" He bellows and runs over to me at full speed. I barely have time to brace myself as he collides with me, giving me a huge hug.

"Woah buddy!" I say, wrapping my arms around him and giving him a huge hug back. "You were great out there kid."

He looks up at me with a smile so big, I'm afraid it's going to get stuck. "You watched?" he asks, eyes wide.

"I was here for the whole thing. I'm so proud of you bud." I clear my throat, trying to dislodge the small lump that has formed.

I look behind Hudson and see Lucy make her way over to us, not breaking eye contact with me. Hudson leans in and gives me another hug before stepping back. Lucy places her hands on his shoulders. "I thought you were out of town."

It's not a question, but a statement.

"I wanted to surprise you guys. I flew in last night so I wouldn't miss it. I didn't want the boys to see me before the game and have them distracted, so I waited." I rub the back of my neck. "I didn't realize how hard it would be to sit back and just watch."

She laughs. "I know what you mean, I don't think I've ever been so nervous for a game as I was for this one."

"I wasn't nervous," Hudson chimes in. "We had this, Mom."

We both laugh and I reach over and ruffle his hair. "That's a great attitude to have going into every game."

Kara comes up to us with Kade in tow. "Kessler, nice to see you again," she says with a big smirk on her face.

I return the smile. "Kara, always a pleasure. Kade, great plays out there my man." I hold my fist out for a bump, which he enthusiastically returns.

"We just came over to say hi and let you know we're heading home for showers and dinner. You guys are welcome to join us. We're having burgers and fries." Kara shrugs her shoulders. "Nothing fancy."

"Actually," I say turning to Lucy and Hudson. "I was hoping you two would join me for dinner?" I ask hopefully.

Lucy looks at Kara, who raises her eyebrows and mouths "do it" to her. She looks back at me, uncertain.

"That would be so cool. Can we please, Mom?" Hudson asks, turning out of his mom's embrace to look at her.

I decide to use this to my advantage. I walk up and put my arm around Hudson. "Yeah, please, Mom," I say, mimicking Hudson and giving her a pouty lip.

She smirks at me and Hudson. "OK, OK. But," she says, looking directly at Hudson, "you sir, need a shower first. No one will let us in with that stench."

We all laugh.

Little does she know that my mom has had that stench in her house plenty of times. But I'm not ready to disclose that's where we're going. I think she'd back out if she knew. Kara and Kade take off and I walk to the dugout with Lucy and Hudson to grab their gear. We grab everything and make our way out of the field and to her car. I reach down and grab Lucy's free hand, lacing my fingers with hers. She looks down at our hands then up at me, giving me a shy smile.

*Progress.*

We throw the gear into the back of her car. Hudson walks to his side and climbs in. I walk around and open her door for her. She pauses and looks up at me.

"Where do you want us to meet you?" she asks.

"Oh no, I'm following you home. I'll wait for you guys to clean up, then I'll drive you."

She gives me a surprised look. "Uh, are you sure? We can just meet you there, it's no problem. That way you won't have to drive us back after dinner."

I lift my hand and lay it on her cheek, running my thumb across it. "Lucy, I have waited all week to see you again. Not being able to be near you during the game was torture. I would love nothing more than to spend as much time with you as I can. So yes, I am sure I want to drive you and Hudson."

She visibly swallows. "Ok, then," she croaks out.

I lean down and give Hudson a wink over her shoulder. "See you soon bud." Lucy gets into her car and I shut the door. I jog over to my truck parked a few spots away and hop in. I follow Lucy out of the lot and onto the road.

About 15 minutes later we pull up to a small light blue cottage type house with a small neat front yard. Rose bushes line the walkway and small colorful flowers fill the spaces between. Lucy and Hudson climb out of the car and make their way to the porch. I hop out of my truck and follow them up the steps. Lucy unlocks the door and it opens into a spacious living room with the dining room and kitchen connected off to the left.

Hudson heads straight down the hallway and into a room off to the right, which I'm guessing is his bedroom.

Lucy sets down her bag on the entryway table and turns to me. "Make yourself at home. There's drinks in the fridge if you're thirsty." She pops a couple of her fingers and fidgets with a ring on her thumb I've never noticed before. "I'm just going to hop in the shower really quick. Uh, where are we going? So I know what to wear, and tell Hudson what to wear."

I step forward and take her hands in mine, quieting her fidgeting. "It's casual, just jeans and a T-shirt will be fine."

She nods her head, but doesn't say anything. I let go of her hands and run my hands up her arm. "Can I hug you?" I ask, realizing I've never had my arms around her.

She lets out a small laugh. "Yes, you can hug me."

I wrap my arms around her back and envelope her into me. She tucks her head right into my chest and wraps her arms around me. I inhale her scent, a mixture of coconuts and vanilla hits my nose. Her body relaxes into me and mine follows suit. We stand there wrapped up in each other for a few seconds. She pulls away and I reluctantly let her.

"I better go shower so we can get going." Lucy heads down

the same hallway as Hudson and stops at the door of his room. She knocks twice, then opens the door. I hear her say something about jeans and a T-shirt, then shut the door and head into another room at the very end of the hallway.

Hudson comes out of his room a few seconds later, clothes in hand, and heads into a door across from his, I'm assuming the bathroom. He shuts the door and a few seconds later I hear water running. Seeing as I have a few minutes to kill I decided to look around the living area. There are a bunch of pictures of Lucy and Hudson throughout the years. Birthdays, baseball games, a few at the beach. Most of them have Kara and Kade in there and I notice I don't see any of people who would be the age of Lucy's parents. I make a mental note to ask her about that sometime, wondering if they're still alive.

I take my phone out of my pocket and take a seat on the couch. I send my mom a quick text letting her know Lucy and Hudson will be joining me. She texts back a few seconds later.

MOM

Oh Kessler! I am so excited to meet them.

ME

Please don't go overboard. I can tell Lucy is nervous, just keep it casual please.

MOM

OF COURSE I will. Casual is my middle name.

I snort. Oh boy. I hope my mom can keep her excitement contained and not freak Lucy out. Scrolling through my messages, I see I have one from Reese.

REESE

Well? How did the team do? Was Lucy surprised?

ME

Nosey aren't we?

REESE

It's the least you can do after I helped you.

ME

The boys won the tournament. It was a battle man. I haven't been that nervous for a game since I was a rookie. I'm proud of them. Made me think about why I love baseball.

REESE

Aww listen to the proud not papa.

ME

Don't be an asshole.

REESE

Too late. And Lucy? Was she surprised?

ME

I don't think I should answer that. Since you want to be a dick.

REESE

Oh come on man, pull the tampon out. Just tell me.

I sigh, I swear I need new friends.

ME

Yes, she was surprised. I'm actually sitting in her living room right now waiting for them to shower so we can go to my parents.

REESE

Awesome man, I'm happy for you.

ME

Thanks dude.

I hear a door open down the hallway, but can't see who it is from the couch. I look up from my phone to see a freshly showered Hudson walking out.

"Hey, bud. Ready for dinner?"

He flops down on the couch at the other end and grabs the remote. "Yeah, I'm starving," he says, turning on the TV.

"I hear ya man, I'm always hungry after a game. Don't worry. We'll have you fed soon."

He nods his head and flips through the channels until he finds one he likes. He's quiet for a few minutes. I think this is the least I've heard him talk since I met him. The silence doesn't last long.

"So, are you my mom's boyfriend now?" He asks still staring at the TV.

I take a few seconds trying to figure out what I want to say. "Would it be OK if I was?"

Hudson doesn't answer me right away. He takes his eyes away from the TV and looks at me. "I guess? She's never had one before, but you seem pretty cool." He shrugs his shoulders and turns back to his show.

I chuckle. "Well thanks bud, I think you're pretty cool too." I pause then add, "I'm not your mom's boyfriend, but I'm working on that."

He nods his head but doesn't say anything further, focused on his show. I hear a door open in the hallway, then see Lucy appear at the entrance. She looks beautiful. I mean, I think she always looks good when I see her, but *wow*. Her hair is in long loose waves around her face. She has more makeup on than I've ever seen her wear and it makes her hazel eyes pop. She's wearing a flowy flower print shirt that billows around her when she moves. Dark jeans and gray ankle boots complete the look. She sees me staring at her and gives me a shy smile. She walks over to where Hudson is sitting.

"Ready to go bud?"

He nods his head and reaches for the remote, turning off the TV I stand from where I'm sitting and we all head towards the door. Lucy is the last to exit and she turns to lock up. We make our way to my truck and I place my hand on the small of her back, needing to touch her. Hudson opens the back door to my truck and climbs up. Lucy reaches for her door, but I stop her.

"Don't even think about it. That's my job," I say, opening her door for her. She climbs into my truck and gives me a sweet smile. The urge to kiss her is so strong, I almost can't stop myself, but it's not something I want to do for the first time in front of Hudson.

I make myself shut the door and jog around to my side and hop in. I back out of the driveway and head in the direction of my parent's house. It's quiet in the truck. After a few minutes of silence, Lucy notices we're heading out of town.

"We're not eating in town?"

I look back in my rearview mirror and see Hudson crashed out in the back. I tip my head towards the mirror. "Someone's out."

Lucy turns around in her seat and breathes out a laugh. "I figured he'd crash at some point. I just thought it'd be on the way home from dinner." She faces forward in her seat and looks at me. "You didn't answer my question by the way."

I smirk at her. "Can't get anything past you, can I Coach?"

"Nope," she says, popping her 'P'

I take a deep breath in, hoping she won't freak out like I think she's going to freak out.

"Before I tell you, I want you to know this is a weekly thing and unless I'm out of town, I cannot get out of it. So with that said. We're going to my parent's house," I say the last part quickly, hoping it'll soften the shock.

It doesn't.

I feel Lucy silently stare at me. I take my eyes off the road quickly to look at her face and see utter shock on it.

"I'm sorry, did you say your parents' house? As in your Mom and Dad. The people who gave you life?"

That makes me chuckle. "Yep, those would be them."

"Kessler," she whispers. "Wha, wh, why?" she finally gets out.

I take one hand off my steering wheel and hold it out, palm up. I can see her look at it out of the corner of my eye, but she doesn't move to take it. I wiggle my fingers. "Give me your hand, and I'll give you your answer."

She places her hand in mine and I give it a squeeze. "One, like I said before. If I'm not out of town, Sunday dinners are mandatory. It's something we've done every Sunday since I can remember. Two, no one will see us there. There's no fans to ask me for autographs and pictures. No one taking photos that will end up on the internet. This way, you and Hudson are protected."

She gives my hand a small squeeze. "Thank you. For thinking this through," she says softly. "Yes, that is a big worry of mine. I don't want Hudson exposed to that," she pauses, "at least, not yet."

Feeling a spark of hope, I bring her hand to my lips and kiss the back of it. Her lips part and she inhales a sharp breath. Goosebumps break out over her arm. A small jolt of satisfaction spreads through me knowing I can make her body react like that with a simple kiss. Before my mind wonders what else I could make her body do, I talk about the game today.

"So, I never pictured you as one to yell at an umpire., I say with humor in my voice.

She groans quietly and puts her free hand up to her face. "Not my finest moment. I'm usually not like that, I swear. That game had me on edge the entire time, and that crap call just snapped whatever thread of calm I was holding onto."

I chuckle. "I'm not going to lie. It was a big turn on to see you get riled up like that."

I sneak a look over at her and see her face flush. I squeeze her hand again. "Don't be embarrassed, it happens to the best of us."

Lucy lets out a sigh and leans her head back against the seat, looking out the passenger window. "This drive is really pretty. How much longer until we're at your parents?"

"About another ten minutes. This is my favorite drive to make during fall. The trees change into different shades of oranges and yellows with pops of reds throughout. I've always thought about getting property out here and building a house when I retire."

Lucy keeps her head on the headrest and tilts her face towards me. "Do you think about retirement? I mean you're not old, but your injury was bad and I know the toll injuries like that take on your body. It's impressive you've been able to make such a fantastic recovery."

I forget she knows all about recovering from injuries like that, being a physical therapist, I'm sure she's seen it all. I feel like I can open up to her about it, and how difficult of a recovery I had in the beginning.

"After my first surgery, I thought my playing days were over." I think back to the dark place I was in and how shitty I was to everyone who tried to help. "I didn't handle not being able to play baseball well. I pushed myself harder than I should have, thinking if I just tried hard enough, I could make my body do what I wanted it to." I shake my head and huff out a laugh. "I caused so much inflammation and scar tissue from pushing myself too hard too early, they had to go back in for a second surgery about four months later and clean it up."

I see Lucy shake her head.

"I know, I was an idiot. Reese and Brent tried talking to me but I shut them out for a while. I shut everyone out actually. After I set myself back longer than I needed to, Coach Dixon came to my apartment one day and had a talk with me. He told me he understood and respected my drive to get back out on the field, but that I was causing more harm than good, not only for myself but for my team." I laugh. "He told me to pull my head out of my ass and put it back on the good shoulders my parents gave me where it belongs."

Lucy chuckles.

"After that, I listened to my body and the therapists, I took it easy and only pushed when I was told I could. The last six months of my recovery were grueling, but I was able to make the progress I needed to get back out where I belonged." I look over at Lucy and see her looking out the window at the scenery passing us by and make the decision to tell her what I also learned while I was recovering.

"I also realized something else during that time. Something I didn't really think I was missing, or needed. I spent a lot of time wondering what I had to show for all my hard work. Yes, I had awards, division championships, money." I pause and lift her hand, placing another kiss to her fingers. She turns from the window and gives me a smile. "But what I didn't have, was anyone to share that with."

"My first game back, the day I met you, I felt something." Her eyes widen slightly, but she doesn't say anything, so I continue, "I didn't realize it until I was sitting at Tony's with you and Hudson what it was that I felt. A want, no, a need, desire, whatever you want to call it, for a family." I pause and take my eyes off the road to look at her. Her lips are parted slightly and she's staring intently at me. Frozen. So I decide to lay it all out there. "I've known you for a little over a week, and you and Hudson are already the first thing I think about when I get up and the last thing to cross my mind before I go to sleep."

Lucy pulls her hand from mine and sets it in her lap. I panic slightly, thinking I've gone too far. "That's infatuation Kessler. It fades," she says quietly.

"No, Lucy. I've been infatuated before, I've had flings and one night stands. What I felt the day I met you, the energy between us, me hearing your voice above all the others. That's not something I've ever experienced, and if you can tell me you don't feel the same way I will drop you and Hudson off after dinner, and never bother you again." I sit there silently praying she doesn't take me up on that.

She's quiet for a few minutes, twisting the ring on her thumb. I can see her worrying her lip out of the corner of my eye. I grip the steering wheel, turning my knuckles white. I shouldn't have said anything yet. It's too soon. I see my parent's long driveway come into view and I slow down and make the turn. I drive slowly up the gravel driveway and park behind my brother's car. I turn the truck off and we sit there in silence.

"I didn't-"

"Can I-"

We both start. We stop and motion for the other to go ahead. Exhaling a small laugh I say, "Please, go ahead."

"I, just. I guess I just need some time to mull this over in my head. I'm not going to lie and say this doesn't all freak me out a little."

I nod, understanding where she's coming from. "If I'm honest, it freaks me out a bit too that I can feel this strongly for someone, in such a short time."

We sit in silence for a few beats, when we hear Hudson stirring in the back seat. I look back and see him yawn and stretch. He rubs his eyes asking, "Are we at the restaurant?"

Lucy unbuckles her seat and turns to look at him. "No restaurant bud. We're at Kessler's parent's house."

"Oh, ok," he says, completely unaware of the weirdness between me and his mother right now.

I unbuckle my seatbelt and open my door. Lucy moves to do the same but I stop her. "No, don't move. I will get your door." I hop out and move to the passenger door and open it. I give her my hand and she takes it and slides out of the truck. She tries to take her hand back, but I hold onto it, not wanting to let go in case this is the last time I get to hold it. Hudson jumps out of the back and looks around.

"Woah, this place is huge. Did you grow up here?" he asks, taking it all in.

I look up at the two-story house with its stone chimney towering above us and memories flood my brain. "Yep, this is home." I put my free hand on his back just below his neck, and guide them both up the walkway to the front door. It opens before we even reach it and my mom walks out.

"You must be Lucy and Hudson," she says greeting us. "I'm Marlene. Kessler's mom." She takes Lucy's free hand and gives it a squeeze then turns her attention to Hudson. "Come in, Come in. The food is almost done. You must be starving after playing so hard today," she says to Hudson, ushering us inside.

We walk in and into the living room, which flows into the kitchen. Off to the right of the kitchen is the dining room. Mom's talking to Hudson about his game and leading him through the dining room and through the sliding door off the back, where I see my brother and dad at the grill. Lucy smirks. "Well I guess I don't have to worry about Hudson."

I chuckle. "Mom loves kids. She's been dying for a grandkid to dote on for years now."

Lucy tries again to pull her hand from mine but I tighten my grip slightly. "Please Lucy, just let me have tonight. Whatever you decide I will respect, but let me have this night with you and Hudson."

She stares up at me and I can see her brain working overtime, but she nods her head and keeps her hand in mine. I take that as a good sign and lead her through the sliding door. We see Hudson talking animatedly to my brother, who is laughing at something he said. My dad is at the grill, flipping what looks like burgers. My mom sees Lucy and pats the seat next to her. "Come sit next to me dear," she says. I reluctantly let go of her hand so she can go sit next to my mom.

I head over to my dad, grabbing a bottle of water from the mini fridge on my way. I gifted my parents an outdoor kitchen for their 30th wedding anniversary, and even though they balked at the idea of me spending my money on them, it's been well utilized.

"Kessler. How's the shoulder?" Dad asks, closing the grill lid and turning to me for a hug.

I return my dad's hug and we pat each other on the back a couple of times. "Hey, Dad. The shoulder's good."

"Burgers should be done in a few minutes. Hope everyone brought their appetites," he announces to the table.

"Thanks honey!" my mom calls to him then turns back to her conversation with Lucy.

Judd has his phone out and is showing Hudson something, and they're both laughing. I pray that it's kid-appropriate.

Dad leans back against the built in counter and crosses his arms over his chest taking in the sight before us. "It's nice to have some more people at family dinner," he says casually.

I take a swig of my water and nod my head. "I'm hoping it becomes a regular thing," I admit.

He looks over at me, eyebrows raised. "Why wouldn't it be? I thought you guys just started dating?"

I grimace and grab the back of my neck. "Yeah, about that.

This is technically our first date. She has reservations about dating me, or anyone for that matter."

Dad gives me a wink. "Well, hopefully we make her change her mind tonight."

I reach over and pat my dad on the back a few times. "Thanks, Dad."

He nods his head, then turns back to the grill to check the burgers. "Burgers are done!" he yells over his shoulder at the table. "Come eat!"

# CHAPTER 10

## Lucy

"I DON'T THINK I COULD EAT ANOTHER BITE," HUDSON says, flopping back in his chair.

"Oh, I'm sorry to hear that because I have stuff to make S'mores for dessert," Marlene tells him.

Hudson sits up in his chair, bumping the table slightly. "Really? I could probably find room for S'mores."

We all laugh and Marlene assures Hudson once the table is cleared and dinner is put away we'll go make S'mores around the fire pit.

Judd reaches over and ruffles Hudson's hair. "Come on bud, let us men go build the fire."

Hudson looks to me for permission. "Go ahead, just be careful and listen to Judd please."

He pumps his fist and gets up out of his chair following Judd to the fire pit out in the middle of the yard.

Marlene gets up from her seat and starts clearing the table. I get out of my seat and start grabbing cups. "Oh dear, you don't have to help," she assures me.

"Please, it's the least I can do after you guys provided that lovely dinner," I tell her. Kessler and Henry move to help but Marlene stops them.

"We have it under control here. Why don't you go supervise the boys to make sure they behave."

Kessler puts the bowl down he had grabbed and turns to me giving me a quick peck on the cheek and follows his Dad down to the fire pit. I stand there stunned, trying to wrap my head around what just happened.

I feel Marlene staring at me and I give myself a mental shake. Marlene doesn't say anything and heads into the kitchen and I follow after her. She pulls containers from the cupboards and we fall into a comfortable rhythm of me emptying food into them. Her taking the empty dishes and rinsing them off before putting them into the dishwasher. I go back out to the table and finish collecting napkins and silverware. I hand Marlene the remaining silverware and discard the napkins. She starts the dishwasher and wipes her hands on a towel.

"Well, now that that's all done I think we deserve a drink. Care for some wine?" she asks moving to a cabinet and taking out two wine tumblers.

"That sounds great," I say and she grabs a bottle of Riesling out of the fridge and pours us both a generous amount.

"Let's go sit on the swing and watch the men for a bit before we join them. We can have some girl talk." We grab our tumblers and head out the sliding door and take a seat on the swing. I tuck my legs up under me criss-cross applesauce style and she pushes off the ground, gently swinging us. We sit in comfortable silence for a minute before Marlene speaks.

"You know I actually had plans to set Kessler up on a date tonight," she starts.

I look at her, eyebrows raised. She holds up her hand. "It's not what you think. I didn't know about you until yesterday. I had this planned for a few weeks, so when Kessler told me he wanted to bring you to dinner, I of course was delighted. A little hurt he hadn't told me he was seeing someone, but he explained that to me too." She looks at me and I turn away, taking a drink of wine. "I see it, you know? Actually, I feel it too, I'm sure everyone does," she says, taking a drink of her own wine.

I give her a confused look. "I'm sorry, I'm not sure I know what you're talking about."

She laughs softly. "I mean the pull between you two. There's an energy when you two are together. I can see that he touches you whenever he gets the chance. I saw the shock on your face when he kissed your cheek. I know you're trying to fight it, but it's not something you can fight."

I take a gulp of my wine trying to figure out what I should say to that, nothing comes to mind so I stay quiet.

Marlene lays her right hand on top of my left one and gives it a soft squeeze before releasing it. "You're the first woman he's ever brought home since high school." She lets that bomb drop.

I whip my head to look at her to see if she's joking, she's not. "But, He's 36," I blurt out.

She lets out a laugh that makes Kessler look up at us, a huge smile on his face. "I'm well aware of how old he is. All I could think about when he told me about you, was 'it's about time.'"

I sit there in stunned silence for a minute not understanding why he's never brought anyone home, and why me, why now?

"When you know, you know dear," Marlene says as if hearing the questions running through my brain. "Henry and I only dated for three months before we got married. I was pregnant with Kessler a month later and 36 years later, here we are." She pats my hand. "Granted I didn't have to worry about Henry being in the spotlight like Kessler is, nor did I have a child's feelings to protect, but Kessler wouldn't do anything to intentionally hurt someone he loved."

I freeze. Love? But, that's not possible. Right? Marlene must see the panic on my face because we've stopped swinging and it slows. "Oh dear," she says. "Lucy, I-"

I jump to my feet before she can finish her sentence. I turn to run to the bathroom, then realize I don't know where the bathroom is. I turn back. "Restroom, I need the restroom. Where is the restroom?" Jesus, can I say restroom anymore?

"Down the hall, first door on your right. Are you ok?"

I nod my head, then dash inside in search of the bathroom. I find it and quickly shut the door, locking it behind me. I set my tumbler on the counter and pace the space a few times. I stop and turn the faucet on cold, letting the water run over my wrists, trying to cool my body that has broken out in a sweat. I take a few deep breaths, trying to calm my racing heart. My heart starts coming down to a normal pace when a knock sounds at the door.

"Lucy," Kessler says through the door. "Are you ok? I saw you rush in the house, when I asked Mom what happened she said I better come talk to you. Can I come in?"

My heart starts racing again and I don't answer.

Kessler knocks again. "Lucy? You're worrying me here, Coach. Let me in."

I turn off the water and wipe my hands on a towel. I turn the lock and the door opens. Kessler's 6'2" frame fills the doorway and I've never noticed before how much taller he is than me. I stare at him taking him in. He stares back at me, uncertainty and concern in his eyes.

"What's wrong? Are you sick? Do you need to go home?" he asks, reaching for my face and feeling my forehead.

"No, I'm-" I start, but stop to clear my throat and continue, "I'm not sick" is all I can manage to say.

"Ok, then what happened?" he asks, taking his hand from my forehead, instantly making me miss the physical contact.

I open my mouth to tell him but the words won't come out. Instead, I find myself closing the distance between us and burying my head into his chest, wrapping my arms around him. I feel his arms come around me and hold me tight. I inhale his leather and spice scent and feel my body relax. He softly rubs my back and we stand there like that for a few minutes. I finally lift my head from his chest and tilt my face to look at him. He looks down at me, and I feel the air crackle between us.

*Hmm, that must be the energy Marlene was talking about.*

"You're so beautiful," Kessler whispers, moving one of his hands from my back, up to my cheek to caress it. I close my eyes and lean into his rough palm. Opening my eyes, I swallow hard when I see him looking at my lips. I lift up onto my toes and he meets me the rest of the way. His warm lips press against mine. I sigh and open my mouth slightly. Kessler matches me and deepens the kiss, sucking the breath from me.

*Holy shit. I'm kissing Kessler. Wait, weren't you just upset because his mom told you he loved you?*

I break the kiss and put my hand on Kessler's chest, pushing back slightly. We both stare at each other slightly out of breath.

"Your Mom told me you love me," I blurt out, not being able to hold it in anymore.

"Oh," he says, realizing why I ran in here.

"Oh? I tell you your mom told me you love me and all you have to say is 'oh'?"

"What do you want me to say Lucy?"

I take a step back and cross my arms. "That it's not true? That she was mistaken?" I uncross my arms and flail them around in the air. "I mean we've known each other for a little over a week, Kessler. Isn't this fast? Crazy even?"

He shrugs his shoulders. "My parents-" he starts to say, but I cut him off.

"Only dated for three months. I know, your mom told me before she dropped a bomb on me!" I say, raising my voice.

Kessler steps forward and places his hands on the side of both my arms. "Lucy, I'm not asking you to say it back. I'm not even the one who said it to you. I am willing to go at whatever pace you're comfortable with. I know you're scared." He pauses. "I'm scared too," he admits.

"Why are you scared?" I whisper.

He grips my chin and lifts my face to his looking directly into my eyes. "I'm scared you'll leave and I know I'll never feel what I feel for you, with anyone else."

Hearing him admit he's scared to lose me loosens a brick in my wall and I can feel them start to crumble down around me. I can feel tears build in my eyes and I blink them back. Pushing all my fears and worries away, I lean forward, closing the distance again between our lips.

This time Kessler isn't as gentle and I can feel his tongue trace my lips asking for permission. I open my mouth and Kessler's tongue invades my mouth. I match his hunger and lift my hand, running it through his hair. I grip the short strands at the back of his head and give them a slight tug. He growls into my mouth and pulls back slightly to nip at my lip. I let out a gasp. I can feel his smile on my lips before claiming them again. We stand there in his parent's bathroom for who knows how long, making out like teenagers. This time he's the one to break the kiss.

"As much as I would love to make out with you all day. I'm sure Hudson is wondering where we went."

*Shit.*

I lean my forehead against his and collect my thoughts.

"Before we go back out there. I need to tell you something." I lean back and look into his eyes.

Apprehension crosses his face, but he stays silent and waits for me to speak.

"I know I've been holding back, but coming here tonight and talking with your mom. Seeing you with Hudson." I shake my head. "You flew home early to watch his game and he's not even your kid." I fight back the tears that threaten to choke me. "I may not be ready to say certain words to you, but I am ready to see where this goes."

"Really?" Kessler says quietly.

"Really," I say nodding my head. He leans down and captures my lips again and gives me a soul searing kiss. I place my hand on his chest and push back, breaking us apart. "We should really head back out there before they send a search party for us."

Kessler laughs and places one last kiss on my lips before turning and opening the door. I grab my wine tumbler and walk out the door. Kessler follows me down the hallway and out the sliding door before I can get any further he grabs my free hand and entwines his fingers with mine. We get to the firepit and I see the makings for S'mores scattered all about. Judd is talking to Hudson and showing him where to place his marshmallow over the fire. The sight brings a warm feeling to my chest. Hudson looks up, sees me, and grins.

"Mom, Judd is teaching me to roast the perfect marshmallow. He says it's all about the heat pocket."

"That's awesome. You better watch it to make sure it doesn't burn."

He turns his attention back to his marshmallow right before it bursts into flames, charring it.

"No!" he exclaims, trying to blow out the flames, but it's too late, the marshmallow is toast.

"No worries bud, we'll just try again," Judd says handing him a fresh stick and marshmallow and taking the burnt one from him.

Kessler leads me over to two seats next to his mom and dad. He moves them so they are closer together and gestures for me to sit. I take a seat next to Marlene and he takes the one on the other side of me and reaches for my hand again once we're seated.

Marlene looks at our hands and back up at us. "So I didn't ruin things?" she asks, her face pinched with worry.

I give her a smile and reach out to give her a reassuring squeeze. "No Marlene, you didn't ruin anything. The complete opposite actually. That was the push I needed to get out of my head and see what's in front of me. So thank you for that."

I feel Kessler give my hand a squeeze and lift my fingers to his lips placing a kiss on them. Marlene puts her hand to her mouth and blinks her eyes a few times like she's holding back tears.

"Mom stop, you're embarrassing me," Kessler says jokingly.

Marlene just waves her hands at him and laughs. "Don't mind me. I'm just so happy."

Henry pats Marlene's hand a few times before getting up and joining Hudson and Judd. Judd switches his dad spots and comes to sit in his seat with his double decker S'more. He takes a huge bite making half the square disappear.

"So," he says around a mouthful of chocolate, marshmallow, and graham cracker. "Are you two finally together or what?" he says motioning between us.

Marlene uses the back of her hand to smack him in the chest. "Don't talk with your mouth full, I raised you better than that. "

I laugh as Judd rubs at the spot on his chest. He swallows what's in his mouth then continues, "Well?"

Kessler looks at me, then back at Judd. "Yep, she's all mine," he says grinning back at me.

"Thank, Fuck," Judd says, earning another backhand from Marlene.

"Juddson Davis, language," Marlene chastises. "Where did I go wrong?" she mutters, shaking her head.

I bark out a laugh, amused by the scene. I hear Kessler chuckle beside me. Judd finishes his S'more and gets up from his seat, walking back to where Hudson is finishing off his second S'more.

"Those look delicious, I'm going to go make one. Want one, Coach?" Kessler asks, getting up from his chair and looking down at me.

I hold up my wine. "I'm good with this, but thank you for asking." He gives me a wink and heads over to the group. I take a sip of wine and take in the scene before me. Kessler reaches for the package of graham crackers, which Judd snags before he can grab them. Kessler hooks his arm around Judd's neck and gets him into a headlock. Hudson howls with laughter. Henry just shakes his head and works on his marshmallow.

"I swear those two will never grow out of messing with each other," she says with warmth in her voice.

I chuckle watching as Judd and Kessler drop to the grass away from the fire pit and wrestle each other. "Have they always been like that?" I ask.

"Oh yeah. Since Judd was old enough to start being the little instigator that he is." She takes a drink of her wine and looks over at me. "Do you have any siblings?"

I take a huge drink of my wine before shaking my head. "No, I'm an only child." Not elaborating any further.

"Oh, that's too bad. As annoying as they are sometimes, having siblings to grow up with and confide in is something I'm glad I have, and my boys."

I give her a small smile and finish off my wine.

"Do you want a refill?" Marlene asks standing, noticing I'm done.

I look at her and back at my tumbler. "I shouldn't," I say

"You don't have to drive and Kessler isn't drinking, so you can have more if you'd like."

I bite the side of my cheek, contemplating, then nod my head in agreement. "OK, but I can get it."

Marlene waves me off. "I'm already up dear. I don't mind." She holds her hand out for my tumbler and I hand it to her.

"Thank you. Only half the amount this time though. I do have to work tomorrow."

"You got it dear," she says walking back to the house.

I lean my head back in the chair and look over at the guys. Kessler and Judd have stopped wrestling around and are now devouring S'mores. Henry is putting more wood on the fire and Hudson is poking a stick in the fire. I let out a sigh. This has been a whirlwind of a day. I went from having doubts about pursuing a relationship with this man, to being in a relationship with him and him telling me that what he feels for me is not something he's ever felt before. He looks over at me and gives me a wink. I feel my cheeks warm.

Marlene comes back out of the house and hands me my tumbler and takes her seat.

"Thank you."

Marlene and I sit there watching the boys joking and laughing around the fire.

"Do you want more kids?" Marlene asks after a few minutes.

I don't answer her right away, thinking about it. Do I? I'm not sure. "I uh, well, I haven't dated in 12 years so I guess I never gave it much thought." I shrug my shoulders.

Marlene pauses her glass halfway to her lips. "12 Years? You haven't been with anyone for 12 years?"

I shake my head and take a generous sip of my wine, silently praying this doesn't go where I think it's going to go.

Marlene sits there in silence for a few beats before taking a sip of her own wine. "Kessler said Hudson's father isn't in the picture. Obviously, there's a reason for it, so I'm not going to pry." She pats my hand. "But I will say this. Kessler doesn't give his heart easily. So please, try not to let your past experiences ruin any future you may have with my son."

I give her a nod, mulling her words over in my head.

Kessler comes over and plops down in his chair next to me as I stifle a yawn.

"We should probably head back soon. Hudson has school tomorrow right?"

I nod and finish the last of my wine. I stand up and stretch. Kessler stands up and takes me in his arms. I wrap my arms around his neck and look up at him. He places a soft kiss on my lips then one on my forehead. "Let's get you two home," he says.

We head over to everyone and tell them we're taking off.

"I should probably head out too," Judd says, gathering the remaining S'mores supplies and putting them back into the Tupperware container. "We have an afternoon game against the Devils tomorrow and I'm starting."

My body tenses hearing the name of the team he's playing against, but no one seems to notice.

"Then we play against you guys on Thursday. Hope you're ready to get your asses handed to you," Kessler says, thumping Judd hard on the back.

"Bring it, Brotato," Judd says, thumping him back just as hard.

"OK you two, that's enough thumping for one night," Marlene says. "We'll walk you guys out."

We all head back through the house and out to the front

porch. Marlene and Henry give Hudson and I hugs. Judd fist bumps Hudson and gives me a hug. Kessler hugs his parents and slaps Judd on the back. We head to the truck and wave our goodbyes as we back out of the driveway. Kessler takes my hand in his and we drive back to my house, Hudson and Kessler joking around and talking about baseball the whole way.

# CHAPTER 11

## Lucy

**ME**
SOS

**MARIE**
Uh Oh, Whats up

**KARA**
You're alive!

**ME**
I need a girls night stat.

**MARIE**
I'm free tonight.

**KARA**
Same. I can ask Mom to watch the boys at our house for a few hours.

**ME**
Perfect. Thanks ladies.

MARIE

No thanks needed

KARA

You're welcome to thank me 😊

I ROLL MY EYES AND CLOSE OUT OF THE TEXT THREAD. After getting home last night, I crashed hard. Not stirring one bit until my alarm rudely woke me up this morning. Thankfully Mondays are my work from home days, so after getting Hudson off to school, I hop in the shower and turn the water as hot as I can handle it.

One rejuvenating shower later, I'm in my kitchen making coffee when I hear a knock at my door. I frown and look at the clock on the stove, 8 am. Weird, I'm not expecting anyone. Maybe it's Kara coming over to get the gossip early. I walk to the front door and open it.

"Kar, I..."

My words die on my lips. Kessler is standing on the other side holding a cold brew coffee from Latte Daze. A wide smile covering his handsome face.

"Wh, what are you doing here?"

He leans down and covers my mouth with his. A sigh escapes, and I lean into the kiss and him. I could get used to this. He pulls back, a sigh escaping his own lips. "Good morning," he says grinning at me.

"Good Morning," I say, grinning back. "What are you doing here? Wait, how did you know I was working from home today?" I know I haven't told him that.

He gives me a smirk. "A little bird told me. Can I come in?"

I step back to let him in and shut the door. He sets my coffee down on the entry table and takes me in his arms, leaning down for another kiss. He teases my lips with his tongue and I open letting him in. I feel a hunger behind his kiss that I didn't feel yesterday. Kessler takes a step forward backing me up until my back is against the door. Moving one hand from my waist, he entangles his fingers in my still damp hair and tugs gently. I lift my chin and he peppers kisses along my jaw and down my neck.

I gasp at the sensation his lips leave. "You taste so sweet," he whispers in between kisses. I hear a groan, and realize it's coming from me. He makes his way back up my neck and back to my lips, taking the bottom one between his lips and sucking on it softly, pulling another groan from me.

*Jesus, get it together woman.*

"Mmm I missed you," he whispers between kisses.

I exhale a laugh and pull back. "You just saw me last night."

"Yes, and it's been 12 hours since I dropped you off, which is too long in my book."

"Needy Nancy," I say, not stopping the wide smile on my face.

He rubs his nose against mine. "I do need you," he whispers. Sending chills down my spine and heat to a place it hasn't been in a long time.

"Oh," is all I say.

*Oh?* My brain screams at me.

*You have a sexy as shit man, practically swallowing you whole and all you can say is Oh? How about "Yes Daddy, please?"*

I snort.

"Something funny?" he asks, grabbing my chin and tilting it back to stare at me.

I shake my head.

"Good. Take me to your bedroom. I want to show you how much I missed you."

*Oh.*

I stand with my back against the door, my legs refusing to move forward even though my brain is yelling at me to move.

"Lucy," Kessler says in a commanding tone. "I won't ask again. Take me to your room."

My eyes grow wide and I feel my core clench at the command.

Finally my legs get the signal my brain is now screaming at them and I take a wobbly step forward and another and another, until I'm grabbing Kessler's hand and leading him down the hallway and into my room. I stop just inside the threshold and turn around, looking up at him. His moss-green eyes are almost black with lust. I lay my hand on his chest and feel his heart thundering behind his shirt.

"I dreamt of you last night," he says, placing one hand over mine bringing it up to his lips. "I couldn't get you out of my mind, even in my sleep. Now that you're mine, I want to worship you, Lucy."

*Say YES!* My brain begs.

"Yes, Kessler," I say, my voice barely audible.

As if he was waiting for my permission, Kessler's lips crash to mine with hungry need. I match his eagerness, and grip his shirt in both fists, bringing him as close to me as I can. Kessler runs his hands down my thin tank top, reaching the hem and pulling it over my head. Next, he reaches for the waistband of my leggings and slips both hands down the back grabbing handfuls of my ass. He groans into my mouth and rocks my hips forward, pressing me against his erection. I let out a moan as his solid mass hits my sensitive clit. Kessler backs me into the bed, and my knees give way as they hit the bed. He reaches down and pulls my leggings off and tosses them to the side. His dark eyes slowly take in my body.

I move to lay my hands over my stomach. "Don't even think about covering yourself up Lucy." He growls, stopping me. He kneels down in front of me and runs his hand up my thighs and over my stomach. "You are the sexiest, fucking woman I have ever laid my eyes on. These," he says tracing over my faded stretch marks, "only make you that much sexier. Don't ever cover yourself in front of me."

His hands roam up the rest of my body and over the dark-green lace bra. He circles one of my nipples and rolls it between his thumb and pointer finger.

"Ahh," I cry out, arching my back off the bed, and pushing my breast further into his hand.

"Mmm, such a responsive, good girl."

I lay back down against the bed as his hands move back down my body. Propping myself up on my elbows to watch him. "You're wearing too many clothes," I say, trying to sit up.

He pushes my chest back down and chuckles. "I'll get there. Right now, I'm taking care of you. Lay back and enjoy the ride, Coach."

I do as I'm told and he positions himself between my legs. He traces his nose up one of my thighs, placing soft kisses as he goes. Heat pulses between my legs. He reaches my lace panties and hooks a finger around each side and tugs them down, tossing them on the floor. He returns to my pussy and runs his nose up the slit. I suck in a breath. He looks up at me with smoldering eyes. He opens his mouth and runs his tongue up my crease, licking me like an ice cream cone, never breaking eye contact.

*Fuck me.*

"So sweet, just like I thought you would be," he says, before returning his tongue to my slip and tracing a path up it again.

He's barely even touching me and I'm ready to combust. I squirm under him, trying to increase the pressure. He smirks up at me and circles my clit with his tongue. Sending me crashing back into the mattress.

"Fuuuck," I groan out, gripping the sheets with one hand and reaching for his hair with the other. Kessler grabs my legs and throws them over his shoulder, tugging me closer, and increasing the delicious pressure. "Yes, yes, so good," I whisper. I can feel pressure already building inside of me.

I push my heels into his shoulders and increase the pressure. Kessler lets out a growl and reaches up and tweaks one of my nipples. I cry out. "Jesus Kessler, just like that." I grind my hips into his face and ride him, pushing myself further to the edge. My grip tightens on his hair making him groan. Kessler moves his hand that's wrapped around my leg and slides a finger inside of me slowly stroking the inside in a come here motion and hitting a spot that has me seeing stars.

"Oh Fuck, Kessler. That's, that's. I'm going to…" I don't even finish my sentence as my orgasm hits. I clamp my thighs down around his face and he continues his pace, not letting up until my aftershocks have subsided and he's licked me clean.

Kessler rocks back onto his heels and stands. He stares down at me giving me a 'cat who ate the canary' look. "I've been dreaming of doing that to you since we had dinner at Tony's," he says, grabbing the bottom of his shirt and wiping his mouth. "Even better than I imagined."

I sit up and grab his joggers, pulling him forward. "Already eager for more?" he asks, cupping my face and running his thumb over my swollen lips.

I shake my head. "Not yet, but I can return the favor." I run my hands over the length of his impressive erection, causing him to let out a hiss. I stroke the outside a few times before pulling his joggers down. He steps out of them and kicks them to the side.

"Take your shirt off," I say, returning my hands to his cock stroking him through his briefs. He does as I tell him and I pause, taking a minute to soak in the beauty that is Kessler. I knew he worked out, but I didn't think he was this fit. I count six toned abs, with a light sprinkling of hair starting from his belly button and continuing down into his underwear. I pull his briefs down and his cock springs free, bobbing with delight. He steps out of them and I return my hands to his cock, stroking the soft skin.

Kessler hisses a breath through his teeth and closes his eyes, tilting his head back. I give it a few strokes, then lean forward and run my tongue around his head, licking up the precum that's leaked out.

Kessler weaves his hand into my hair and grips tight, making my scalp prickle and my eyes water slightly. "Fuck Lucy," he grinds out through his teeth. "You need to stop or I'm going to embarrass myself." I chuckle and lean forward to do it again, but he stops me. "I'm serious Lucy, I need to be inside you. Now."

I nod and climb back onto the bed. Kessler bends down and reaches into his sweats, grabbing his wallet, he pulls out a condom. Ripping the foil with his teeth, he gives himself a few strokes before rolling it on. I never thought of that being a turn on, reading several scenes like this in my smut books. How wrong I was.

Kessler stalks towards me and crawls on to the bed and over my body. He captures my lips with his giving me a slow deep kiss. Pulling back he gives me a devilish grin and flips me over onto my stomach. I let out a yelp, and start to get to my knees. I feel a sharp *smack* against my ass, and the sound echoes off the walls. Kessler's hand pushes me back down to the mattress.

The vibration from his hand makes my clit throb, begging for another release I know isn't possible. I've never come more than once. He runs his hand over the spot he spanked me, soothing the slight sting. He leans his body over me and whispers into my ear, "I'll tell you if I want you on your knees baby."

*Fuck me.*

Kessler places kisses from my shoulder, down to my outer

hip as he moves back down my body. Getting back into position behind me, he grips my legs where my hip and thigh meet, pulling me up, just slightly. He releases one of my hips and runs a finger through my sensitive lips.

"Fuck baby, you're dripping for me." His voice growing hoarse. I turn my head to look at him and he smacks my ass again. "I didn't say you could look at me yet." His hand soothing the spot again. I put my head back down on the mattress and wait for Kessler to tell me what to do next. I hear him whisper, "Such a good fucking girl."

I let out a small moan as I feel Kessler run the tip of his cock up and down my slit, teasing me. I move my ass back against him, getting impatient. He chuckles. "Eager are we? Be a good girl and I'll reward you" My walls clench and I'm shocked by how much I'm turned on by the praise.

Just when I feel like I can't take it any longer, he pushes the head of his cock in slightly. I inhale a sharp breath. "Fuuuuck," I breathe out, as he lets me adjust. He drops his grip on my hip and pushes me completely flat. Laying over the top of me, he places his hands on both sides of my shoulders and slides further inside on me.

"God, you're so tight, Lucy... I'm going to have a hard time controlling myself." His voice straining.

"So don't," I say, pushing back against him, sending him deeper inside me. I haven't been with anyone in 12 years, but Kessler has me so worked up, I push past the discomfort.

He growls into my ear. "Be careful what you wish for, baby, you might just get it."

"Promise," I ask, pushing back again, sending his full length inside me. "Yes," I hiss.

He growls again and bites down on my shoulder. I gasp and tilt my head to the side, opening my neck to him. He runs his nose up the side of my neck and places soft kisses back down. Sending shivers through my body.

"I wanted to go slow with you the first time, Luce, but I can't hold back. You feel too good."

I turn my head to look at him. "Fuck me, Kessler," I say, pushing up to my forearms and back into his cock. He gathers my hair into a sloppy ponytail and holds it in one hand. He lays the other on the bed anchoring himself, and starts pumping into me.

"Yes," I moan, letting the sensation roll through me.

"Fuck, Lucy, you're so fucking tight," he groans, increasing his speed.

The slight pressure of my clit against the bed as he rocks into me is driving me crazy. "More Kessler, I need more."

He lets go of my hair and reaches around and takes one of my breasts in his hands. He rolls my nipple between his fingers driving into me harder. "Yes, just like that Kess." I can feel the pressure building again inside of me. Taking me by surprise.

"Jesus baby. I don't know how much longer I can hold on. Are you close?"

"Yes," I whimper, the pressure building higher inside of me.

Kessler suddenly stops and I let out a protest. He grabs my leg and pulls it around flipping me over onto my back. He places one of my legs over his shoulder. "I want to watch you come undone," he says, siding back into me and filling me back up. I arch my back and let out a deep moan. He starts grinding into me harder and harder until all that you can hear is the headboard hitting the wall and flesh pounding against flesh.

"Oh fuck, Kessler. I'm, I'm almost there," I cry out.

"Grab your tits, Lucy. Let me see you play with those beautiful nipples."

I grab my breasts and roll my nipples between my fingers. The sensation brings me closer to my release. Sweat starts to prick at my skin and my mind blanks. My breath grows ragged and I'm not sure how much longer I can hold on. I tilt my head back and close my eyes.

"No," Kessler growls. "Look at me."

My eyes snap back open and I look into his lust filled eyes. He reaches down and circles my clit.

"Shit. Fuck. Kessler. I'm, oh God, I'm there," I call out.

"Let go, Lucy," he says, increasing the pressure on my clit and sending me right over the edge.

"Kessler," I cry out as my orgasm rips through me.

"Right there, Lucy." His voice tight, finding his own release.

Kessler drops my legs and lays over my body. Finding my lips, he gives me soft kisses while continuing to slowly pump into me drawing out the last ripples of pleasure from our bodies. I cup his face and look up into his eyes. "Wow," I say with a smirk.

"Wow," he says, smirking back.

"Where's your bathroom?" he asks, rolling off of me. I motion to the door across from my bed and watch as his chiseled ass cheeks walk away from me. Laying back in bed, running what just happened through my head. I hear the door open and see Kessler come out with a washcloth in his hand. He leans down and carefully runs the washcloth over me. After I'm cleaned to his satisfaction, he tosses it in the laundry bin and crawls back onto the bed with me, tucking me into his side. I let out a contented sigh and lay my head on his chest.

"So," I say, tracing circles onto his impressive chest. "Not that I'm complaining, because two orgasms is nothing to complain about, but what was that all about?"

His chest shakes with a silent laugh. "I told you, you're mine now and I couldn't wait another second to claim you."

"And a little bird told you I'd be home?" I ask, propping myself up on my elbow, giving him a look.

"Mmmhmm."

"This little bird wouldn't happen to have a name that starts with a 'K' would it?"

"I can't reveal my sources."

"Right, of course not."

"Actually, besides bringing you coffee and claiming you, I did have something I wanted to ask you," Kessler says, rolling to his side and propping his head up on his elbow.

"And what might that be?" I ask, using my free hand I reach up and use my finger to lightly trace the scar on his left shoulder.

"I want to take you and Hudson to my brother's game tonight." My finger freezes mid stroke on his scar. "I rarely get to see him play unless we're the ones playing against him. I thought it'd be a fun first official outing for all of us." Kessler stares at me hopeful.

"I uh, I can't. I already made plans with the girls." Thank god I already made plans with the girls.

"Oh," he says, disappointment in his voice.

"I'm sorry, maybe next time?" I say.

"Yeah, of course. Where's Hudson going to be during your girl's night?"

"Kara's. Her mom lives with her, so they'll be supervised."

"Do you think I could still take Hudson? Kade can come too. We can have a guy's night." He looks at me with that hopeful look, yet again.

A warm feeling spreads over my chest. I lean forward and give him a kiss. "I think that would be perfect. Let me check with Kara, I don't think she'll care, but I'll ask." I look at the clock on my nightstand and groan. "I hate to fuck and run, but I do have to get some work done today."

"Lucy," Kessler says, eyes darkening. "That mouth. If we had more time, I'd put it to work."

I clench my thighs together, turned on by the suggestion.

*WTF! I just had TWO orgasms, I can't seriously want more.*

We both get out of bed and find our clothes that we carelessly tossed around in the moment. Once dressed, I stand there awkwardly, not knowing what to do. Kessler finishes pulling his shirt over his head, much to my disappointment, and looks over at me. He walks over to me and takes me in his arms. Tipping my chin up, he gazes into my eyes. "Hey, don't over think this ok? You're my girlfriend, I'm your boyfriend. Nothing else."

I nod, knowing it's easier said than done.

"Come on, walk me out." He links our hands together and we walk to my front door. "I'll pick Hudson and Kade up at four."

I nod. "I'll text Kara as soon as you leave to run it by her."

He leans down and gives me a slow kiss. "Bye," he whispers after pulling back slightly, leaving a couple inches between our lips.

"Have a good day," I whisper back.

He closes what little gap is between us and gives me another kiss. I giggle and push him back, breaking the kiss. "You better go before we end up naked in the doorway."

He wiggles his eyebrows at me and I give his shoulder a light shove. Kessler leans in, giving me one last quick kiss before turning and jogging to his truck. I lean my head on the door frame and watch him drive away.

I blow out a breath and close the door. Boy, do I have a lot to tell the girls tonight.

I LEAN BACK and close my laptop just as I hear the front door open. Getting up, I peek my head out of my office and see

Hudson dumping his backpack on the floor and head to the kitchen.

"Hudson," I call from the doorway. He stops halfway to the kitchen and looks down the hallway at me.

"Yeah?"

"Backpack." I nod my head towards the object in question. He huffs and turns around, picking his backpack up and hanging it up on the hook six inches from where he dropped it. "Thank you."

He doesn't say anything and turns back towards the kitchen. Grabbing my phone, I shut the door to my office and join him in the kitchen. Taking a seat at the breakfast bar, I wait for Hudson to finish finding a snack before I tell him about Kessler's plan.

"So," I start, "Judd has a game tonight."

"Yeah I know," he says around a mouth full of peanut butter and pretzel so it sounds like "ah I mow."

I shake my head and continue "Kessler came by this morning, he wanted to see if we might want to go," I say, leaving out the other reason. Hudson pauses, pretzel mid way to his mouth.

"Really!? Are we going?"

"Well," I say, drawing out the word. He looks at me expectantly. "Kara, Marie, and I are having a girl's night."

His shoulders droop and he shoves the pretzel into his mouth.

"But." Hudson's eyes shoot to me. "You, Kade, and Kessler are going to go and have a guy's night."

Hudson lets out a whoop and fist pumps the air. "I'm going to go tell Kade!" he says, tearing out of the kitchen and into the backyard that connects to Kara's. I can hear him yelling Kade's name through the open door.

My phone starts vibrating and I look down to see Kara's name.

"Is Kade as excited as Hudson is?" I ask before hearing another loud whoop from the backyard.

Kara laughs. "Does that answer your question? I'm heading over now. See you in a minute."

I hang up the phone and see Hudson and Kade talking animatedly through the window. Kara appears at the gate connecting our backyards holding two bottles of wine in her arms. Oh we are definitely in for some dishing tonight. Kara makes her way through the sliding door and immediately goes to the fridge to put the wine away. She closes the fridge and turns, leaning across the island and propping her chin on her hand.

"Sooo, how's Kessler?"

"Uh, fine I guess," I say, giving her a questioning look.

"Mmmhmm, I bet," she says, smirking at me.

"What's that look for?" I ask

"Oh, no reason." she says nonchalantly. "You just have this glow to you." She looks out the sliding door to see where the boys are at. She lowers her voice and adds, "You know that post sex glow."

I let out a gasp. "How in the…"

"HA I KNEW IT!" she screams pointing her finger at me. She lowers her voice and says, "I thought I saw his truck leave your house this morning."

"It doesn't pay for you to work from home." Kara has her own business as a graphic designer, which means she has the luxury of working from home. Which today is unfortunate for me.

"Oh, yes it does," she says, giving me a smug look.

The boys come back through the sliding door ending our conversation.

*Thank God.*

Kara gives me a pointed look and I know we will be talking about this later once Marie gets here.

"When is Kessler going to be here?" Hudson asks, practically bouncing around the kitchen.

I look at my watch. "In about 20 minutes."

"Should we wear our jerseys?"

I shrug my shoulders "If you want."

Hudson and Kade look at each other, as if having a silent conversation, then nod their heads at each other. Hudson races to his room and Kade turns and runs out the back door. Kara and I laugh and shake our heads.

20 minutes and two jersey changes later, the boys are sitting in the living room playing video games, waiting for Kessler. I hear a vehicle pull up in my driveway and a few seconds later a knock sounds at my door.

Before I can even get off my stool to answer it, the boys have both abandoned their controllers and race to the door. Hudson flings it open to reveal Kessler standing there with a bouquet of flowers in one hand and a boyish grin on his face.

He holds out his free hand and gives them each a fist bump. "Boys, are we ready to watch some baseball and stuff our faces with hot dogs and nachos?" Both boys shout out 'yeah' and pump their fists in the air. Kessler chuckles. "Love the enthusiasm."

He looks over at me and I make my way over to him, fighting a wave of shyness that's come over me. He moves past the boys and meets me halfway. "These are for you," he says handing me the flowers and leaning down to give me a kiss.

Mmm, I've missed these lips, even though I just kissed him this morning.

We hear gagging behind us and break apart looking towards the door. Kade and Hudson are both covering their mouths, pretending to throw up.

"Ok, knock it off you two stooges," Kara says from her seat at the island.

I laugh and nod my head towards the TV. "Shut the game off and put the controllers away so you guys can get going."

We hear "so gross" and "I'm never having a girlfriend" as they clean up their mess and head back to the door.

"Thank you for taking them tonight. I know they are going to have an absolute blast." I take my flowers and lay them on the island. "Try to limit the amount of junk food though please, I don't need Hudson missing practice tomorrow. Oh, that reminds me." I walk over to the entry table and grab my purse. "I'll give you money for his stuff." I'm digging in my purse for my wallet when I feel Kessler come up behind me and hands grab my purse.

"Absolutely not," he says setting down my purse. "I got it."

"But," I start.

Kessler puts his hands on my arms. "No. I invited the boys, I'm paying." His voice says that's final. I stare up at him and swallow, his alpha voice doing things to me downstairs. I feel my cheeks heat a little and a little smirk crosses his face. "We better get going, I'm sure traffic is going to be a nightmare." He leans down and gives me another kiss, this one a little harder than the last.

The boys groan beside us and I can feel Kessler's lips turn up in a smile before he pulls away. He walks over to the door and drapes his arms across the boy's shoulders. "Boys, one day you're going to find a girl who completely turns your world upside down. When you do, I hope I'm there to gag when you guys kiss." He turns and gives me a wink, then ushers the boys out the door and into the truck. He honks his horn twice and gives me a wave as they drive off.

Kara sighs from behind me. "You guys are so freaking cute."

I shut the door and make my way back to the kitchen to take

care of the flowers. "It almost feels too good to be true Kar," I say, grabbing a vase and filling it with water. I trim the ends of the flowers and arrange them in the vase. They're the same kind he had sent to my office. I inhale the sweet lily scent and sigh.

Kara's smiling at me from across the island. "What? Do I have something on my face?" I ask, reaching up and swiping at my cheeks.

She shakes her head, her smile growing bigger. "I'm just so happy for you."

I walk around the island and sit down next to her, bumping her shoulder with mine. "Thanks, Kar." I give her a sad smile. "I want you to be happy too."

She waves me off. "Don't worry about me. I had the love of my life. I'm content with how life is now. I have you, my mom, and the boys. I don't need anyone else."

I put an arm around her shoulder. "Not even, oh I don't know, an ice cream man?" I tease.

Kara barks out a laugh and gives me a small shove. "Nope, I am not going there."

I'm about to question her more when there's a knock at the door. Kara hops off her stool and practically runs to the door. "That must be Marie!" She flings open the door revealing Marie with two boxes of pizza from Tony's.

"Sorry I'm late," Marie says, setting the pizza down on the island. "What did I miss?"

"Oh nothing," Kara says, grabbing plates from the cupboard.

"Kara has a thing for Kessler's ice cream man," I announce.

Marie's head whips over to Kara, who's sending daggers my way. I blow her a kiss and grab the wine from the fridge and glasses from the shelf.

"Let girl's night begin, we have a lot to cover ladies!"

# CHAPTER 12

## *Kessler*

WE GET TO THE STADIUM WITH SOME TIME TO SPARE, SO we load up on all the snacks and take our seats behind the plate. The boys are stuffing their faces with food, chatting, and having a good time. I take my phone and text Lucy, letting her know we made it. "Hey boys, hold up your hotdogs and say 'cheese'." I point my phone towards them and take a picture, sending it to her.

**LUCY**

They look like they're having a blast. Thanks again Kess. 🤗

ME

Anything for you Lucy. I hope you have a good time with the girls.

**LUCY**

Oh I am. 👶

I laugh, I think Lucy has already started in on the wine. I go to put my phone in my pocket when it vibrates again, indicating another text. I open the screen and it's a selfie of Lucy taking a drink of her wine and winking. I look closer and notice she's not drinking the wine, but licking the rim of the glass. My cock stirs as I immediately imagine her tongue somewhere else.

*Jesus.*

I sit forward in my seat, trying to hide the boner Lucy just gave me. I look to the side to make sure the boys don't see my phone, their attention is on the field. I click reply.

ME

> Lucy. You just gave me a boner, in public. The things I want to do with that mouth...

LUCY

> The things I'd like to do to you with that mouth. 😈

*Shit.*

If we don't stop this, I'm going to have a full on erection, in public.

ME

> Lucy, I really don't want to go to jail for public indecency.

LUCY

> 😔 ok, ok. I'll stop.... For now. 😉

*Fuck, this woman.*

I put my phone away and count backward from 20, trying to refocus my brain. Thankfully the announcer comes on the speaker introducing the starting lineup, indicating the game starting. We stand up and cheer as the Jackals are announced. The Jumbotron pans over to where I'm sitting.

"Look at that folks, big brother Davis is here to cheer on Judd," the announcer says.

The crowd cheers and I give a wave back, a sense of pride filling my chest. Judd was the typical little brother, always wanting to tag along and do what I was doing. So, when I started playing baseball, it was only a matter of time until Judd wanted to also. When he became old enough to actually pitch to me and help me practice my catching, I knew he'd be something.

Standing here today, listening to the crowd cheer, not only for me, but my brother too is such an unreal experience. Getting to share that with Hudson, who seems completely in awe of it all, well that's just icing on the cake

Hudson appears on the screen and I give him a nudge, jolting him out of his trance. He gives a small, shy wave to the camera before it pans back to the field and the Devils lineup is announced.

The crowd boos, Hudson and Kade included and the tension in the stadium amplifies with every smug grin the opposing team gives the camera. The Devils are not a popular team here. They're known for being rough and playing dirty. They hold the highest record of fights in the MLB. We play them next month and no one is really looking forward to it.The National Anthem starts and we all stand.

Once it's over the crowd grows loud as Judd takes the mound. He's been on fire this season and is one of the top five pitchers in the league. I'm proud of the work he's put in, even if he has been partying a little too much lately, in my opinion. I'll have to talk to him about it. I'd hate for him to throw this all down the drain by doing something stupid. I shake my head and focus on the game, now's not the time to mull over that.

IT'S the Bottom of the 9th and the Jackals are down by one. Judd was taken out in the 6th after pitching a hell of a game. With two outs, their left fielder, Tucker Jones, is their last hope. Tucker is one for three tonight, so the odds could go either way for him. The Devils closing pitcher, Wayne Feldman, hasn't been making it easy though.

The whole stadium is on their feet. The boys are at the fence clinging to it like a life raft. Wayne sends the first pitch over the plate, it looks good but curves off at the last minute. Tucker swings and misses. Strike one. The boys groan and grip the fence tighter.

Tucker brushes it off and re-positions himself. Wayne nods and launches another curve towards the plate. This time, Tucker doesn't swing, and the ball hits the outside of the plate, resulting in a ball.

The energy in the stadium is tense as we wait to see if we're heading to an extra inning. Wayne takes his position, nods, and throws a fastball straight over the plate. Tucker swings and connects with the ball. A collective gasp makes its way through the stadium. It's a line drive towards the shortstop, who looks like he might not make it to the ball. The crowd amps up, thinking they have a base hit, but at the last minute, he dives, making the catch and ending the game.

The boys deflate against the fence and turn walking back to their seats. While we wait for some of the crowd to thin out, I turn to the boys.

"We can't win them all guys, you know that." They both nod, faces still sullen.

"I'm going to tell you what one of my coaches told me a long time ago. Sometimes the only thing we can control in a game is how we react to our losses, so take a minute to be disappointed or sad, but then brush it off and look towards the next one."

The boys nod again, taking in the advice I gave them. I look around and see that the crowd has thinned out a bit. "Come on, let's congratulate Judd on his pitching."

The boys and I make our way to the family area after the game.We swung by the merch store first and I bought Judd's jersey for the boys. I texted him to meet us here after the game. I see him make his way down the hallway and raise my hand towards him. He looks up and gives me a nod letting me know he sees me. He stops and signs a few autographs before making his way over to us.

"Hudson, what's up broski?" he greets Hudson, giving him a fist bump. "Who's your friend?" motioning to Kade.

"This is my best friend Kade. Mom's having a girl's night with Aunt Kara, so Kessler said Kade could come with us and we could have our own guy's night."

He gives Kade a fist bump too. "Nice, Did you guys have a good time?"

Hudson and Kade nod enthusiastically.

"What are your plans now?" Judd asks, looking over to me and giving me a fist bump too.

I look at the time on my phone. "I actually need to get the boys back, it's getting late and they have school tomorrow." The boys groan. Judd and I chuckle.

"Look at you playing dad and being responsible." Judd teases and slaps me on the shoulder.

Hmm, I guess I never put much thought into being Hudson's dad if things progress like I want them to with Lucy. I give him a smirk and a shrug. He raises his eyebrows at me. "Really?" he says, not having to say anything more. I already know what he's asking.

"I mean." I shrug again. "Yeah."

The boys look back and forth between us, scrunching their faces, like they're trying to understand the bro code we're speaking in.

Judd stares at me, mulling it over, then nods his head."Awesome bro. I'm happy for you," he says, coming in to give me a hug and a slap on the back.

"Thank Judd," I say, returning the hug and back slap.

Kade leans over and whispers to Hudson. "What just happened?" Hudson shrugs his shoulders in response.

Judd opens his mouth like he's going to say something else, but something catches his eye over my shoulder. He raises his hand and I turn to look to see who he's waving to.

Jared Cox, shortstop for the Devils. I'm not a huge fan of his. I've heard mixed things about his attitude and treatment of women through the grapevine. Judd came up through the minors with him though so I don't say anything.

"Judd, what is up my brother from another mother," Jared says, greeting Judd with a handshake.

"Nothing much, just saying 'hey' to Kessler and his girlfriend's son and his friend," Judd says.

Jared turns to me and holds out his hand for a shake. "Kessler Davis, nice to finally meet you," he says. "Judd talked a lot about you when we went through minors together. How's the shoulder?"

I take his hand and give it a shake. "Shoulders good, thanks for asking."

"Girlfriend huh? I thought I read in a recent article that you said you didn't have time for dating?" he says, giving me a smirk. Something about that statement rubs me the wrong way. Maybe it's the tone he's using.

I give him a shrug. "When it's the right person, you make the time."

"Right," he says as if he doesn't believe in that bullshit. I admit, I didn't either, until Lucy. He nods to Hudson and Kade. "Who are these two?"

I place my hand on each of their shoulders and introduce them. "This is Hudson, Lucy's son, and his friend Kade."

Jared freezes mid fist bump, staring at Hudson. Judd and I exchange a look and look back at Jared.

"J, you good?" Judd asks Jared.

Jared blinks then takes a step back, dropping his hand. "Uh, Yeah, yeah. I uh." He shakes his head. "I'm actually not feeling that great. I'm going to have to take a rain check on going out," he says. He looks at Hudson again and takes another step back. He turns and heads off the same way he came. "I'll text you," he calls over his shoulder before disappearing down the hallway.

"That was weird," Judd says, still looking in the direction Jared went.

"Yeah. Weird," I agree. Something niggles at the back of my mind, but I'm not sure what to make of it.

"What's wrong with him?" Hudson asks, both boys looking at me.

I shrug. "Who knows bud. It's late, let's get you guys home."

The boys and I say bye to Judd and head out towards the parking lot. When we step out of the entrance I hear "Hey, that's Kessler Davis!" I look to my left and a bunch of paparazzi start screaming my name and rushing towards us taking pictures.

"Kessler, who are the kids?" one yells.

I shield the boys the best I can and usher them to the truck.

"Are they from the Little League team you were photographed with?"

"What are your names, boys?"

"Is something going on between you and that female coach?"

"Don't answer them," I tell the boys and keep shoving them towards the truck. I hit the button on my key fob and the boys rush to the back and open the doors, scrambling in. One guy reaches us first and tries to open the door Hudson just closed.

I slam my hand against the door and tower over the guy. His black greasy hair is slicked back and he has a sharp point to the end of his nose, making him look like a shrew. "Don't even fucking think about it," I growl

He slinks back and points his camera at me, snapping off a few pictures. "Chill out man, I just wanted to ask the boys a question."

"BACK THE FUCK OFF!" I yell. I turn to the group. "Get a fucking life, all of you." I turn and climb into my truck and slam the door. I put my key in the ignition and the engine roars to life.

"Boys, seatbelts," I say, looking at them in the rearview mirror. They nod and click their seatbelts in place. I put my own on and throw the truck in gear. Security has made their way to the commotion by now and has cleared a path for me to get out of here. I nod to one of the security officers and he gives me a two finger wave. The boys are quiet in the back seat. Once I'm on the freeway and have calmed myself down a bit I check on the boys.

"You guys ok?" I ask, hoping that didn't freak them out.

"That was crazy," Kade says, looking at me in the mirror.

"Do you think we'll be in the paper?" Hudson asks.

"Maybe Suzie Jenkins will talk to you now that you're famous," Kade teases Hudson.

"Shut up!" Hudson says.

I let out a sigh of relief and laugh. Doesn't look like it bothered them too much.

"So," I say, signaling to get over in the other lane. "Who's this Suzie?" I ask.

"Only a girl that Hudson has been drooling over since third grade," Kade says.

"Have not!" Hudson denies, elbowing Kade in the side.

They start arguing with each other in the back seat, I chuckle and shake my head. To be 11 again.

WE PULL into Lucy's driveway about an hour later. The boys talked and teased each other the whole way home. They scramble out of the truck and run into the house. I walk in the front door after them and see Lucy and Kara lounging at opposite ends of the sectional, empty wine glasses on their respective side tables.

A show is paused on the TV and the boys are both talking a mile a minute, telling them all about the game and showing their jersey's I bought them. Lucy looks over at me and gives me an adoring smile, making my heart stutter in my chest. Her cheeks are flushed and her eyes are a little shinier than usual, probably from the alcohol. I grin at her back and walk over, taking a seat next to her on the couch. I give her a kiss on her temple and wrap an arm around her. She leans into me and sighs.

Kara tosses the throw blanket back she had on her lap and gets to her feet. She stretches and lets out a yawn. "Well mister, we should probably head home and get some sleep, it's late," she says to Kade as she wraps an arm around his shoulder. "Tell Kessler thank you."

"Thanks a lot Kessler," he says. "I had a lot of fun tonight, even when those people with the cameras chased us."

I feel Lucy's body go rigid against my body and sit up. "What?" she asks, looking between me and the boys.

"Yeah, it was crazy. We were leaving and walked out the gate and all these-" Hudson pauses and looks at me. "What did you call them? Pepperonis?"

I can't help but chuckle. "Paparazzi."

"Yeah, Paparazzi. All these Paparazzi people were shouting and taking our pictures. It was nuts," he finishes and plops down in the spot Kara just abandoned.

Lucy's quiet and Kara's giving her a look I can't interpret. "Yeah, then Kessler yelled at them when we got to the truck and they tried to open our door. It was crazy," Kade chimes in.

"You can tell me all about it at home. We need to get you to bed." She gives Lucy another look and then looks at me. "Thanks again Kessler, I owe you one."

I hold my hand up. "No need to thank me. It was my pleasure, we had a blast."

Kade and Kara say their goodnights and head out through the patio door, walking along the lighted walkway. I look over at Lucy and point my thumb over my shoulder. "Does their backyard connect to yours?" Lucy looks at me with unfocused eyes, like she's thinking about something else. I tilt my head a bit and wave my hand in front of her face. "Lucy?"

She sucks in a breath, and her eyes refocus, looking at me. "Sorry, what? I wasn't paying attention."

I stare at her a moment, before repeating my question. "Oh, yeah we put in a gate between our yards a few years ago. It's so much easier than walking around the block."

I look over at Hudson, who's almost asleep. Then back at Lucy, who's picking at her cuticles. I place a hand over hers, stopping her. She looks up at me, worry and something else in her eyes. Fear? "Are you worried about what happened after the game? Because I would never let anything happen to the boys. You know that right?"

She turns her hand over and slips her fingers between mine.

"I know, its, I..." She stops looking at Hudson. "Let me get him to bed, then we can talk. Ok?"

I nod my head and watch as Lucy shakes Hudson awake. He yawns and stands. He mumbles a goodnight to me and Lucy guides him down the hallway. A few minutes later, Lucy comes out and sits back on the couch, snuggling into my side.

We're both quiet for a few minutes before Lucy speaks. "It's not that I didn't think the boys weren't safe with you. I just, it's." She sighs and continues. "I'm just not comfortable with the publicity. I know you're probably used to it by now, but I'm not and I didn't think it would be that bad." She untucks herself from my side and I can feel her not only pulling away physically, but maybe distancing herself emotionally too.

"Hey," I say softly, grabbing her chin and turning her face to look at me. "It's not usually that bad, ok? There's just been an uptick lately because I'm coming back from my injury and the whole thing with me being at the tournament and practice before that." I cup her cheek and close the distance between us giving her a gentle kiss. "I will fix this," I whisper.

*I'm calling Dale as soon as I leave. But I'm not leaving until I feel she's ok.*

She nods her head and leans her forehead against mine. I move and give her a kiss on her forehead and envelop her into my chest. She melts into me and circles my waist with her arms. In this moment all I want to do is tell her how much I love her, but I know she's not ready to hear those words.

Lucy yawns into my chest and I look at the clock on the wall and see it's well past ten o'clock. "You should probably head to bed. It's getting late." She nods into my chest, but doesn't make an effort to move. I chuckle and grip her arms pulling her back to look at me. She gives me a small sleepy smile.

*God, she's just so fucking beautiful.*

I stand and pull her to her feet. She stretches and gives me an amazing view of those perfect breasts I had my hands and mouth all over just this morning. I grab her hand and lead her to the front door.

"I wish you didn't have to go," she whispers, leaning against the door frame.

I cup her cheek and look down into her hazel eyes, that have turned more green with the burgundy top she's wearing. "I know, and I would love to stay, but I know it's too soon for that."

She gives me a smile and a nod. "I know, and thank you for understanding that."

I lean down and give her a slow kiss, teasing her lips open with my tongue. She opens her mouth for me and I tangle my tongue with hers. She moans softly into my mouth. I pull back and give her a smirk. Her eyes are dark with hunger. "That's for teasing me earlier," I say.

Her cheeks flush and she covers her face with one hand. "I can't believe I did that. I blame the wine and peer pressure."

I pull her hand from her face. "I thought it was fucking sexy as hell, and if I wasn't out in public and with your son, I would have been more than happy to play along." Her flush grows deeper. "You're the sexiest woman I have ever laid my eyes on Lucy." I kiss her again. I need her, but I know I can't have her right now. Not with Hudson down the hall. We break apart, slightly breathless. I take a step back. If I don't leave now, I'm not going to leave at all.

"Goodnight, Coach."

"Goodnight, Kessler."

I force myself to get into my truck and drive away. Once I'm on the road, I use my Bluetooth and call Dale. He answers on the second ring.

"Hello?" his voice heavy with sleep.

"Dale, it's Kessler. Sorry to call so late, but we need to do something about the pap's harassing me."

"Just a minute," he says. I hear shuffling on the other end, and him having a muffled conversation with Mary, his wife. A few seconds later he comes back onto the line.

"Ok, Kessler, now what's going on?"

I relay what happened in the parking lot back to him. I can hear him taping on something on the other end. Probably his keyboard. "Shit," he mutters.

"What?"

He lets out a sigh and I can imagine he's leaning back in his chair scrubbing a hand over his eyes. "There's a video of you threatening one of the paps. Tell me you didn't threaten this guy Davis."

"Does it show that he tried to open the back door to my truck where the boys were?" I ask, my hands gripping the steering wheel so tight, my knuckles are white.

"No, it doesn't," Dale says, his voice flat. "Come by tomorrow morning before you head to the clubhouse and we'll draft up a press release."

I nod my head, even though he can't see me. "Ok, great Dale. Thanks."

He's quiet for a few beats before he says, "I know you like your private life private Kessler, but we're going to have to get ahead of this, and the only way I can think of doing that is to have you and Lucy go public with your relationship."

I open my mouth to object but he stops me first.

"I know, I know, it's giving them what they want, but if we can lay all the facts out there first, they can't speculate and print any more lies."

I let out a sigh. "Ok, Ok. I know you're right. But tomorrow is just about releasing the truth about what happened at the game. I need to talk with Lucy first before I publish that we're together."

And if I know Lucy like I think I do, that's not going to be an easy thing to convince her of.

"Ok, but don't wait too long. There's already an article online trying to guess who the boys were. It's only a matter of time before they find out."

I clench my jaw so tight I feel like I might break a molar. "Ok, I'll talk to her tomorrow. Thanks Dale. Tell Mary sorry for the late night call."

Dale chuckles. "No need to be sorry Kessler, that's why you pay me the big bucks," he jokes. Dale is worth every penny if he can make this stop. I disconnect the call and pull into the parking garage to my apartment. Once I get inside. I toss my keys onto the entry table and head to the fridge. I grab a beer and pop the top, chugging the whole thing down. Lucy is not going to like this, and I don't want to lose her because of it. I scrub a hand down my face and put my bottle in the recycling then head to my room. I'm exhausted and I need to try to get some sleep before shit hits the fan tomorrow.

I'M SITTING in Dale's home office bright and early the next morning. Mary, being the amazing hostess she is, left a pot of freshly brewed coffee and blueberry muffins she baked yesterday before leaving us to our task.

I'm on my second muffin and third cup of coffee as Dale reads over the statement again, making sure it's clear and to the point. He sits back in his chair and takes off his glasses, pinching the bridge of his nose. "I think that'll do it. I'll send this off to the team and let them take care of the rest."

I crumble up my muffin wrapper and toss it in the trash. "Thanks Dale." I check my phone and stand. "I should head to the field."

Dale stands and comes around his desk and claps me on the back. "I'll walk you out." He walks me to the front door and opens it.

"Tell Mary thanks again for the muffins and coffee." I shake his hand and turn to leave.

"Kessler," he calls when I'm halfway down his steps.

I turn back and look at him. "Yeah?"

"If Lucy is as important to you as you say she is. Don't let this stuff come between you and your relationship with her. At the end of the day, what's most important is your family. Not the opinions of strangers."

I nod and give him a wave then head to my truck. I'm not the one we have to worry about letting it come between us. I climb into my truck and pull up my call log and dial Lucy's number. It rings twice before she picks up.

"Hello?" she puffs out.

"Good morning, beautiful. How did you sleep last night? Dream of me?" I tease and wiggle my eyebrows even though she can't see me.

She huffs out a laugh. "Hi, handsome. I slept like shit." She pauses, panting then continues, "Sorry to report no good dreams." Then more panting.

"Lucy, what are you doing? You sound out of breath." My cock stirs.

*Jesus.*

Why does my mind always go there?

*Because she's hot as fuck.*

I adjust myself and merge onto the freeway.

"I needed to clear my head so I got up early and went for a run," she pants out.

"What's going on?" I ask. "I know the paparazzi thing freaked you out last night, but I told you I'd take care of it and I did. I just left my agent, Dale's house, and we drafted a press release about what really happened. And the boys are minors so legally they can't release their photos without consent, which they don't have.

More panting.

"Ok. Yeah, that–that makes me feel better. Thank you Kessler."

I debate mentioning what Dale suggested about us going public, and decide it'd probably be better if I talk to her about that in person. I turn off onto my exit, but take a right instead of a left towards the field. "Where are you right now?"

"About three blocks from my house. I'm cooling out now," she says, her breaths not sounding as labored. "Why?"

I turn into her neighborhood and drive in the direction of her house. I drive slower than I normally would, looking down the streets. Up ahead I see a figure in a green sports bra and matching workout pants, walking in the direction of Lucy's house. I drive past her and pull my truck over. I hear her gasp through my speakers and I get out of my truck and walk straight to her. Her eyes are wide and I take her in my arms and kiss her hard. She's still for a second before melting into my arms and matching my eagerness.

"What are you doing here?" she asks, breaking the kiss.

"I missed you," I say simply and kiss her again.

She pushes back against me. "Kessler I'm all sweaty," she says into my lips.

"I don't care," I tell her, kissing the rest of her protests away. I hear a laugh in the back of her throat as she melts back into my embrace. We stand there making out like teenagers, when the neighbor's sprinklers turn on, spraying us. Lucy lets out a shocked squeal and runs out of the stream of water. I follow her laughing. "Well, that's one way to cool the fire," I joke, wiping away the water that's dripping down my face.

She laughs and shakes out her arms. "I think I have a towel in my truck," I say linking my fingers with her and walk to my truck. I open the door and reach into the back grabbing a towel. I wipe my face off and offer her the towel. She takes it and wipes her arms down, then hands it back to me. I toss it back in my truck and close the door.

"Want a ride back?" I ask.

"No. Thank you, but I should finish cooling out my muscles. I have a busy day and don't need my muscles cramping up on me."

I nod my head and reach for her hand, pulling her to me. She takes a step forward and circles her arms around my neck. I lean down and give her another kiss. I don't think I'll ever get tired of kissing her soft perfectly plump lips. She lets out a soft sigh and pulls back.

"As much as I would love to keep kissing you, I need to get home and shower before work." She looks at her watch, it's one of those digital ones that track everything.

I give her one more quick kiss before I reluctantly let her go. She walks backward a few steps before turning and jogging off. I watch as her perfect ass jogs away. I climb into my truck and for the second time this morning, I adjust myself before throwing my truck into drive and head toward the field.

# CHAPTER 13

## Lucy

"Ok!" I yell and clap my hands together. "Great practice guys, I'll see you Friday." The boys head for the dugout, grab their gear, then head towards their respective vehicles. I finish gathering stray balls and make sure all the other gear is put away. Heading into the dugout, I see Tommy still here, joking around with Hudson and Kade. I look around and notice the only cars left are mine and Kara's.

"Hey Tommy, is your mom running late again?" I ask, even though I already know the answer. Tommy's mom is notorious for being late for pickup. I've offered to drop him off on our way home before, but she bit my head off and told me she didn't need my help and that as a single mom I have enough of my own to worry about. Tommy gives me a sheepish look and nods his head.

"Ok, no worries. We'll hang out until she gets here." Tommy is a great kid, a little shy, but I've never had any issues with him. I don't want him to feel guilty for his mom's actions. I nod my head towards the field. "Why don't you guys go practice some hitting until Linda gets here"

The boys grab a bat and a couple balls and go out onto the field. I take a seat on the bench in the dugout and Kara sits next to me. "You don't have to stay," I tell her.

Kara looks at me and rolls her eyes. "Please like I'd leave you to fend for yourself when the she-devil gets here."

I chuckle. "Thanks, I really didn't want to deal with her alone." Linda is... unpredictable and you never know what mood she's in. I think there's more going on at home than we know, so I try to cut her a break. Kara says she's just a bitch, and that she's unhappy with her life, so she has to make everyone else miserable too.

I only ever see her husband at games and he's usually on the phone. Linda's always staring at him like if she could, she would shoot daggers at him with her eyes. I don't understand why people stay together sometimes, but it's not my place to judge. I check my phone for the score of Kessler's game and see that they won by two tonight. I'm about to send him a text congratulating him on the win when I feel Kara nudge my arm. I look up at her.

"Incoming," Kara says, nodding to the parking lot where Linda's pulling up in her white Land Rover.

"Tommy, your mom's here!" I call out to him, and put my phone away. I'm hoping if he gets his gear and heads over to her, she won't get out of the car. He's halfway to the dugout when we hear a car door slam and see her trudging over to us. *Damn it.* We grab our stuff and meet her halfway to the parking lot.

"Sorry I'm late, I just lost track of time," she says apologetically, sliding her oversized Gucci glasses into her perfect blonde hair and giving me a smile that shows her perfectly straight white teeth. Hmm she's in a good mood today. She falls into step with us as we make it to our vehicles.

"No worries, it happens," I tell her, planting a smile on my face. "Have a good night. See you Friday, Tommy." Tommy gives us a wave and climbs into the car after putting his gear in the back of his mom's car. I expect Linda to follow suit but she stays at the back of her car looking at me. I close the hatch on my SUV and give her a small wave.

"So, I actually wanted to ask you, Lucy." She comes closer and gets next to me lowering her voice. "Are you dating Kessler Davis?"

"Oh, uh, I really don't like to talk about my personal life Linda," I tell her.

"Oh come on," she says, nudging my shoulder with hers like we're best friends.

Fun fact, we're not.

"You can tell me, we're friends. Our kids have played base-ball together for years." Before I can say anything she continues. "Oh you know what, why don't you guys come to our house for dinner this weekend and introduce us? That would just be so much fun." She slides her sunglasses back down and walks to her door, leaving me standing there speechless. She twiddles her fingers at me over the roof of her car and calls out, "I'll text you later this week. Bye!" then backs out of her space and drives off.

Kara appears at my side. "What the fuck was that?"

"She asked if I was dating Kessler, then invited us over to dinner," I say, dumbfounded.

Kara snorts. "Like that's going to ever happen."

I shake my head, still trying to wrap my brain around what just happened. "She's crazy."

"Agreed," Kara says, laughing as she walks back to her car. "Better you than me," she calls out before getting in.

I open my door and give her the finger over my roof before climbing into my own vehicle. I look over and see her cackling through the window.

"What's Aunt Kara laughing at?" Hudson asks.

I shake my head. "Nothing bud, she's just a nut."

"I'm hungry, what's for dinner?" Hudson asks as we pull out into traffic and make our way home.

"How about breakfast for dinner? Pancakes, eggs, bacon?" I suggest.

Hudson nods his head.

A few minutes later we turn down our street and I see a familiar truck in my driveway. My stomach erupts in butterflies.

"Kessler's here!" Hudson announces, sitting up in his seat.

I laugh. "I can see that." I pull up beside his truck and Hudson scrambles out of my car and over to the porch where Kessler is sitting in one of the chairs I have out there. I sit in my car for a second and take him in. His hair is wet, like he just got out of the shower and he's wearing cargo shorts and a faded Silverbacks T-shirt. He says something to Hudson that makes him laugh and my heart skips a beat. He makes us both so happy. He makes time for us. I mean he played a freaking game today and even though I know he's probably exhausted, instead of going back to his place, he's here, with us.

*Because he loves you, moron.*

And I think I may love him too. The thought terrifies me, but not as much as the thought of him not being in our lives does. I know I need to tell him. Everything. But now isn't the time.

He looks over at me and I realize I'm still sitting in my car lost in my thoughts. I take a deep breath and climb out of my car. I walk over to them and give Kessler a big smile. "Hey, I didn't think I'd see you tonight." I dig my keys out of my purse and hand them to Hudson. He heads to the door and unlocks it, leaving it open and heading inside. Kessler comes over to me and wraps me up in his arms. I sigh and lean into him and wrap my arms around his back, breathing in his spice and leather scent. I feel him place a kiss on my head, then lay his chin on top of it.

"I didn't want to go home to an empty apartment, I hope this is ok?" he says into my hair.

I pull back and look up at him. "Absolutely. Have you eaten? We're just making breakfast for dinner." I shrug my shoulders. "Nothing fancy."

He leans down and captures my lips with his, giving me a long slow kiss. ˏWhen he pulls back he looks into my eyes. "Sounds perfect."

He takes my hand and we walk into the house. I set my stuff down on the entry table and I can hear the shower running in Hudson's bathroom. "I'm going to go change, make yourself comfortable" He nods and I head to my room and quickly change out of my practice clothes and into leggings and a tank top. I walk back to the kitchen and see Kessler sitting at the island. I get the bacon and a baking sheet out and turn the broiler on, on the stove.

"Need any help?" Kessler asks, looking at me from across the island.

"No, I got it. You just sit back and relax. Oh, congratulations on the win today, I wasn't able to catch the game, but I looked up the score after practice." I slice the bacon package open and start laying the strips on the sheet.

He stares at me, eyebrows scrunched.

"What?" I ask. "Is there something on my face?" I use the back of my hand to wipe at my face.

"What are you doing?"

I pause and stare back at him. "Cooking the bacon?" I say, like it's obvious.

"By putting it under the broiler?" he asks like it's the most insane thing he's ever heard of.

"Uh yeah? How do you cook bacon?"

"In a pan," he says, like it's obvious.

I roll my eyes at him, "This is much faster, trust me." I grab the sheet and put it under the broiler and turn the exhaust fan on.

"Whatever you say, Coach." Kessler says, giving me a smirk. I smirk back at him and wash my hands before grabbing the stuff for pancakes and putting it on the island along with the mixing bowl and griddle. We fall into a comfortable silence as I move around the kitchen making dinner. Like this is a normal Tuesday night for us. Hudson comes out a few minutes later and sits next to Kessler at the island. They talk about Kessler's game and Hudson tells him about practice.

After we eat, and all the food is put away, which wasn't much between the two bottomless pits, I'm rinsing dishes and putting them in the dishwasher. Hudson and Kessler are back at the island. Kessler tried to help me do dishes but I shooed him out to go hang with Hudson.

"So are you guys going to get married?" I hear Hudson ask Kessler. The plate I was rinsing slips from my hand and shatters in the sink.

"Shit," I mutter, turning off the water so the pieces don't go down the drain.

"Are you ok?" I hear Kessler ask, his chair scraping back from the island.

I wave him off. "I'm fine, the plate just slipped." Not paying attention to the shard I'm grabbing, I feel a pinch and a burning sensation. I look down to see blood pouring from my finger. "Fucking shit," I say, turning the water on and running my finger under it.

Kessler appears at my side and grabs my wrist. "Here," he says, taking paper towels that he grabbed and wrapping them around my finger, putting pressure on it.

"Thanks."

"No need to thank me, Coach. Now go sit down and keep pressure on your finger and I'll clean this up and finish loading the dishwasher." I open my mouth to protest, but he lays a finger across my lips and gives me a pointed look. "Go."

I roll my eyes at him, but do as he says and take a seat next to Hudson.

"You good, Mom?" he asks, looking at the bloody paper towel that's wrapped around my finger.

I give him a reassuring smile. "I'll be fine, bud. It's just a cut."

He nods and looks at me expectantly. "Sooo are you going to answer my question?"

"Uh-" I start. I was hoping he'd forget. I look over at Kessler, who's stopped loading the dishwasher and is leaning back against the sink, legs and arms crossed looking at me. I look back at Hudson. "It's, um, it's early in our relationship, sweets. We have to get to know each other better before we decide that." I look back over at Kessler and raise my eyebrows, waiting for him to agree with me. He just gives us a smirk and shrugs his shoulders, turning back to the sink.

"Ok, is he going to live with us? Jenny Baker's mom got a boyfriend last year and even though they're not married, he moved in with them."

What are kids talking about these days? I move to pinch the bridge of my nose, but remember I'm trying to keep from bleeding out through my finger. Kessler shuts the dishwasher and comes to the island and leans his arms across it. "Would you like it if we did live together?" he asks Hudson.

*Um, what?*

I stare at Kessler as he reaches across the table and grabs my hand with the towel. He gently unwraps the towel and looks at the cut.

Hudson looks at me then at Kessler and shrugs his shoulders. "I mean yeah, it'd be cool."

Kessler nods his head and looks at me. "The bleeding has slowed and it's not too deep, you won't need stitches. Where's your Band-Aids?"

"I'll get them," Hudson says, getting out of his chair and going down the hall to his bathroom.

"Grab the ointment too, bud," I call down to him.

We hear a muffled "K'" down the hallway.

I turn to Kessler and smack his arm with the back of my free hand.

"Ow," he protests. "What was that for?"

"What do you think it was for? Why did you ask him if he'd be ok with you moving in? We *just* started dating." I'm whisper shouting and I can feel my breaths coming faster. I just realized today that I might be falling in love with this man and I haven't even told him yet, now we're discussing moving in, with Hudson.

*What is going on?*

"Hey," Kessler says, taking my chin and tipping it towards him so I'm looking at him. "We're just having a conversation. I'm sure Hudson has a bunch of questions about this since you've never dated anyone."

I take a deep breath and let it out. He's right. This is new. To everyone, and the only way to get through it is open communication. I nod at him and we hear Hudson come out of the bathroom with the box of Band-Aids and the antibacterial ointment.

"Thanks, bud," Kessler says, taking the stuff from Hudson. I go to take my hand back but Kessler stops me. "Let me bandage you up. You take care of people all day. Let someone take care of you for a change."

I swallow and nod, letting him bandage me up. Hudson sits back down in his spot watching Kessler.

Well might as well try this open communication thing. "Hud," I say, waiting for him to look at me. When he does, I continue, "I know you have a bunch of questions about Kessler and me, and I want you to be able to ask us anything." Hudson looks at Kessler, who's wrapping my finger with the bandage, and back to me.

"So are you moving in?" he asks again.

Kessler gathers the garbage from the bandage and chuckles. "Not yet, bud."

*Yet? So he wants to?*

I shove those thoughts aside and turn back to Hudson.

"But," I say. "How would you feel if he stays the night sometimes?"

Hudson looks between Kessler and me and shrugs his shoulders. "I guess it'd be cool."

"Great, now that that's settled, I have something I need to talk to you and your mom about," Kessler says. Hudson and I both turn to look at Kessler. "As you know, I went to my agent, Dale's house, this morning and we sent out a press release about what happened yesterday at the game," he says, looking at me.

I nod my head and he continues, "He suggested in order to get ahead of the press and keep them from printing misinformation, that we go public with our relationship and release our own statement." All I can do is stare at him. I knew it'd come out eventually, I mean we couldn't keep it a secret forever. There have been whispers after he showed up to the boy's tournament. But I thought we'd have a little more time. That I would have more time to get used to this, and talk to Kessler about the one thing I've held back.

Kessler reaches across the island and takes my uninjured hand and gives it a squeeze. "I know it's a lot and it's over-whelming, but I think it's a good idea. We can keep it straight-forward. That we met at the meet and greet for the team, we hit it off and started dating, simple as that."

*Or not so simple as that.*

"Ok," I hear myself say, even though I'm still lost in my thoughts. "What do you need us to do?" I ask.

He clears his throat. "Dale and I thought it'd be a good idea for you two to come to my game on Thursday, when we play against Judd and his team. My parents will be there and you and Hudson can sit with them. Actually," he holds up his finger, "I'll be right back." He goes to the front door and slips his shoes on, then disappears out the door. I assume he's going to his truck.

I turn to Hudson. "You ok with all this? I'm not going to do it if this bothers you."

Hudson shrugs his shoulders again and looks at me. "I like Kessler, Mom. He's cool and you're different around him."

I frown and scrunch my eyebrows. "Different how?"

"I don't know. Happier I guess?"

"I was happy before Kessler too, Hudson." I don't want him thinking I wasn't happy when it was just the two of us, because I was.

"Yeah, but you smile a lot more now and he makes you laugh. It's not bad, Mom. Don't worry so much," he tells me. As if it's just that simple.

Kessler comes back in the door and kicks his shoes back off. He's carrying a bag with him and he sets it down on the island between Hudson and I. He reaches into the bag and pulls out two Silver and Teal jerseys. He hands one to Hudson and one to me. I unfold mine and flip it to the back. Davis is written on the back with his number 22. "We can't be dating and you not wear my jersey." He rubs the back of his neck, looking unsure."I've never asked a woman to wear my jersey before."

I can't help the smile that breaks out over my face. I stand, setting the jersey on the counter. I lift up onto my tiptoes and wrap my arms around his neck. Kessler slips his arms around my waist and I place a quick kiss on his lips. "I love it. Thank you."

"So you'll wear it Thursday? If-if you agree to do this, that is."

"I already have one of your jersey's," Hudson says, we both look at him and he's slipped the jersey over his head. "Mom bought me one when I became the main catcher for the team. She said if I wanted to be a catcher I might as well learn from the best one in the league."

Kessler turns back to me and I can feel my face heat. "Best in the league huh?"

I shrug my shoulders. "That was before you got old," I tease.

He gives me a sinister smile and leans down and whispers into my ear. "You didn't think I was too old yesterday morning." His breath sends shivers down my spine and goosebumps break out over my body.

"I'm going to go show Kade," Hudson says hopping off the chair and heading out the back door, completely oblivious to Kessler and I.

Once Hudson is gone, Kessler descends on me. He kisses me hard making me moan into his mouth. His hands roam down my back and over my ass. Cupping both cheeks, he lifts me up, making me squeal. "Kessler, your shoulder!" I protest.

"My shoulder is fine," he says as he plants kisses down my neck. "I've been wanting to do this all night." I let out a soft groan and run my fingers through his hair. Kessler makes his way back up my neck and captures my lips again. I nip his bottom lip and he pulls back to look at me, eyes dark with desire. "Lucy," he says, voice strained. "I want you so fucking bad."

"Just a second," I tell him and hop off the counter and grab my phone.

I need you to keep Hudson there for at least 10 minutes. Please.

KARA

Say no more girl. I got you.

I smile and put my phone down on the counter. Thank God for good friends. I walk over and grab Kessler's hand and lead him down the hallway to my bedroom.

"What are you doing?" he asks, standing in my room.

I turn and shut the door then turn back to him. "We have ten minutes," I tell him. I walk him backwards until the back of his knees hit my bed. He collapses down and I crawl over him and kiss him. He grabs my hips and grinds me down his length, letting me feel how hard he is, making me whimper.

"Fuck," he groans into my mouth. I break our kiss and slide down his body, stopping at his waist. He props himself on his elbows to watch me with hooded eyes. I unbutton his shorts and slide my hand down over his thick erection. Kessler sucks in a breath. A moan sounding in the back of his throat. Knowing we only have ten minutes. I get to work. I pull at his shorts and Kessler lifts his hips, allowing me to pull them off. I repeat the process with his briefs and his cock springs free and bobs on his stomach, a bead of precum already glistening on the tip. I kneel down between his legs.

"Lucy," Kessler's voice strains. I look up at him through my lashes and give him a mischievous smile. Taking his cock in my hand, I swipe my thumb over the tip and put it in my mouth. Sucking it clean. "Fuck," Kessler whispers. I lean forward and swirl my tongue around the tip making Kessler's head fall back and groan. He's so big, I have to wrap one hand around his base and stroke it as my mouth glides down the top of his length. I use my other hand to cup his balls and gently massage them.

I swirl my tongue over his tip before sucking him back into my mouth. Kessler uses one hand to grab my hair, while holding himself up with the other. I continue my rhythm while Kessler whispers words of encouragement, letting me know how much he likes it. I can feel his balls tighten as his words die off and his grip tightens on my hair. "Fuck, Lucy. I'm almost," he pants, not being able to get the words out. "Lucy, I'm going to cum." I let out a hum and increase my pressure on his base. He throws his head back and groans out my name, hips bucking into my mouth. I swallow down every last drop and when he's done pulsing into my mouth, I detach my lips with a 'pop'.

Kessler collapses back onto the bed panting and I sit back on my heels and wipe my mouth with the back of my hand. I get up and lay on the bed next to Kessler propping my head up on my hand, a satisfied grin on my face. He looks over at me and grins back. "Wow," he says, propping himself up on his elbow and leaning forward to give me a kiss. He pulls back and looks me in the eyes "You're amazing, you know that?" I feel my cheeks redden at the complement. "I don't think I have time to return the favor." Regret in his voice.

"I don't need you to return the favor," I tell him. I sit up and walk to my bathroom to fix my hair. When I come back out Kessler is dressed and sitting on the edge of the bed. I walk over to him and his arms go around my waist. I lean down, kissing him softly, and I pull back. "And, the answer to your question earlier is yes," I say.

He looks at me confused for a minute, before it clicks in his brain. "You'll go to my game Thursday?"

I nod. "Officially, as your girlfriend."

A grin breaks out over his face and he crushes my lips with his. I giggle into his mouth kissing him back. I don't think I've ever been happier.

# CHAPTER 14

## Kessler

IT'S GAME DAY AND I HAVEN'T BEEN THIS NERVOUS FOR one of my own games in a long time. Knowing Lucy is going to be here watching me play and cheering me on, not as a fan but as my girl is doing something to me. The fact that she even agreed to do this and come out in public as a couple makes me love her even more. She's stepping out of her comfort zone and putting herself out there for me.

I feel something hit the back of my head and fall to the floor. It's a roll of athletic tape. I turn around and see Brent laughing at me from across the locker room

"What the fuck dude," I say, throwing it back at him. He catches it easily in one hand and tosses it up in the air, catching it again.

"Are you off in your own little world over there? I called your name twice," he says, throwing the tape back up in the air and catching it again.

I scrub a hand down my face and scratch my beard, it's

getting long and I need to trim it. I haven't had the time or energy between practice, games, and spending time with Lucy and Hudson. "Sorry man, just got a lot on my mind."

He nods his head at me. "You good?" Brent may love busting my balls, but I know he'd be there in a heartbeat for me if I needed him. That's why he's one of my best friends.

I nod back at him. "Yeah man, I'm good."

The rookie looks over at me giving me a cocky smirk. "Hey if you need to sit this one out, I'd be more than happy to fill in for you tonight, just say the word man."

I huff out a laugh. "Nah man, I'm fine."

*Fat chance in hell.*

My phone buzzes with a text and I see it's Judd. I open it and it's a picture of him flexing in the mirror.

**JUDD**
Need tickets to the gun show?

**ME**
🙄 put a shirt on, no one wants to see that.

**JUDD**
That's not what the chick I was with last night said

**ME**
Was she blind? Because that would explain a lot.

**JUDD**
👍

**ME**
🙂 Good luck out there today dick.

**JUDD**
You too ass hat.

Ah, brotherly love. I click over to my text thread with Lucy and send her a quick text.

> ME
>
> Can't wait to see you tonight 🥰

I'm surprised when she texts me back so quickly. She must be in between patients.

> LUCY
>
> Can't wait to watch that fine ass all night.

Oh, flirty Lucy is out to play. I've noticed the more comfortable Lucy gets with me and our relationship, the more she's been opening up, and I like what's under the layers she's hid.

> LUCY
>
> autocorrect* I mean I can't wait to watch *you* play tonight 😊

I laugh

> ME
>
> I think the first message was correct.

> LUCY
>
> 🙈 I plead the 5th.

> ME
>
> I spoke to Charlie. She's going to meet you at the ticket booth and bring you and Hudson to me so we can take the picture on the field.

Dale and I thought it would be best to get a picture before the game so he can send out the statement before the game even starts. I send her Charlie's number since I won't have my phone on me out on the field.

ME

Just send her a text when you get here.

LUCY

Ok. I gtg, my last patient is here. 😷 I'll see you soon.

I put my phone back in my locker. Lucy seems to be taking this in stride, which helps settle my nerves. Reese sits down at his locker, distracting me from my thoughts.

"You good man? You seem antsy," he says, nodding to my leg that I didn't even notice I was bouncing up and down.

I stop it and lean forward, taking a breath. "Yeah man, I'm good, just ready to get this thing going."

"Well, we have a bit, wanna go jog off some nervous energy?"

I nod my head and we both head off to the gym off the locker room. We jump onto treadmills next to each other and start at a brisk walk, warming up our muscles.

"So," Reese starts. "How are things going with Lucy? I know you're going public with your relationship. How's she handling that? How are you handling that?"

I blow out a breath and let my lips flap. "Things are great with Lucy. I know we've only been officially together for what? Four days? But I feel like I've known her forever. If I'm not with her, I want to be. We actually talked to Hudson the other night about me staying the night sometimes." I laugh thinking back to the conversation with them the other night. "He asked if we were going to get married–Lucy broke a dish in the sink."

"What did you say?"

I shake my head. "Nothing, Lucy cut her finger on the plate and I figured it wouldn't be a good time to say that's what I intend to do."

Reese whips his head around to look at me and stumbles, he grabs onto the handle to keep from eating shit. I chuckle and increase the speed on my treadmill to a slow jog.

"I'm sorry, what did you say?" Reese asks, righting himself and increasing his speed too.

"I know it's crazy, but that's where I see this relationship going. When we were at my mom's for dinner the other night, it just felt...right. Like this is where they belong. With me."

Reese is quiet for a beat like he's mulling something over. "Are you sure this isn't just new relationship feelings? I know it's been a while since you've been with anyone."

I get where he's coming from, it's been at least two years since I've dated anyone, but I know what I feel, and it's not what I've felt for anyone before. I tell him as much. I shake my head. "No, this is real. I've never felt this way about anyone before. She's it for me."

I slow my treadmill down to an easy walk. The nervous energy dissipates and leaves me much calmer. Maybe admitting my feelings to someone was what I needed.

Reese slows down with me. "Well then I'm happy for you man. I can't wait to get to know her better. And I better be the fucking best man at your wedding. Brent can fuck right off."

I laugh. "I think my brother would have something to say about that. Plus I have to ask her first and we are definitely not there yet."

We walk for a few more minutes and hop off, each grabbing waters from the fridge and chugging them down. Heading back to the locker room, I stop Reese at the doors. "Hey, can you not mention anything I told you back there to anyone? Brent can't keep his mouth shut to save his life and I don't need anything getting back to Lucy and freaking her out. I already feel like I'm pushing it on how fast we're going."

Reese claps me on the back. "Your secret's safe with me bud."

"Thanks," I say, opening the door to the locker room.

We head to our lockers and suit up.

WE'RE out on the field stretching, making sure we stay warm before the game. Fans are starting to fill the stands and I check the entrance for what seems like the hundredth time looking for Lucy and Hudson. I'm just about to turn back when I see Charlie make her way out of the dugout with one of the team photographers, followed by Hudson, then Lucy. Lucy steps onto the field and we lock eyes.

Seeing her in my jersey and knowing my name is on her back sets my blood on fire. I make my way over to them, my eyes on Lucy the whole time. The closer I get the bigger her smile gets. When I reach her, I take her into my arms. She places her arms on mine and stares up into my eyes. The air crackles between us, like it has since the day we met. Every-thing else fades into the background as I lean down and whisper into her ear.

"You look so fucking sexy with my name on your back."

Lucy shivers and softly chuckles. "Kessler, we're in public. People are looking." Her eyes flit around us.

I grip her chin between my thumb and finger and tip her head back, so she's looking at me. "Let them look," I say, leaning down and sealing my lips over hers. She's stiff at first. I move my hand to the back of her neck and deepen the kiss. She sighs and relaxes into me, moving a hand from my arm to the front of my chest.

I hear some whooping in the distance, and someone clears

their throat, breaking us apart. Lucy's cheeks turn a deep red color and she tucks her face into my chest. I chuckle and wrap my arm around her back and turn us toward Charlie and Hudson. Charlie gives me a smirk and Hudson looks like he'd rather be anywhere but where his mom is making out with her boyfriend.

"Let's get a couple of shots of you three at home plate, then we can get Lucy and Hudson to their seats," Charlie says.

We nod and pose at home plate. The photographer takes a few shots, then lets us know he's got a few good ones to work with. "We'll pick out the best ones and send them over to Dale for approval. The article will be released right before the game starts," Charlie says, clicking through her phone.

"Thanks Charlie," I tell her and she nods in response and stands by the dugout entrance, waiting to take Lucy and Hudson to their seats.

I look at Hudson, who's looking around, watching all the pregame stuff in awe. An idea strikes me and I turn to Lucy. "Can I take Hudson?"

She scrunches her eyebrows. "Take him where? You have a game soon."

"To do pregame stuff with me, hang out in the locker room." I lift a shoulder. "Guys bring their kids all the time."

"But he's not your kid," she says quietly in disbelief.

I run my hand down her back resting it at the dip at the bottom. I give her a look before saying, "Not yet, Lucy. But those are just minor details. I love that kid like he's mine and that's all that matters."

Tears well up in Lucy's eyes and she tries hard to blink them away, but one escapes and runs down her cheek. I swipe it away with my thumb and lean down to give her a soft kiss. When I pull back I make the decision to tell her.

I swallow and cup her cheek, looking into her shiny hazel

eyes. "I mean it Lucy. I love you two more than I thought was ever possible." Her lips part and eyes grow wide. "I know you're not ready to say it, but I can't hold it in anymore. You and Hudson, you guys are mine, my future. I know we've only known each other a few weeks, but that energy we feel between us, not everyone gets that and I'm not letting that go."

Lucy swallows and nods her head. "I think Hudson would like that," she says, giving me an answer to my original question.

I nod and give her a quick kiss on her cheek. "Go find your seat with Charlie. I'll send Hudson back to you when we're done." Lucy turns and walks over to Charlie, still in a dazed state.

Charlie gives me a questioning look. "I'm going to take Hudson for pregame stuff, can you come get him when it's time?"

She gives me a nod then heads off with Lucy.

"Where's Mom going?" I hear Hudson ask behind me.

I turn to him and sling my arm around his shoulders. "She's going to go to her seat. We're going to hang out for pregame stuff."

"Really?" he shouts in excitement.

"Yep, let's introduce you to some of the guys you don't know."

I look back over my shoulder one more time where Lucy disappeared. I hope I didn't move too fast. But I can't help what I feel with her. Hudson lets out a whoop and we head off towards my team. I push my worries to the back of my mind and focus on my time with Hudson.

# CHAPTER 15

## Lucy

I'M SITTING IN MY SEAT BEHIND HOME PLATE WATCHING Hudson and Kessler in a dazed state. He told me he loves me.

*No shit*, my inner voice says in a snarky tone.

I shake myself out of my trance and grab my phone to text Kara. I'm opening my text thread when I hear a familiar voice calling my name.

"Lucy!" I hear and turn to see Marlene and Henry making their way to me.

I stand and Marlene greets me with a tight hug that instantly makes everything better. I return her hug, not realizing how much I missed her.

"Where's Hudson?" she asks, looking around me.

"Oh, uh-" I point to the field where Hudson and Kessler are tossing a ball around with a few of his other teammates, laughing and having a good time.

Marlene's hand moves to her chest. "Oh, isn't that just a sight," she says. She turns back to look at me, eyes red-rimmed.

I feel my eyes sting again and nod my head, not trusting my voice to speak.

"Now quit hogging the girl and let me get a hug in," Henry says moving past Marlene for a hug of his own. "Enough with the waterworks, you two," he jokes, releasing me. "This is a happy day. Let's enjoy it."

We both chuckle and take our seats. Marlene's chatting with me about her neighbors down the road from her having to sell their place because it's become too much work for them. A thought pops into my head about how nice it would be if we could buy their place and live closer.

*Wait, what!*

We? Two seconds ago I was freaking out about him telling me he loves me and here I am thinking about how nice it would be for *us* to live closer to his family. What the hell is going on?

Marlene's looking at me expectantly, like she just asked me a question. I give myself a mental shake and pull myself back into the conversation. "I'm sorry, what did you say?"

She chuckles and nods to my phone in my hand. "I said your phone went off dear, but you looked like you were lost in your thoughts."

"Oh, yeah. I uh, just remembered something I have to take care of tomorrow at work. I'm sorry," I tell her, apologizing for lying, but she doesn't know that.

"No need to apologize dear, you're a busy woman."

My phone beeps again, then again. "Sorry, I'll switch it to silent."

"Sounds like someones trying to get a hold of you," Marlene says. "Go ahead and check it."

I unlock my phone and quickly check my notifications. I set my Google alert to notify me whenever Kessler's name comes up in the media. I have one notification from that and three texts waiting for me. I click on the group text from Marie and Kara first.

> KARA
>
> GIRL! THAT PICTURE!
>
> MARIE
>
> It's 🔥
>
> KARA
>
> I think I'm pregnant from just looking at it.

What are they talking about? I hit the Google notification and see it's the 'Official Announcement' Kessler's team released about his relationship with me. I scroll down and suck in a breath. "Holy shit," I whisper.

"What's that dear?" Marlene asks, turning back to me.

I turn my phone towards her and show her.

She pulls her glasses down from the top of her head and takes my phone. "Oh my." She looks at me with a mischievous smirk, then back down at the phone. "Well, there's no mistaking you two are in a relationship now, is there?" She scrolls down then hands me back my phone and adds, "I'll have to ask Kessler to get me a copy of both of those to add to our wall of family photos."

I take back my phone and look at it again, noticing the second picture. The picture I originally thought was going to be in the release. It's of the three of us, posing like a happy family. Kessler and I have a hand each on Hudson's shoulders and our other arms are behind each other's back. But that first photo.

*Shit.*

Kessler has me in an embrace and is looking at me like he wants to devour me. I shift in my seat and cross my legs, trying to ease the ache that's formed. Kessler's not even near me and he's doing things to my body I've only ever read in books.

I click over to my text thread with the girls.

ME

> I didn't even know they were taking pictures yet when that photo was taken.

KARA

> Well there's definitely no question about who you belong to.

I laugh. No there is not. I couldn't deny it even if I wanted to. The more I think about it, the less it scares me.

MARIE

> I never took Kessler as the possessive type...

I think back to what he told me on home plate. About Hudson and I being his.

ME

> I'm learning when it comes to the people he loves... he's very protective.

My phone rings not even 20 seconds after I send that text. Kara. I excuse myself and walk down away from Kessler's parents.

"Hello?"

"Don't *hello* me. Did you just say LOVE!" Kara shouts through the phone.

I pull the phone back from my ear a bit and chuckle. "Hi to you too, Kara."

"Shut up and answer my question."

"I'm sorry, was there a question in there? I couldn't tell over all the shouting."

"Lucille Elenor Carver, do not be cheeky with me. Spill."

"Ew, don't full-name me." I let out a sigh and relent. "Kara, he told me he loves me. More specifically he said he loves

Hudson and me and that he thinks of Hudson as his." I hear her gasp.

"Hold on," I tell her and pull my phone away from my ear and take a picture of Hudson and Kessler out on the field and send it to her.

"I just sent you a picture."

I hear her shuffle the phone. "How adorable is that?" she says. "What did you say back to him?"

I sigh. "Not what I know you wanted me to say. I told him Hudson would like going onto the field with him."

"Lucy!"

"I know, I know! I just... Kara. Isn't it too soon?"

Kara lets out a heavy sigh. "Lucy, I don't think time has anything to do with it. He's already proved to you, a couple times now, that he's in it for the right reasons. Trust him, put your heart into this, and keep your head out of it."

"People are going to talk," I say, my stomach turning at the thought of other people's opinions. I've tried hard to not care about the opinions of others, but this situation brings back all the insecurities I've tried so hard to overcome.

"Fuck 'em! Let them talk. If they're negative, they're just jealous because you have what they want."

I let out a laugh. "This is why you're my best friend. You tell me all the hard things I don't want to hear, but need to. Thank you Kar."

She blows a raspberry into the phone. "That's what I'm here for. Now go watch your man play."

I end the call and make my way back to Marlene and Henry. I take my seat and Marlene raises her eyebrows. "Everything ok? You looked a little frazzled down there."

I give her a smile. "Everything's good. My best friend was just talking some sense into me."

She nods and pats my hand. "Those are the best kind of friends."

We're quiet for a moment and I mull over my conversation with Kara. "Marlene?" I say, feeling I need her opinion on this.

"Hmm?" she says looking over at me.

I pop my fingers and fidget with my ring on my thumb. "You don't think Kessler and I are moving too fast, do you? I mean, I know you and Henry were married within three months of meeting each other, but..." I shrug my shoulders. "These are different times."

It's not Marlene who answers me though, it's Henry. He leans forward to look at me, his eyes so much like Kessler's, but with more wrinkles around the edges. "Lucy, if I've learned anything in my 60 years on this Earth, it's this–the amount of time doesn't matter. What matters is the actions that happen in the span of that time. Does he show up for you and Hudson? Does he treat you right? Has he ever for one second made you think you're anything but important to him?" he pauses, letting his questions sink in.

He's right. I know he's right. I'm just scared that this could all come crashing down and I won't survive the fall.

When I don't say anything Henry continues, "Don't let your fear take over, Lucy. I see how my son looks at you, that love doesn't come around often." He grabs Marlene's hand and gives it a squeeze. "And not everyone is lucky enough to find it, so when you do, you hold on and don't let it go."

I wipe at a tear that's somehow found its way onto my face. "I thought you said no more waterworks," I say letting out a laugh.

Marlene and Henry chuckle. "You're right. Enough mushy crap. There's no crying in baseball."

I let out a gasp. "That's my favorite baseball movie!"

Henry laughs. "I knew Kessler had good taste."

We spend the rest of warmups discussing our favorite baseball movies. We're in a disagreement over which Major League movie is the best when I see Charlie and Hudson make their way towards us. He takes a seat on the other side of Henry and Charlie takes a seat next to me.

"So, did you see the announcement?" she asks, looking hesitant.

I nod. "I did. I was... shocked you chose two pictures."

She bites the corner of her lip. "Yeah, well, it wasn't me who chose it. I sent everything we had to Kessler's agent Dale, and he made the final decision." She shrugs her shoulders. "No one can question if you guys are dating."

I let out a laugh. "That's pretty much what Marlene said."

"So you're not mad? I figured you'd be upset. Kessler mentioned how hesitant you were to be in the public when he and his agent arranged this."

"I was upset at first, but I'm quickly realizing if I'm going to be with Kessler, there's some things I can't control. Public opinion being one of them."

Charlie lets out a breath and nods. "I'm so glad you feel that way, because we're a sold-out crowd tonight and I was notified that because of the announcement, you will be on the Jumbotron at some point tonight."

*Shit.*

WE'RE in the 8th inning and it's been a scoreless game. Kessler raised his mask and winked at me in the first inning, which the Jumbotron caught, causing the crowd to erupt in cheers. Since then all focus has been on the game, thankfully. Kessler's catching and hitting are on fire tonight, but the other team's defense is on point too, making it difficult for us to score. Marlene joked it's because he has someone to impress, which makes me blush.

The Jackals starting pitcher has pitched an amazing game, but he's starting to fade. Duke Keller is walked and next on deck is Kessler. The Jackals manager comes out and Judd is brought out to replace him. The whole stadium erupts in a cheer and everyone gets to their feet. Nothing like a good sibling rivalry. A grin spreads across Kessler's face as he makes his way to the plate.

Judd has a matching grin on his face as he winds up for the first pitch. He sends a slider down into the bottom corner of the strike zone for strike one. Kessler's been having a hard time with outside strikes thanks to his shoulder, and his brother is capitalizing on that. Judd takes his position again and releases another slider. This time he over snaps his wrist and gets ball one. Kessler taps his bat on the plate and re-positions himself. Judd takes a visible breath and winds up, sending a fastball right across the plate. Kessler swings and misses. Strike two.

Kessler calls for a time and steps out of the box, taking a few swings. I send up a silent prayer to the baseball gods as he steps back into the box and swipes at the dirt with his foot a couple times before he positions himself. Judd gives him an ear-to-ear grin before releasing another slider. This time Kessler's on it and the sound of the crack echoes through the stadium. The stadium holds a collective breath as we all watch the ball sail high and far, right over the right field wall. Cheers erupt and Marlene and I scream, hugging each other. Henry gives Hudson a high five. Kessler makes his way around the bases. When he hits home base, he looks right at me, kisses his hand and sends it my way, giving me a wink.

The inning ends with Judd striking out the last two batters, bringing us to the top of the 9th. If we can keep them from scoring, we win. Jace Friday, our closer, comes in. The crowd goes wild. If Kessler can keep him dialed in, no one will score. The cutter on this kid is deadly.

We start the inning with a strike-out and a base hit. Not bad, but not great. If we can't get the next two out, we're in for a battle. Jace throws two balls and the batter hits two fouls. Kessler calls for a time and jogs to the mound. He has a quick conversation with his pitcher, covering his mouth so the other team can't read their lips. Watching him in action all night has got me all riled up, knowing he's coming home to me. I'm surprised they're not hosing me down with how hot I am.

Kessler gives Jace a tap on the ass and jogs back to his position behind home. He takes his position and Jace's next pitch is a beautiful cutter, the batter doesn't even swing. Whatever Kessler said to him helped. The last batter makes his way to the plate and the stadium is on their feet again. Jace shakes off the pitch Kessler calls for. Kessler sends another sign and Jace nods, liking the decision.

The runner on first keeps creeping away from his bag, trying to get a head start for a steal. Jace sends a fastball over the plate and the batter swings and misses. Strike one. The runner on first tags up on his bag and starts creeping back out towards second. Jace sets up and lobs another pitch over the plate. The runner goes and Kessler snaps the pitch up and jumps to his feet. Jace ducks and Kessler launches the ball straight to Brent. Brent catches the rocket Kessler sends him and back tags the runner as he slides into second.

"OUT!" the infield umpire shouts. The stadium shakes as we all scream in celebration. Marlene and I are hugging and jumping with joy. Charlie is taking video of the stadium for the social media page. The Jackals call for a play review, but the stadium doesn't care, we know he's out and we're celebrating.

Kessler's teammates rush him. I grab Hudson and give him a hug.

"That was AMAZING!" Hudson yells over the noise of the crowd.

"That's why he's the best bud." We stand at the fence watching the celebration. Kessler breaks free and looks over to us. I send him a kiss and he catches it, placing it over his heart. In that moment, I know, he's mine too.

# CHAPTER 16

## Kessler

I'M BACK.

My shoulder didn't pull once tonight and I made a perfect throw down to second. My girl and her son were in the stand watching me. My parents by her side. Life can't get any better. Well, it can, but we're not there yet.

I rush through my after game ritual, eager to see Lucy and Hudson. I make my way out of the locker room, receiving fist bumps and back slaps as I go. Before I can escape through the doors, Coach Dixon calls to me.

"Davis! Got a minute?" he calls out in his gruff voice.

*No, I don't.*

"Yeah, sure Coach," I say instead, and make my way to his office.

I step into his office and he motions for me to shut the door. "Take a seat," he says.

I sit in one of the chairs in front of his desk, waiting for him to speak. I was intimidated by this man when I first came up to the big leagues. He's not so much big in stature as he is in presence. At barely six feet, he carries himself with an air of self assurance that dictators wish they had. His hair has gone from graying to completely gray in the years I've known him.

He clears his throat. "I just wanted to congratulate you on the good game tonight. I know you've been struggling and it looks like you're finally back on track." He pauses and drums his fingers on his desk a few times. "Whatever you're doing, keep it up."

I nod my head. "Thanks, Coach." He watched me struggle with the reality that I may have to retire. He was the one who told me to get my head on right and figure my shit out. I know he's probably as relieved as I am that my comeback is paying off. "Anything else?" I ask, bouncing my leg up and down, eager to head out.

He shakes his head and I all but jump out of my seat and head to the door. "Kessler," he says as I'm pulling open the door.

"Yeah?" I ask looking back at him.

"I hear your brother's going to be a free agent soon."

I nod.

"See where his head is at with that," he says, giving me a look.

I nod. "Sure, Coach."

He gives me a nod "Now get out of here, go celebrate with your family."

I leave his office and make my way to where Lucy and the rest of my family are waiting. I haven't played ball on the same team as my brother since we were in high school. I'm lost in my thoughts when I push open the door to the family area. Cheers erupt when I step through and I push my conversation with Coach Dixon to the back of my mind. Hudson rushes up to me talking a mile a minute.

"Kessler! That was the most exciting game I've ever seen in

my life! You killed it!" He looks at me like I hung the moon and I never want that feeling to go away. I set my bags down and open my arms for a hug. He rushes forward and I squeeze him tight. Pretty soon he's going to be too 'old' for hugs. I need to get them in while I can. I look up and see my mom and Lucy watching us with matching expressions. Eyes glossy, but not letting the tears escape.

I release Hudson and my dad comes over giving me a back slap and a hug. "Great game, Kess," he says, choking on emotion of his own.

"Thanks, Dad," I whisper past a lump that's formed in my throat.

"Hey, I thought there was no crying in baseball?" Lucy says jokingly, coming up to us.

My dad barks out a laugh and raises an eyebrow at me. "She has jokes now."

I look between my dad and Lucy, feeling like I've missed something. My face must say the same thing because Lucy says, "I'll fill you in later," as she tucks herself into my side and wraps an arm around my waist. I lean down and place a kiss on the top of her head, inhaling her coconut and vanilla scent.

My mom comes up to us and I move out of Lucy's embrace to give my mom a hug. "Oh, Kessler," she whispers, choking back her tears. I chuckle and give her a kiss on her cheek.

"There is a lot of crying in baseball apparently," I joke. She pulls back and lightly smacks my chest, chuckling. She backs into my dads embrace and I pull Lucy back into mine.

I look around and can't help but think this is what I've been missing in my life, and now that I have it. I'm never letting it go.

Judd comes through the doors and Hudson runs up to him, giving him the same excited chatter he gave me. Judd laughs and gives him a fist bump and ruffles his hair. They make their way over to our group and my parents greet Judd with hugs.

Judd looks at me and gives me a shit eating grin. "Nice hit, brotato." He holds out his fist for a bump.

I return the bump with my freehand. "Thanks. Your pitching was alright," I tease. I decide to talk to him in private about what Coach said to me. There's no need to discuss this in front of our parents until we know more. I don't want to get my moms hopes up of Judd possibly moving home. Even though he only lives a little over an hour away, I know she would like him closer.

Judd rubs his hands together. "I'm starving, let's go eat." He grabs his bag and heads to the exit.

"Yeah, I'm starving," Hudson says, rubbing his stomach and following Judd out the door.

"How can you be hungry? You pretty much ate the entire snack bar," Lucy says with a laugh. I entwine her fingers in mine and grab my bags with my other hand, following the group.

Judd turns around and walks backward. "We're growing boys, Mom," he says, patting his flat stomach.

Hudson turns around. "Yeah, Mom, we're growing boys," he says, copying Judd.

Laughter erupts in the hallway and they turn back around and walk through another door. Lucy shakes her head, adding, "We are in so much trouble when he's a teenager. He's going to eat us out of house and home."

I stumble and quickly catch myself. I pull Lucy to a stop and stare down at her, dropping my bags.

"What?" she asks, scrunching her eyebrows. "Did you forget something in the locker room?"

I don't answer her, instead I grip her face with both hands and continue to stare at her, trying to wrap my head around the words she just said. "Did you mean it?" I ask.

She raises an eyebrow. "Mean what, Kessler?" She lifts a

hand grabbing one of my wrists, her other hand resting on my hip.

"That we're in trouble when Hudson is a teenager. That means you're thinking about the future. A future with me?" I say, hope blossoming in my chest.

She bites the corner of her lip and looks off to the side. We're the only ones in the hallway. My family either did not notice we're not with them, or they did and decided to leave us to our conversation. Either way I'm not leaving the hallway until I get an answer.

"Lucy?" I question, desperate for an answer.

"Yes," she says. She looks up at me with a smile that ignites her eyes. "I had a conversation with your dad during warm ups. He made me realize what we have–" she pauses and cups my cheek, "what we have is worth taking risks for."

I back her into the wall and capture her lips with mine. A low moan sounds from her throat. I reach down and grab both her legs, picking her up. She wraps her legs around my waist and I brace myself against the wall with one arm. She opens her lips allowing me to deepen the kiss, plunging my tongue into her mouth, fucking her mouth with my tongue. She pulls at the hair on the back of my head and I release a growl into her mouth.

A door slams down the hallway and we both startle and look where the noise came from. An intern looks at us like a deer in the headlights. "Uh, s-sorry, I didn't know anyone was down here." He turns around and heads back to where he came from.

Lucy covers her face with her hand, stifling a laugh. I chuckle into her neck and pull back, setting her back down to her feet. She straightens her shirt and hair. "We better catch up with the others," she says, linking my fingers with hers.

I lean down and give her one last kiss before letting her lead me down the hall. "We'll talk more later," I tell her.

"There wasn't much talking going on just now," she teases.

We meet up with the others and they make no indication that they were even missing us. Security meets us at the exit. Charlie arranged for them to escort us to our vehicles, knowing the press release would cause an uptick in swarming paparazzi and she was right.

"Keep your heads down and don't answer any questions," I tell Lucy and my parents. They nod and we exit the doors. Blinding flashes immediately surround us. Followed by a sea of voices shouting questions. Judd wraps an arm around Hudson's shoulders and leads the pack to the cars. My dad wraps his arm around my mom, who's holding a hand up to protect her eyes from the flashes. We follow, I wrap my arm around Lucy and try to shield her as much as possible with my gym bag and body. Security surrounds us and tries to create a human shield. Paparazzi stick their cameras between gaps and snap pictures as quickly as they can.

It's slow going but we eventually make it to our vehicles. I make a note to thank Charlie for thinking ahead and suggesting my parents and Lucy park close to my truck. I open Lucy's door for her and she climbs in. I jog to my truck and hop in. Hudson, Judd and my parents climb into my parents' vehicle and we all make our way out of the lot as quickly as possible. Heading to Tony's for dinner.

TWO HOURS and three extra large pizzas later and we've shut Tony's down. Tony closed a little earlier than normal to visit with us and we've taken over the party space. Judd, Hudson, and Kade are at the back playing on the air hockey table. Lucy called Kara on her way here and invited them to dinner.

Tony and my dad are chatting away, trading cooking advice. My mom, Marie, and Kara are talking about their plans for their flower beds this year. Lucy's tucked into my side lying her head on my shoulder. She chimes in every once in a while, but for the most part she quietly observes.

I place a kiss on the top of her head. Lucy tips her head back and gives me a sleepy smile. I place a finger on her chin and tip her head back a little further and give her a soft kiss. I pull back and run my nose along hers. We hear gagging from the game corner and Lucy giggles and hides her face into my shoulder.

"Leave them alone boys," my mom calls to the corner, making them snicker.

Kara stands and stretches. "Well we should probably head home. I have an early client meeting tomorrow." She turns to my mom. "Marlene, it was lovely to meet you."

Mom stands and gives her a hug. "We'll all have to have a girl's day and go to one of my favorite nurseries."

"I would love that, I know my mom would love to meet you too," Kara says returning the hug. She turns to Lucy and gives her a wide grin. "Want me to have Hudson over for a sleep over tonight? They don't have school tomorrow," she ends in a sing-song voice.

"Yes," I say, answering for Lucy.

Kara and my mom giggle.

Lucy slinks down into her chair and covers her face. "Kessler," she says into her palms.

I shrug. "What?"

Kara pats Lucy's shoulder. "Just make sure your curtains are closed babe." She gives me a wink.

"Oh my God, please just take me now lord," Lucy mutters, her face going from red to magenta.

"Kade, Hudson, let's go!" Kara says, gathering her purse and slinging it over her shoulder

The boys come over, Judd bringing up the rear. "Where are we going, Aunt Kara?" Hudson asks.

"You're spending the night at my house tonight since you boys don't have school, and you would be going there anyways in the morning. Now you can sleep in," Kara says in one breath. "We'll swing by and grab your stuff before we head to my house."

"Ok," Hudson says. He turns to Lucy and me. "Night, Mom. Night, Kessler."

Lucy stands up and gives him a hug and a kiss on the head. "Not too much junk food, ok? And Listen to Aunt K, when she says bedtime, no negotiating," she says, giving him a pointed look.

"Yes, Mom," he mumbles. He returns her hug and holds out his fist to me for a bump.

I return it and give him a side hug. "Sleep tight bud. I'll see you tomorrow."

He nods and heads off with Kara and Kade.

My parents say their goodbyes to Tony and Marie and give Lucy and me matching hugs.

"See you Sunday," my mom says releasing Lucy.

"Can I bring anything?" Lucy asks, backing into my arms.

"Just yourself, dear."

Judd comes up last and holds his fist out for a bump. "Broski, see you tomorrow." I return the bump. "Lucy, when you decide you want to be with a real man, you know where to find me," he says, giving her a wink.

Lucy chuckles.

I let out a growl, making everyone laugh.

Marie and Lucy say their goodbyes with promises of another girl's night soon. I pulled Marie aside earlier and paid for dinner. So we gather our things and climb into our vehicles and head to Lucy's house.

# CHAPTER 17

## Kessler

WHEN I PULL UP TO LUCY'S HOUSE SHE'S ALREADY OUT of her car and in the house. I get out of my truck and walk to the door. I don't know if I should knock or just walk in. I'm about to knock when the door opens revealing Lucy in nothing but my jersey.

*Holy Fuck.*

Blood rushes to my cock, making it press against my jeans.

She looks up at me shyly and grabs my hand backing away from the door, pulling me in.

I walk into the house and close the door behind me, kicking off my shoes. I pull her to my chest and give her a long hard kiss. She glides her hands up my arms and locks them around my neck, pulling me to her. Reaching down, I glide my hands over her plump ass and pick her up into my arms.

I carry her down the hall and to her bedroom, laying her gently on her bed. She props herself on her elbows and looks at me, her eyes are matching pools of black, rimmed with green. I reach behind me and tug my shirt over my head, tossing it to the side. I unbutton my jeans and step out of them next, leaving me in just my briefs. Her eyes greedily take me in. She pulls her bottom lip into her mouth and rakes her teeth over it as her eyes glide over my body.

"Like what you see?" I ask, crawling over her and planting both knees on the side of her hips. She nods, laying back as I cover my body with hers. Running her hands up my torso and over my chest, she gently uses her nails to scratch a path back down, making me shiver. I dip my head and brush my nose along hers. "I've been thinking about this since I saw you walk out of the dugout in my jersey," I whisper. I flick the top two buttons of the jersey open and gently trace a path down between her breasts. She sucks in a breath and pushes her chest into my touch. I repeat the path, teasing her.

"Kessler," she says, almost pleading. "I need you."

I place soft kisses along her jaw and down her neck, continuing my path to the top of her breast. I look up at her. "You'll have me, but I'm going to take my time worshiping every inch of you tonight." Moving my jersey to the side, I expose one breast. Cupping it in my hand, I suck it into my mouth. Lucy runs her fingers through my hair on the back of my head and pulls at the strands. She arches her back, pushing her breast further into my mouth.

I reach down and release another button. Then move my hand over to her other breast, rolling the nipple between my fingers, causing her to gasp. Her grip tightens on my hair, almost painfully. I move to her other breast and repeat my pattern of licking and sucking while rolling her other nipple with my hand. She inhales a deep breath through her nose and makes a whimpering sound in her throat. I can feel her clench her thighs together, needing pressure.

Releasing her breasts, I unbutton the last two buttons on the jersey and it falls open. I pull back to take in the sight and I don't think I've ever seen anything more sexy in my life. Lucy lays there half-naked in front of me with just my jersey and teal lace panties. My cock throbs at the sight. She gives me a mischievous smile and reaches between us, rubbing my cock through my underwear.

I close my eyes and let out a hiss, rocking into her touch a few times before I place my hand over hers, stopping her. "As fucking good as that feels baby, I'm not done with you yet." I lean over her and pin her arm to the bed, kissing each of her breasts. Placing a trail of kisses down her soft stomach until I reach the top of her underwear.

I stand up and grab her ankles, pulling her to the edge of the bed. She lets out a little squeal and giggles. Kneeling down I place my hands on both sides of her hips and tug her underwear off, revealing her glistening pussy.

I leave a trail of kisses up and down each of her thighs before moving on to her center, where I place a kiss at the top before licking a trail down the slit. She plunges a hand back into my hair, and her hips push off the bed and into my face, trying to find release. Gripping her hips with my hands, I anchor her to me. I lick up and down a few more times, teasing her. She lets out a frustrated groan before I relent and latch my lips around her clit, sucking it into my mouth.

She lets out a moan, tightening her grip on my hair. "Fuck, Kessler." I release her clit and swipe my tongue up and down her beautiful pussy. I trace my tongue around her clit before making my way down and sliding my tongue inside. I repeat this pattern a few times, making her squirm. "I need more Kessler," I hear her plea. Pushing her legs open more, I lick up and down her pussy one more time, then insert a finger inside her. Her walls immediately clench around my finger, trying to pull me deeper. She lets go of my hair to grab her beautiful breasts, pulling and plucking at her pert nipples.

"That's it Lucy, make yourself feel good," I encourage. She arches her back as she continues to play with her nipples, letting out little mews of pleasure. Her walls clench around me again and I insert another finger inside her, increasing my pressure. Sealing my lips around her again, she places a hand back into my hair, pulling my face closer. I work her pussy with my fingers and mouth, letting her ride my face. Her moans grow louder and her movement becomes erratic. "Kessler, I, I'm." I suck her clit hard into my mouth and I feel her walls clench as she comes undone around me.

When she finally comes down from her high, she props herself up on her elbows. "I think it's your turn," she says. I get to my feet and she sits the rest of the way up and reaches for my underwear. She tugs them down, and my cock springs free. I step out of my underwear and kick them to the side. Lucy reaches forward and runs her thumb over my tip, spreading the pre-cum that's leaked out, making me suck in a breath through my teeth. She glides her hand up and down my shaft a few times, making my balls clench. Placing a kiss on my tip, she sucks me into her mouth so hard, I see spots.

"Lucy," I groan. "You, I, you have to stop," I tell her, pulling back. Her mouth detaches with a 'pop'. "If I'm going to come, it's going to be inside you," I tell her, my voice strained. Reaching over to the nightstand and I grab one of the condoms laying on top. I roll it on quickly and move back between her legs. Motioning for her to move back on the bed, she complies.

I lay down over her and cup her face, giving her soft kisses. Lucy reaches down between us and grips my cock in her hand, slowly stroking it as I move my tongue in and out of her mouth. I sit up and pull one of her legs up and place it over my shoulder. Keeping eye contact with her, I line myself up with her entrance and slowly ease in. She breathes out a moan. I give her a minute to adjust to me before moving my hips again. "Fuck that feels so good," she whispers.

I rock into her, making her throw her head back. "Yes," she groans. I release her leg and move over her, gathering her up in my arms so I can kiss her while I rock into her. Her hands move up my back and over my muscles. I set a lazy pace, enjoying the way she feels wrapped around my body. "Kessler," she says, voice thick. "I need you to move faster."

I get an idea and pull back, making her protest when I pull out of her. "What are you doing?" she cries out.

I sit with my back against the headboard and reach my hand out to her. "I want you to take what you need," I tell her. She moves to me and I guide her onto my lap. She sinks back down onto me and we both let out a groan. She grips my shoulders and starts her pace, riding me. Pulling her mouth to mine, she wraps her hands around my back and I move my hands down to her hips to help her grind into me. She whimpers into my mouth.

I can feel her walls start to clench, another orgasm building inside of her. Releasing her lips, I move my mouth to her breasts and latch my mouth around one of her nipples, licking and sucking. I move a hand to her other nipple, rolling it between my fingers. "Fuck Kessler, I'm almost there," she whispers, reaching down between us and circling her clit.

I can feel my own orgasm building and take her breast out of my mouth to take her face in both of my hands. "Look at me Lucy," I command. She blinks and looks at me, her pupils dilated with passion. "I want to watch you as you come around my cock." I pull her mouth to mine and kiss her hard. Her pace increases as she chases her orgasm. The walls of her pussy have my cock in a death grip and I know she's there.

Letting go of her lips, I watch as she throws her head back

in a moan of pleasure. She rocks her hips again, sending me over the edge with her. "Fuuuck," I groan, grabbing her hips and pounding her down on to my cock, chasing my own release. She falls forward onto me, tucking her face into my neck. Lucy wraps her arms around my back, gripping on for dear life as we chase the last waves of pleasure.

We both sit there wrapped in each other's arms, chests heaving, trying to catch our breath. She pulls her face from my neck and kisses me hard. I remove my hands from her hips and caress the back of her head with one, tangling my fingers into her now messy ponytail. I pull back and look into her eyes. "I love you so much, Lucy." She stares back into my eyes, the fear I usually see in them when I say those words, isn't there. "I'm going to spend the rest of the night showing you how much you mean to me," I tell her, pushing her lips to mine for another kiss.

Once I've deposited the condom in the trash and brought a washcloth out to clean us up, we lay in bed, Lucy snuggled into my side. She's tracing slow lazy patterns onto my chest and shoulder. She lets out a sigh and I grab her hand from my chest and give her fingers a kiss. "What's that sigh for?"

She props her head onto her hand, pulling her hand out of mine, cupping my face. She looks at me, her eyes moving back and forth between mine. "Just thinking," she says, still looking at me.

I turn on my side, mimicking her position. "Care to share?" I ask, intrigued.

Lucy's face turns a slight shade of red, like she's embarrassed, and shakes her head. "No, I just have a lot running through my brain. It's not important." She bites her bottom lip, pulling it into her mouth. Looking off to the side.

Gripping her chin, I pull her lip out from between her teeth and turn her face to look at me. "Hey, whatever you're thinking, it's important. Tell me, please?" I move my hand down to her hip. I don't like that she feels like she can't tell me things. I want her to feel like she can tell me anything, without judgment.

Lucy takes another breath. "I uh, was talking to your mom today, she was telling me about some neighbors of hers having to move. The Peterson's I think?" she pauses, looking to me for confirmation.

I nod. "Yeah, They live one driveway over from Mom and Dad. They've got to be in their late 70's if not early 80's."

"Yeah, well when I heard her say they're selling, I thought how nice it would be for us to live next to your parents." She stops and shakes her head. "I can't even tell you I love you, but here I am moving us in together."

My heart pounds in my chest at the words coming out of her mouth.

*She's thinking of the future. Our future.*

I clear my throat making her eyes shoot to mine. "You don't have to say anything you're not ready to say," I tell her, caressing her cheek.

She sits up moving out of my grasp. She crosses her legs and pulls them to her chest, wrapping her arms around them. "That's the thing, Kessler. I, I'm." She huffs and lays her cheek on her knees.

My heart is ready to leap out of my chest. I sit up and pull her into my lap. She wraps herself around my body and we rest our foreheads against each other. "Kessler," she whispers.

I pull back and look into her eyes. "Yes, baby?"

She looks back and forth between mine, a smile touching her lips. "I love you."

My lips crash to hers and my heart soars at hearing those words leave her lips. I pull back and look at her. "Say it again."

She lets out a laugh. "I love you, Kessler Davis."

I descend back down on her lips and spend the rest of the night showing her how much I love her too.

I'M BEGINNING to hate away games. I don't like leaving Lucy, everytime I leave it gets a little harder. The bright side to it is I've uncovered Lucy's naughty side. Getting to video chat with her at night had been an experience. But when we're not video chatting, I'm texting her every chance I get. I just can't seem to get enough of her.

I bought more of the books she likes by Amelia Morgan and have been reading them in my spare time and texting her about them. It seems to make her happy that I'm actually showing interest in one of her hobbies, something I'm sure she's never experienced before.

ME

I caught Brent nose deep in my book today after morning warm ups.

LUCY

*eyes emoji* what part did he read?

ME

Judging by his reaction... THE part.

LUCY

😳 NO!

ME

Haha Oh yeah. He screamed like a girl and threw the book like it was on fire when I asked him what he was reading. I thought he was having a stroke with how red his face was.

LUCY

> Oh, poor Brent. Should we send him a 'get well' basket?

ME

> I think I need to get him a therapy appt. He still hasn't looked me in the eye.

LUCY

> 🌀 Oh, no, poor Brent.

I spot Reese and Brent coming up the stairs and shoot one last text off to Lucy.

ME

> Here he comes, let's see if he sits with us cool kids. Love you Coach.

LUCY

> Kessler Davis be nice. Love you too. Good luck today 🌀

I pocket my phone and look up at Reese and Brent making their way down the aisle. Reese tips his chin in greeting and sits down next to me. "Sup man? How's your girl this morning?"

A wide grin spreads across my face. "She's perfect, man."

Grinning back at me, he claps my shoulder. "Yeah yeah, rub it in." He looks at me and tips his head towards Brent who is sitting in the seat behind us, silent for once, and gives me a wide grin. I match it and we both turn in our seats, poking our heads over the backs.

"So Brent, Kessler told me something interesting happened in the locker room this morning."

Brent's face turns red and his eyes shoot up to Reese's face. "Fuck off, Reese," Brent says grumpily.

I raise my eyebrows at the grumpiness in Brent's tone. "Now now, Brent. That's no way to talk to your elders," I tease. Brent's

27, almost ten years my junior, and eight Reese's. He's like our little brother and we treat him as such, including busting his balls.

"Do we need to have a talk about the birds and the bees?" Reese asks.

I clear my throat. "You see when two people love each other very much…" I start.

"Not necessarily," Reese chimes in. "I've had some incredible hate sex."

I raise my fist to Reese and he bumps it in return.

"Are you two assholes done?" Brent asks, still not meeting my eyes.

A sliver of guilt slides through me, and I decide to cut him some slack. "Ok, ok. I'm done. We're just busting your balls dude. Seriously, it's not a big deal. They're just books Lucy likes to read and I thought I'd read some of her favorites along with her. So I can talk to her about them." I shrug. "They're actually pretty good, and the sex scenes are icing on the cake if you know what I mean," I tell them, wiggling my eyebrows up and down.

"Nice." Reese raises his fist to me this time and I bump it back. Brent rolls his eyes and focuses on his phone.

"Come on, weren't you just busting my balls a few weeks ago about watching porn on my phone?"

"That's not, I didn't…" Brent lets out a sigh. "Can we just forget it please?"

Reese and I give eachother a look, then look back at Brent. "Nope," we both tell him at the same time.

I tip my chin at him. "Spill, what's going on?"

Brent shakes his head, not wanting to answer.

"Come on dude, it's us," Reese says.

Brent looks around the bus, then back at us, muttering something under his breath.

"I didn't catch that," Reese says, cupping his hand over his ear.

Brent closes his eyes and heaves a sigh. "I had a boner," he whispers through clenched teeth.

*Don't laugh, don't laugh, don't laugh.*

I almost make it, but I sneak a look at Reese, who side eyes me, making us both bust up laughing. Brent pulls the hood of his sweater over his head and starts to get up from his seat, but Reese stops him before he can make it into the aisle. "Dude, wait. We're, we're not laughing at you."

"Sure as fuck seems like it," Brent grumbles. Flopping back into his seat and crossing his arms over his chest.

I shake my head. "No, I swear we're not. I'd be concerned if you *didn't* get a hard on from reading those books, especially the part I know you read."

Brent squints his eyes at me, like he's not sure if I'm trying to trick him.

Without giving too much away about my sex life, because that's no one's fucking business, I tell Brent, "Let's just say those scenes have been *beneficial.*"

He looks at me for a minute, then his eyes widen with understanding. "*Oh.*"

"Yeah," I reply.

Reese fist bumps my shoulder. "Old man has still got it."

I deadpan him. "You're only two years younger than me."

He lifts a shoulder. "Hey, two years is two years."

I roll my eyes and look back at Brent. He's taken his hood off and seems more relaxed now. I hold out my fist. "Are we good now?"

Brent returns the bump. "Yeah man, we're good."

I nod, moving to turn back around in my seat. Before I do, Brent asks one last question. "Hey, you think I could get the name of that book?"

# CHAPTER 18

## Lucy

### THREE WEEKS LATER

THE DAYS HAVE BEEN FLYING BY SINCE THE NIGHT I TOLD Kessler I loved him. He's been on the road for away games half of those days, and while I miss him, it's not as bad as I thought it was going to be. He video-chats Hudson and me whenever he gets the chance. We've even gotten each other off over video-chat, and it was one of the hottest things I've ever experienced. I clench my thighs together just thinking about it.

He's coming home today from a four day stretch of away games.

*Home.*

When Kessler is here, he's here.

At my house.

He only goes to his apartment to grab his mail or more clothes. I've even cleared out some closet space for him and a couple of drawers in my dresser.

I asked him why we don't ever stay at his apartment. He told me his apartment has always just been a place to sleep, that my house felt like coming home. So here is where we stay.

Hudson likes that he's here too. A little bit of sadness creeps in because I know he's missed out on having a dad, but that was never in my control. Thinking of Hudson's other DNA provider makes my gut twist. I need to tell Kessler about him. The longer I wait, the harder it gets. I know I need to do it soon, before the media digs too deep and he finds out from someone that isn't me.

I'm lost in my thoughts, and I must not hear the front door open. A pair of big hands grab my shoulders, making me shriek. I jump out of my office chair and whip around. My fist colliding with a solid and familiar chest.

"Whoa there, killer. It's just me," Kessler says, circling my wrists with his hand and pulling me to his chest, shoulders shaking with laughter.

"Jesus, Kessler. You scared the shit out of me." He releases my wrists and I step into him, encircling his waist. Laying my head on his chest, I inhale his spice and leather scent, and release a sigh. "I'm so glad you're home," I say into his chest.

His arms wrap around me and I feel his lips on my head. "It's good to be home, Coach," he says into my hair.

We stand in each other's embrace for a few seconds. I pull back and tip my face to look up at him. His handsome face stares back at me, green eyes boring into mine. "I've missed you," I whisper, lifting onto my tiptoes. He meets me halfway and covers my lips with his, giving me soft, slow kisses.

Our kisses quickly grow hungry. Kessler runs his hands over the curve of my ass and lifts me effortlessly into his arms. "Mmm, I've missed these lips," he says, backing me into the wall and thrusting his hips into mine. I can feel something else that missed me through my thin leggings.

"We have 20 minutes until Hudson gets home." That is all I have to say. Kessler sets me down and tugs my leggings and underwear down and off my feet. He stands and pulls his own pants and briefs down, and steps out of them.

He kneels down and lifts one of my legs over his shoulder, causing me to lean upper back against the wall. Kessler runs his tongue through my slit. "Mmm, already wet and ready for me," he says, dipping his tongue back in. I let out a soft moan and tip my head back. Resting it against the wall, I reach down and run my fingers through Kessler's chocolate-brown hair.

Kessler sucks and licks until I feel the pressure of an orgasm starting to build. I tighten my grip on his hair, pulling his face closer. Using his other hand, he inserts one, then two fingers inside of me, matching the rhythm of his mouth. The sensation is almost too much, and my breathing increases. "Kessler, fuck," I say, voice strained. "Just, just like that." I can feel my orgasm on the edge, just as I'm about to come, he pulls back. "No!" I cry out.

Kessler stands and muffles my protest with a kiss, letting me taste myself on his lips. "I want us to finish together," he says, lifting me and carrying me into my bedroom. He sets me down and walks to my nightstand, grabbing a condom.

I start to walk to the bed, but he stops me. "No, I want you against the wall, don't move." His stern command sends shivers through my body. I back up to the wall and watch him roll on the condom, then stride back over to me, his thigh muscles flexing with each step. "Like what you see?" he asks when he reaches me.

"Always," I tell him, running my hands under his shirt and tugging it off, revealing his glorious body. I lightly scratch my nails down his chest and over his well defined abs, sending a wave of shivers through him.

He pulls my tank top off and flicks the front clasp of my bra, making my breasts spring free. He takes one in each hand massaging one as he sucks on the other. "10 minutes," I say, reminding him that time is not on our side. He releases my breasts and crushes my lips to his. He picks me up again and lines himself up with my center. Looking me in the eyes, he slowly enters me, stretching me. I suck in a breath, relishing in the fullness.

"Hold onto me, Lucy. I'm not going to be gentle," he warns. I lock my arms around his shoulders and he pins me up against the wall. Kessler pounds into me over and over with a force I've never experienced with him. The sound of skin slapping skin and our ragged breathing fills the room. The pressure of an orgasm builds low in my belly.

"Kess, yes, I'm, I'm close," I tell him, digging my nails into his shoulder.

He growls into my shoulder and bites down, sending heat straight to my core. I cry out as Kessler reaches between us and circles my clit. "That's it baby," he whispers into my ear, "come for me." And I do–my orgasm hits me so hard, I see spots. Kessler slams into me a few more times, before he reaches his own release.

Kessler gives me a kiss and eases out of me, going into the bathroom to take care of the condom. I follow him in and grab a washcloth, cleaning myself up. I rinse it out and hand it to Kessler. He cleans himself off and tosses it in the laundry.

We're pulling on the last of our clothes when the front door opens. We both pause and look at each other. "You uh, might want to go fix your hair," Kessler says, motioning to my head. "You literally look like you just had sex." I reach up and touch my messy ponytail. Kessler walks out into the living room while I freshen up.

I walk out to the end of the hallway and see Kessler and Hudson at the kitchen island. A bag of pretzels open between them and a jar of peanut butter is being passed back and forth. I lean up against the wall and rest my head on the edge, taking in the scene. Kessler looks over at me with a grin and gives me a wink.

I'll never get over the sight of them together.

I make my way to the island and grab a pretzel out of the bag. Kessler holds the peanut butter jar out to me and I take a healthy scoop out of it and shovel it into my mouth.

"Oh, hey, did you see the new pictures Mom put up?" Hudson asks Kessler before shoving another pretzel in his mouth.

"Mo. What 'ictures?" Kessler says around a mouth full of food.

Hudson hops down from his chair and walks over to our picture wall. There's three new additions to the growing collection. He points at the pictures I added last week. "These ones."

Kessler follows him over and looks at the ones he's pointing to. The first one is of us at Hudson's tournament, the one Kessler surprised us at. The second one is the picture we took of all three of us when we announced our relationship. And the third, well, that one is my favorite. It's the picture I didn't know was being taken, and it's gone a bit viral. Someone put a caption with the picture saying "Get you a man who looks at you like you're his last meal."

Kessler's eyes land on the last picture and he looks back at me, heat in his gaze. I drop my gaze, feeling my cheeks heat. "I, uh, gave your mom copies of them when we were there Sunday."

Hudson and I went to Sunday dinner at Kessler's parent's house, even though he wasn't there, and it wasn't awkward one bit. Marlene welcomed us with open arms and never looked back, unlike my parents.

As if he knows what I'm thinking, Kessler comes over to

where I'm standing, my eyes shoot to him, following his movements. He stops next to me and leans his hip on the island. Grabbing a handful of pretzels out of the bag, he pops one in his mouth. He finishes chewing and swallows. "I've noticed I haven't seen any pictures of your parents anywhere," he says quietly.

I look over his shoulder at Hudson, who has made his way into the living room and is starting up his game system, then back at him and shake my head. "I'll talk to you about that later," I whisper back.

Kessler nods and leans down, giving me a peck on the cheek. He heads over to the couch and plops down next to Hudson, grabbing the extra controller off the coffee table and challenging Hudson to a race.

"Oh hey, I forgot to mention, I'm taking you out tonight. Hud, you ok with hanging out with your Aunt Kara and Kade for dinner tonight?"

Hudson shrugs and gives a mumbled answer too immersed in his game. Kessler gives me a wink while I stare at him dumbfounded.

"I already cleared it with Kara. You have an hour to get ready, but you're so beautiful you won't need an hour." He gives me a wink before turning back to the screen.

I shake myself out of my shock. "Uh, what. What should I wear?"

Kessler looks over his shoulder at me from the couch. "Whatever you want, Coach. It's casual."

I laugh and shake my head. Men are always so helpful in that department. Grabbing my phone I hit Kara's contact.

"Girlfriend," Kara says in greeting.

"Girl, casual date night clothes–aaand go."

WE'RE in Kessler's truck heading downtown, but that's the extent of my knowledge of where he's taking me.

After talking to Kara we decided on a cute pair of cream safari shorts and a sage green tank top, since it's finally getting warm enough to wear such things and not freeze my tits off. I decided to finish it with a simple pair of strappy sandals. Kessler is dressed similar in a pair of dark-gray cargo shorts that make his catcher's ass look biteable and a soft-gray shirt that make his moss green eyes pop.

"You gonna tell me where we're going yet?"

He looks over at me and gives me a wink. Reaching across the console, he grabs my hand and places a kiss on my knuckles, sending shivers up my arm. "Nope. But we'll be there soon."

I take my hand back and cross my arms giving him a little hmph, pretending to pout.

Kessler chuckles. "As much as I love seeing those pouty lips, I'd like to see them somewhere else, but that's not on the agenda right now, Coach."

I can feel my cheeks heat at the suggestion. Even though he's talked dirty to me several times, I still blush when I hear them come out of his mouth.

We make a turn and I notice we're at the exit to the stadium. Turning, I look at Kessler. "Are we going to the field?"

He replies with a smirk and nothing else.

We pull into the player's lot and Kessler hops out of the truck. He walks around the front and opens my door, holding out his hand. I take it and hop down. Hitting the lock, he keeps my hand in his and leads me towards the entrance. "Why are we here? Did you forget something in your locker?"

"You'll see."

We enter the building and Kessler leads me down the maze of hallways to the gate that leads us out onto the field. We step out onto the dirt and there's a giant tote bag and a picnic basket sitting on home plate. My feet freeze and Kessler stops a couple steps ahead of me once he's realized I've stopped.

"Lucy?" he questions, coming back to my side.

I look at the basket and back to him. "You're taking me on a picnic?" I whisper, my throat clogging with tears.

Kessler cups my cheek. "Hey, why are you crying?"

I inhale a deep stuttering breath, trying to calm myself. "That's, I. It's just so romantic," I croak out.

Kessler laughs. "Just wait until you see what all I have planned." He wipes a single tear that's escaped down my cheek with his thumb. "Come on, let's have our much needed date night."

Leaving me where I stand. Kessler walks over to the picnic basket and tote and grabs them, tucking them into the dugout. He comes back and grabs my hand, leading me over to the batting cage. Opening the gate he leads me in. "I thought we'd hit some balls before dinner, while we still have some light left."

My face cracks into a grin. "I would love that."

I choose a bat from the many hanging on the fence and Kessler walks over to the pitching machine and turns it on. "We're gonna start you out slow, to get you warmed up." I nod my head and take my position. The machine sends a ball my way and I take a swing, missing it completely.

"Is it too fast?" Kessler asks, moving to adjust the machine.

"No, I got it. Let's try it again." I settle into my stance again, waiting for the pitch.

Kessler drops his hand and crosses his arms across his chest, watching me.

The pitch comes again, and again I swing and miss. I let out a frustrated growl.

Kessler jogs over to me. "Here, let me help." His arms come around mine, and I inhale a deep breath, breathing him in. His breath moves the hair that's fallen loose from my ponytail, tickling my neck. I turn my head slightly, our noses nearly touching. The pitching machine sends a ball our way, but neither of us are paying attention, lost in the moment with each other. "That's strike three," Kessler whispers.

"Looks like I'm out," I reply, sliding my nose against his. I shift slightly in Kessler's arms and release the bat.

Kessler turns me around to face him and picks me up, backing me against the fence. I feel the chainlink dig into my back, but the pleasure of his kiss outweighs the pain. I groan into his mouth and my tongue tangles with his. We may have had sex as soon as Kessler got home today, but that seems to have done nothing to curb his appetite for me. He rocks his hips against me, showing me how much I turn him on. I nip at his bottom lip, making him growl. "Lucy, don't start something we can't finish. Even though it looks like we're alone, we're still in public" His dark eyes tell me he'd love nothing more to devour me right here, right now. I sigh, knowing he's right. I give him one last kiss and he lets me down to my feet.

Kessler turns around, adjusting himself through his shorts. I giggle, reaching up to fix my now messy ponytail. He walks over to the now empty pitching machine and shuts it down. Picking up the forgotten bat, I hang it back up where I got it from. I don't even ask Kessler if he wants to bat, knowing he needs to rest his shoulder for his next series of games.

Kessler takes my hand in his and we exit the cage, making our way back over to the dugout. The sun is close to setting, casting the field in shadows. "Are we gonna eat in the dark?"

Not saying a word, he leads me over to center field. Opening the tote he pulls out a blanket and spreads it out. Next he pulls out three fluffy pillows and sets them behind him. Kessler sits down on the blanket and pats the empty space next to him. I kick off my sandals and sit criss cross on the blanket next to him. Kessler opens the picnic basket and pulls out various containers, a bottle of wine, and a bluetooth speaker.

I raise my brow at him. "When did you put this all together?" Because this spread is not spur of the moment material.

Kessler lifts a shoulder. "I had some help."

"Apparently."

"Charlie may have helped me in gathering all the stuff, and left it here for me."

I stretch out and lay back against the pillows, groaning softly. "Remind me to send Charlie a thank you. These are the softest pillows I've ever laid on." I snuggle into them more. "Seriously, what are these made of, clouds?"

Kessler leans back with me and lets out a groan of his own. "These are coming home with us."

I nod in agreement. Too relaxed to speak. Kessler laces his hand with mine and we lay in silence as the field grows completely dark around us. Crickets begin their nightly serenades and I can't remember the last time I laid out in the dark just listening to the sounds of the night.

Kessler's alarm goes off on his phone and the bright outfield lights pop on, bathing us in fluorescent light. My stomach lets out a grumble, making us laugh. Kessler lets go of my hand and sits up, reaching for the containers. "Let's get you fed before you get hangry."

I snort. "I do not get hangry."

Fun fact. I get hangry.

Kessler lets out a snort of his own. "Yeah and I'm the King of England. You missy, get hangry. I almost lost a hand last time we waited too long to feed you."

"Whatever," I grumble, not willing to agree, even though I know he's right.

Reaching into the basket, Kessler pulls out paper plates and passes one to me. I take it and open the container closest to me. The smell of Tony's pizza greets me, making my mouth water instantly. "Oh, come to mama," I say, putting two huge slices on my plate and passing the container off to Kessler.

He chuckles and puts two slices on his own plate. We lapse into silence, both inhaling our pizza. Once we've finished off our slices, we set the plates to the side, letting our stomachs settle. Kessler opens the bottle of wine and takes two glasses out of the basket, pouring us each a glass. The wine is sweet and surprisingly cold on my tongue. Charlie is definitely getting a thank you basket or something for pulling out all the stops for us.

Reaching for the bluetooth speaker, Kessler hits a button on it and then grabs his phone, connecting it to the speaker. He scrolls through until he finds the song he's looking for and hits play. Notes from a piano streams out of the tiny speaker, and "How Long Will I Love You" by Ellie Goulding surrounds us.

Kessler takes my glass and sets it on top of the basket with his. Getting to his feet, Kessler holds out a hand to me asking, "Can I have this dance?"

My heart catches in my throat as I take his hand, letting him pull me to my feet. We step off the blanket and Kessler wraps one arm around my back and holds my hand in his other. Placing my free hand on his shoulder, I lay my head on his chest and we sway back and forth with the music. I close my eyes listening to Kesslers chest rumble as he hums along with the music.

When the song ends, I pull back and look up at Kessler, silent tears streaming down my face. Giving me a soft smile, he leans down and kisses each of my tear stained cheeks before reaching my lips. I open up for him, tasting the salt from my tears on his tongue.

Pulling back before we get carried away again Kessler looks into my eyes, his deep moss green, boring into my hazel ones. "Thank you so much for tonight Kessler. This is the best date I've ever had," I whisper to him.

"This is just the beginning. I will give you the world if you let me, Lucy." And I believe every word he tells me. This is what true love feels like and I've never felt like I do when I'm in his arms, or when he's looking at me when he doesn't think I notice.

Raising my hand to his lips he places a kiss to my knuckles and leads me back over to the blanket. He pulls me down with him and we lay back against the heavenly pillows. I'm tucked into his side, laying my head on his chest.

We lay in silence for a few minutes, before I ask a question I've been curious about. "Have you thought about what you want to do once you actually do retire from baseball?"

My question is met with silence. Sitting up, I prop my head up on my hand and look at him. Kessler takes a deep breath, then lets it out. "I don't really know. I became somewhat interested in how the body heals when I was rehabbing from my injury." He shrugs. "Maybe I'll open a facility for injured athletes to go to for rehab."

That actually wouldn't be a horrible idea, he could staff it with physical, and massage therapists. Have a gym in one section, a small pool for low impact water therapy in another. A sauna and hot tub area. I start building a blueprint in my brain of the perfect layout for a rehab facility. I'm so engrossed in the details, I don't hear Kessler ask me if I'm ready to go until he sits up and is staring at me expectantly. "I'm sorry, what did you say?"

"I asked if you were ready to head out. There's a couple of

staff that stayed late to turn off the lights and lock up when we're done and I don't want to make them stay later than they already have for us."

I scramble to my feet. "Oh, of course, I didn't realize anyone was waiting on us." We pack up the picnic and head to the truck.

We're heading back to the house when Kessler asks, "What were you thinking so hard about back there?"

I shake my head. "You're going to think it's silly."

"Try me."

Smiling, I look out the window. "I was thinking about the perfect layout for your rehab facility." I laugh and raise a shoulder. "I can't help it, it's the PT in me."

Kessler reaches for my hand, entwining his fingers with mine. "I don't think it's silly," he says, giving my hand a squeeze. "Maybe it's something we can do together when it's time for me to hang up my mitt."

I nod, even though it's dark in the truck and lose myself in the details of the perfect facility the rest of the way home.

THE NEXT NIGHT, I'm sitting in bed massaging a knot out of Kesslers shoulder while he reads my favorite Amelia Morgan book. He surprised me with a signed special edition last week before he left. I'm still a little shocked that he's reading them, but he told me he actually enjoys the stories she writes. We text back and forth discussing them when he's on the road.

Kessler chuckles, dragging me from my thoughts. I peek over his shoulder. "What part are you at?"

He leans back against me, making me lay back into the stack of pillows behind me. I wrap my arms around the front of his chest and set my chin on his good shoulder. He holds the book up so I can see what he's reading. "Oh, I love this part. Tina getting shit on by that bird is, muah, chefs kiss," I say kissing my fingers.

Kessler laughs. "I gotta say, the things Miss Morgan comes up with are hilarious. Makes me wonder how she thinks of these things."

I shrug. "I think I read once that it's a mixture of things she reads in articles and life she's experienced. Which is why I'm a reader and not a writer."

He turns his head slightly to look at me. "What do you mean by that?"

I side eye his side eye. "Well, up until I met you, my life was pretty plain and simple. Work, baseball, friends. Nothing exciting worth writing about."

Kessler closes his book and rolls to the side, propping his head on his hand. "And what about family?"

I cast my eyes down and pick at the invisible fuzz on the blanket. "Kara and Marie and their families are my family," I tell him. I know I said I'd tell him about my parents later, I was just hoping he'd forget. It's not something I like to talk about. Kessler covers my hand with his. I look up and see him staring at me, patiently waiting.

I turn his hand in mine and trace the lines, staring at the grooves. "I grew up well off, never wanting for anything, material, at least. I don't think I ever heard my parents tell me they loved me. So when I found out I was pregnant, my mother was less than supportive about it. She demanded I get rid of Hudson, or put him up for adoption. I went to my dad thinking maybe he'd help me talk to my mom about it, help me make her see that it isn't as bad as she was making it out to be. We were never super close, but he's the reason I love baseball. He used to take me to games when I was a kid. I thought what bond we shared from that would be worth something." I pause and take a breath, memories of that day unburying themselves. "He barely looked at me, standing in front of him, begging him to help me talk to my mom. He was too busy looking through the paperwork on his desk." I can feel the prickles of tears forming behind my eyes, and I blink a few times to clear them.

"Hey," Kessler says softly, taking his hand out of mine and sitting up. He tips my chin up, so I'm looking him in the eyes. "We don't have to talk about it if it's too painful. I never want to do anything to cause you pain."

I sniff and shake my head. "No, it's ok. I've had a lot of time and therapy to come to terms with what happened. It's just been a long time since I've had to talk about it."

Kessler pulls me into his lap and lays his head on mine as I rest my body into his. "Ok, but if you want to stop at any point, just let me know, and I'll never bring it up again, unless you want to."

"Ok," I tell him quietly. I lay there soaking in the comfort of his body before I continue. "When my dad finally looked up from his work, his eyes told me what I felt my entire life, and his words just solidified it." I swallow, taking in a deep breath and letting it out. Trying to keep the pain at bay. "He told me my mother just didn't want me making the same mistakes she made, and that I should listen to her and just terminate the pregnancy and move on with my life." My voice cracks and I can feel Kessler's arms tighten around me, like he's trying to absorb my pain for me. Silent tears run down my cheeks faster than Kessler can wipe them away. Finally he just gives up trying and wraps me tight in his arms and gently rocks me back and forth.

I'm not sure how long we sit in silence. My past flooding my thoughts, but when my tears finally slow, I continue, "Once I got over the shock of being told I was a mistake and that my parents never wanted me, I told them I wouldn't give Hudson up. They told me they would cut me off and I wouldn't make anything of myself being a single mother. Which of course, just fueled my need to prove them wrong. I was already working for Tony, but I had to move out of the apartment my parents were paying for. Thankfully Tony let me stay in the apartment over the restaurant. He didn't even charge me rent. He told me it was nice to have another person starting a family use it like he and his wife had when they first moved here and couldn't afford anything else."

"Thank God for Tony," Kessler whispers into my hair, placing a kiss on my head.

"Thank God for Tony," I agree. "I went back to my parents a few weeks after I had moved out of my apartment. I don't know why, maybe to give them one last chance?" I shake my head. "I don't know what I was expecting, but I went anyway, hoping maybe they'd had a change of heart and they would want to be involved in their grandchild's life." I huff out a laugh "I was wrong. When I got there, they had left for vacation and had the housekeeper box up all my stuff and put it in the garage. We had the same housekeeper since I was ten and I felt closer to her then I did my own mother at times. She told me to let her know what I wanted and she would arrange for someone to deliver it to me, since my car at the time, which surprisingly my parents let me keep, wouldn't fit all of it. I went through my stuff and decided if I was going to start fresh I may as well start completely over. I took the clothes I had left and my old stuffed bunny I had when I was a kid and left the rest behind."

"And look at the beautiful life you've created without them," Kessler says.

I nod. "I have made a great life for Hudson and me. I never wanted him to go one day questioning if he was loved."

"There's no doubt in my mind he knows how much he's loved," he tells me, squeezing me tight in a hug.

My eyes grow heavy and a yawn escapes, Kessler reaches over and hits the switch on the light, casting us in shadows. Stretching out on his back, he places a hand behind his head and opens his other for me. I snuggle into the crook of his arm and trace the lines of his well defined stomach with my finger. He pulls his hand from behind his head and laces his fingers with mine, stopping my pattern. Bringing my hand to his lips, he kisses the back of my hand.

"Thank you for trusting me with this," he whispers into the darkness.

I lift my head and look at him. Streaks of moonlight softly light his features, so I can just make out the contours of his face. "I trust you with everything, Kessler," I whisper back.

And I mean it. I don't know how, but in the short time I've known this amazing and confident man, he's earned the trust I never thought I would give to someone again. Which is why I know I have to tell him about Hudson's father. But after the revelations of my past tonight, I am so physically and emotionally drained, I can barely keep my eyes open.

Tipping my chin, Kessler gives me a soft kiss on the lips, whispering, "Get some sleep, Coach."

And I drift off wrapped in comfort and safety.

# CHAPTER 19

## Kessler

AFTER SHOWING LUCY HOW MUCH I LOVE HER IN THE shower this morning, twice, I head out to the living room while she finishes getting ready for the day. My game isn't until tonight, so I'm not due at the field until this afternoon. Hudson's still sleeping, so I turn the TV on to ESPN, instead of one of our shows we've been binge watching when I'm home. Heading into the kitchen, I pull out stuff for breakfast. My favorite thing about being home on the weekends is that we do family breakfast when we can. If I was in my apartment, I'd just have a shake or an omelet.

I'm grabbing the pancake mix out of the cupboard when I feel arms wrap around my

middle from behind. I set the mix on the counter and turn to see a fresh faced Lucy staring up at me. A warm feeling spreads across my chest, I don't think I'll ever get used to how beautiful she is. No makeup, hair down and air drying from our shower. Her hazel eyes have taken on a deep green color today, from the burgundy shirt she's wearing.

I cup the back of her head and trace my nose along hers, teasing her lips with mine. She giggles and I capture it in my mouth. A door opens down the hall and a groan and "gross" follows a few seconds later. Lucy pushes back, giggling. "Sorry Hud," she says, moving out of my arms and over to the fridge.

"I'm not," I say, teasing Hudson. He just wrinkles his nose at me and plops down onto the couch. "Trust me, bud, one day, you're going to meet a girl who is going to make you want to kiss her for the rest of your life, and then you won't think it's so gross."

"God, I hope that's a long time from now," Lucy mutters, placing the bacon on the counter. That's another thing I love about this woman, she's not afraid to eat, and she can really put away the bacon. I move to grab a baking sheet out of the cupboard, but Lucy beats me to it and shoos me out of the kitchen. "Go watch one of your shows with Hud, I got this." I place a kiss on her temple and join Hudson in the living room.

"What should we watch today?" I ask, grabbing the remote and sitting on the opposite couch. I'm about to switch it off of ESPN when a familiar face comes onto the screen. Jared Cox. His profile picture from the Devils pops up on the screen, followed by a video clip of flashing cameras and him covering his face leaving a police station. I turn the volume up to hear what the reporter is saying.

"Sources say Cox was charged with driving under the influence, reckless endangerment, and resisting arrest. It's also rumored that he was on an illegal substance at the time of his arrest. His bail was set at $100,000, which his attorney posted this morning."

"Hey, we met him at Judd's game," Hudson says.

A crash sounds in the kitchen, causing both Hudson and I

to whip our heads around. A stunned looking Lucy is standing in the middle of easily a dozen broken eggs. She's not looking at the mess on the floor though, she's starting into the living room, at Hudson.

Smoke starts billowing from the stove and I jump up off the couch to take the bacon that's burning out of the stove. The smoke alarm goes off before I make it two steps from the couch. The alarm seems to snap Lucy out of whatever trance she was in, she steps forward to grab an oven mitt off the counter, slipping on one of the broken eggs and crashing into a cabinet.

When I reach her, she waves me off, pointing at the stove. I turn the broiler off and take the now charcoaled bacon out of the oven. I wave a towel in front of the smoke alarm until silence greets our ears. When I turn back to Lucy, she's sitting with her back against the cabinet, her eyes bright with unshed tears. Her trembling lips, pinched between her teeth, trying to hold her emotions back.

I kneel down on my knees beside her. "Hey, it's only bacon," I say softly, not understanding why she's so upset. That only seems to send her over the edge and she bursts into tears, hiding her face in her hands. Not knowing what else to do, I sit down and pull her into my lap. Her sobs muffle into my chest, as she wraps her arms around me.

Hudson comes quietly into the kitchen with a horrified look on his face. "What's wrong with Mom?" I don't have a good answer for him, since I'm wondering the same thing myself, so I just shake my head. He looks around the kitchen and grabs the roll of paper towels and the garbage can and starts cleaning up the broken eggs.

Lucy's sobs start to subside, but I don't make an effort to move, I just keep rubbing small circles on her back. She finally lifts her head and uses the neck of her shirt to wipe her nose. Her eyes are red and swollen and sadness reflects back at me. I use the pads of my thumbs to wipe the tears from under both of her eyes. "I'm sorry," she whispers, voice hoarse from crying.

"There is nothing to be sorry for," I tell her. "It was an accident. And look, Hudson has it all cleaned up," I say nodding to where Hudson is pulling out the mop to clean up the sticky egg residue.

Lucy hiccups. "Thank you, Hud," she squeaks out, and a fresh round of tears start. Covering her mouth with her hand she scrambles out of my lap and rushes off down the hall, the soft 'click' of her bedroom door following her.

Hudson gives me a wide eyed look. I get up from the floor, give him a reassuring pat on his back and help him clean up the rest of the kitchen.

"SOMETHING'S OFF WITH LUCY," I tell the guys as we're sitting in the locker room. It's been a few days since the 'egg incident' and Lucy hasn't been quite the same since. I tried to get her to go to breakfast afterwards, but she said she wasn't hungry and to just take Hudson. We brought her back her favorite breakfast, buttermilk biscuits with sausage gravy and bacon, but she only ate a couple bites out of it before putting it away.

Reese looks up from his phone when he hears the concern in my voice. "What do you mean?"

"I don't know." I tell them about the kitchen incident and how she just completely lost it.

"I'd probably cry too if I wasted delicious salty pork," Brent says, tossing his bag into his locker and plopping down into his chair.

Reese throws a half empty water bottle at him. "Shut up, Brent," he says nodding to me.

"What's up?" Brent asks, cluing in that I'm actually worried.

"I don't know, that's the problem." I run my fingers through my newly shortened hair, tugging at the ends. "She's not eating like she normally does, she's quieter than normal, she's just... I don't know, distant?"

Reese twists his chair back and forth, his fingers steepled at his chin. "Did something happen before this?"

I lift my shoulders and let out a sigh. "I mean, yeah. She revealed some pretty heavy stuff about her past the other night, but we were good after that. She seemed happier, like a weight was lifted off her shoulders." I shake my head. "I heard her throwing up last night, when I asked if she was sick, she said she was fine and that she just must have eaten something that didn't agree with her." I shake my head. "I don't know, she just doesn't seem 'fine' like she says she is."

"Maybe she's pregnant," Brent says, flipping the water bottle Reese threw at him earlier, trying to get it to land right side up.

I stare at him, all thoughts in my head screeching to a halt.

"Jesus fuck, Brent," Reese mutters, pinching the bridge of his nose. "Did you have to mention that before the game?"

"What!? It would explain why she's emotional and throwing up. Maybe she's afraid to say anything since they haven't been together that long."

"Yeah, but now he's going to be distracted during the game and wondering if it's true."

I drag myself from my racing thoughts. "He's right here," I tell them. "And I'm good, I'll be good." I clench my fist, trying to stop the shake that's started.

Reese claps my shoulder. "Just talk to her man, it's probably nothing."

I nod, hoping he's right, but deep down, I know he's not.

I STARTLE out of my sleep, echoes of a noise fading with my dream. I reach for Lucy, but the space beside me is empty and cold. I look towards the bathroom, but it's dark too. Rolling over, I tap my phone screen, 1 am. Scrubbing a hand down my face, I scratch my beard and yawn. We lost our game, my head wasn't in it and it showed. I made errors I hadn't made since I was a rookie. I couldn't block out what Brent said in the locker room. By the time I got home, Lucy was passed out in bed and I didn't have the heart to wake her knowing she hadn't been herself lately.

A noise sounds down the hall and it vaguely sounds like the noise I heard in my dream. I throw my legs over the side of the bed and walk out into the hall. I see the blue glow of the TV in the living room and the lights are on in the kitchen. Scratching my chest, I make my way towards the noise. I stop at the end of the hallway, taking in the sight before me.

The sliding door leading to the back yard is open, the wind is causing the hanging plant in the corner to knock against the wall, the sound that woke me from my sleep. I look around, but there's no Lucy in sight. I hear a door open behind me and I turn, thinking it might be Lucy.

Hudson appears out of his room bleary eyed, rubbing the sleep from them. Yawning, he sees me and quietly pads over. "What's going on?" he asks, looking around.

I scratch the back of my head. "I'm not entirely sure bud. The pot hitting the wall woke me up, and I came out to find this," I tell him, motioning to the scene before us.

"Oh," he says, yawning again. "Mom must be sleep walking."

I raise my eyebrows. Looking down at him I ask, "Does she do that alot?"

Hudson shrugs his shoulders and walks into the living room, turning off the TV. "It's only this bad when she's, like, super stressed." He nods towards the open sliding door. "She's probably outside watering the plants. That's what she does when she's stressed, she gardens, or runs."

I lightly clap my hands down on his shoulders, turning him back to the hallway. "Why don't you try to go back to bed. I'll get your mom and turn everything off."

He nods and heads back to his room, he makes it halfway to his door before he turns and looks back at me "Kessler?"

"Yeah, bud?"

"Don't try to wake her up, it's not good to wake up people who sleep walk."

I tip my chin at him. "Got it. Thanks, Hud."

He nods and goes to his room, closing the door behind him.

I let out a sigh and scrub my hand down my face again. I knew something was eating at Lucy.

I walk outside onto the back patio. Turning towards the sound of running water, I find Lucy. She's standing barefoot, watering her geraniums in her light blue short sleep shorts and matching tank top, nothing else. Goosebumps rise on my arms from the gust of wind. I don't know how long she's been out here, but she's got to be cold.

I walk over to her and gently place a hand on her shoulder. Her skin feels like ice. She turns and looks at me, a blank expression in her eyes. It's weird seeing her awake, but knowing she's not. I try to take the hose from her hands, but her grip tightens and she pulls it away from me and moves down to the next plant, muttering something I can't make out.

I huff out a sigh and grip the back of my neck. I'm going to have to convince her to go back to bed herself. Walking over to her again, I place both hands on her shoulders and softly whisper into her ear, "Lucy, you're getting cold, let's go back to bed."

She stands there unfazed by my words, watering her damn geraniums.

Sliding my hand down to hers I cover it with mine. "We need to get some sleep, Luce. Your plants have plenty of water," I tell her in a soothing tone.

Her hand releases the trigger on the nozzle and she turns her head to me. "Cold?" she questions.

*Thank fuck.*

"Yes, Lucy. You're getting cold. Let's go to bed baby."

She drops the hose and turns back to the house, going through the sliding door.

After turning the water off, I follow her into the house, locking the slider behind me. I head back to the bedroom, turning off the lights as I go. I stop at Hudson's room and quietly open the door. Peaking in, I see him laying on his back, one arm slung over his face, softly snoring. Satisfied he was able to go back to sleep, I close the door and head into our room.

When I get there, Lucy is on top of the covers curled onto her side in a ball. I notice her feet are dirty from being outside barefoot, so I go into the bathroom and grab a washcloth. Running it under warm water, I go into the bedroom and gently wipe her feet off. After I've cleaned them the best I can, I pull the covers out from under her legs and pull them up her body, tucking her in.

I wipe my own feet off and toss the rag into the dirty clothes hamper before laying back into bed. Pulling the covers over myself, Lucy turns and snuggles into me. I suck in a breath at the chill of her body. Wrapping my arms around her I pull her into my body as close as I can, trying to use my body heat to warm her up. She lets out a sigh, mumbling an "I love you" into my chest.

I place a kiss on her head. "I love you too, baby. I just wish you'd talk to me," I whisper into her hair. She lets out a soft snore in response.

I lay there for hours listening to her softly snore, wondering if what Brent said is true, or if there's something else bothering her. Sleep finally takes over and I drift off with Lucy on my mind.

# CHAPTER 20

## Lucy

I**T'S** **ALREADY** **LUNCH** **TIME** **AND** I **PLOP** **DOWN** **AT** **MY** desk, lying my head down. My eyes feel like sandpaper and my head is pounding. When I got up this morning, Kessler was already awake, watching me. His worry lines were in full force when he told me he found me outside watering my plants last night. I haven't slept walked like that in a long time. Normally if I do, it's going out to the living room and falling asleep on the couch, or moving things around in my room or kitchen, not the level of chaos I caused last night.

I rearranged everything in the kitchen cabinets and it took us a few minutes to find where I put things in my state last night. Hudson found my phone in the fridge with the grapes, which I had been frantically looking for in my room, where I had plugged it in last night. I tried to make a joke out of it, but Kessler didn't laugh, instead he just watched me with worried eyes.

I know I need to tell him what's going on, but with his team playing the Devils in a four game series, starting tonight, I decided to wait. I don't want anything else affecting Kessler's game, especially since he seemed distracted in his last game and played like shit.

Sighing, I sit up and grab my phone. Opening my text thread to the girls I type out a message.

ME

So apparently with my stress at an all time high, Hurricane Lucy hit the household last night.

KARA

Uh oh, what did you do?

MARIE

Not again...

ME

Yep, I decided my kitchen wasn't satisfactory and rearranged EVERYTHING in it, put my phone in the fridge, turned as many lights on as possible, then went out back and watered every living thing.

I yawn, exhausted from just reading everything I did last night. Finding out Hudson unknowingly met his father has really sent me into a tailspin. Maybe if I tell Kessler I have something I need to talk to him about after he plays the Devils, it'll help release some of the stress.

*But it'll stress him out not knowing.*

Ugh.

KARA

Girl, WTF, you need to talk to Kessler, this is eating you alive.

MARIE

I agree with Kara, this isn't healthy.

ME

But he's playing the Devils TONIGHT what if it messes with his game.

KARA

Your weirdness is already messing with his game. *sigh* look I wasn't going to say anything, but he texted me and he's really worried about you.

I read the text, guilt eating me up and swallowing me whole. I knew he noticed something was off about me. I've been so wrapped up in figuring out when would be a good time to tell him, and wondering if he'll look at me differently, that I didn't even think about what it was already doing to Kessler.

ME

Shit, what did he say

KARA

I'm not going to tell you what we discussed. I'm just going to tell you he really loves you Lu, and you need to be honest with him. He WILL NOT judge you for this.

MARIE

I agree Luce, I've known both of you for a while and you're letting your past and fear of rejection affect the amazing relationship you have now.

KARA

Becoming a nut doctor has benefited us Marie.

MARIE

Jesus, Kara. a psychologist helps everyone, not just the 'Nuts' as you so delicately put it.

I snicker, Kara loves busting Maries balls over becoming a psychologist, but she does it out of love. We're both tremendously proud of her. While her family is supportive of her following her dreams, they don't quite agree WITH her dream. Tony wants one of his kids to take over the restaurant, but so far, none of them have really shown any interest.

My phone buzzes with another text pulling me from my thoughts.

KARA

> So, what are you going to do Luce?

I sigh, making a decision.

ME

> I'll tell him... tonight, after he gets home from his game.

MARIE

> We'll be here if you need us. Just be honest and open with him. There is nothing you need to be ashamed of.

*Easier said than done.* I think to myself.

I know it's been 11 years, but the embarrassment and shame I felt that day still leaves a residual mark on me, making my already dismal appetite disappear.

ME

> Thanks...

A knock sounds at my door making me jump. "Uh, come in?" I look at my clock, and see I have another few minutes of lunch left.

My door opens and Kessler's handsome face peeks around the corner. "Mind if I come in?" he asks, looking just as tired as I feel, dark circles shadowing his eyes.

"No, please," I say, motioning him in. I stand from my chair and walk around my desk, perching on the corner. He comes the rest of the way in and I spot an iced coffee in his hands.

He closes the door behind him and walks to me, holding out the coffee. "I thought you'd need this to get you through the rest of your day."

I take the coffee from him and immediately suck down a third of it. Sighing I look up at him. "Thank you, I needed that." I set the coffee down and take a step towards him. He opens his arms to me and I close the gap between us, tucking myself against him. I inhale his scent and let out another sigh, feeling myself relax a fraction.

His arms close around me and I feel his chest expand with a sigh of his own.

"I'm sorry," I whisper into his chest.

"You have nothing to be sorry about," he tells me

I pull back and look up at him. "Kara told me you texted her." His eyebrows raise and I hold a hand up. "She didn't tell me what you guys talked about, she just said you were worried." I drop my gaze to his chest. "I, I." I stop, swallowing the words I want to say. This isn't the time or place for it. I look up at him and give him a small reassuring smile. "Everything will be ok. I promise."

Kessler pulls me into his arms and gives me a hug and kiss on the head. "Ok," he says into my hair. "I have to get going. I just wanted to bring you this on my way to the field. I'll miss you tonight."

We have practice so, unfortunately, *but not really,* we'll be missing Kessler's game tonight. I wouldn't have gone if we didn't. I don't want to be anywhere near the Devils when they're in town.

I nod into his chest not trusting my voice at the sudden rush of emotion. He steps back, gives me a kiss on the cheek, then he's gone.

AND I'M LEFT with the feeling that all is not right.

THAT FEELING CARRIES over into practice later that night.

Someone forgot their mitt, thankfully I have extras. Boys run into each other in the outfield trying to catch a pop fly. Joey jammed his thumb warming up. It's one minor shit show after another. With 20 minutes left of practice I make the decision to cut practice short and just let the kids hang out until their parents show up.

Kara sits next to me in the dugout while we watch the boys play around, tossing balls to each other. "You doing ok?"

I shrug my shoulders instead of answering. I feel off, and I can't explain it. Like something bad is on the horizon and there's nothing I can do to stop it. I have to wonder if it's because I've failed to tell Kessler the truth, or if it's something bigger.

Kara nudges me with her shoulder. "He's going to understand," she says, trying to reassure my fears.

"I know, but is he going to judge me for it? Is he going to decide I'm actually all those things Jared called me years ago? I'm mean Jesus, what are the fucking odds. My baby daddy and my boyfriend are both famous MLB players." I shake my head and take a deep breath, forcing back the tears threatening to fall. "I can't keep this from Hudson any longer either." I look over at Kara. "Hudson met him at the game Kessler took the boys to."

Kara lets out a gasp and covers her mouth. "And you're just telling me this now?" she nearly shouts.

"I just freaking found out about it the other day!" I reply, closing my eyes and thumping the back of my head against the dugout wall.

"What happened?"

"Nothing that I know of. That's the morning I lost my shit and ruined breakfast. I wasn't exactly in the state of mind to ask questions," I remind her.

Kara blows out a breath. "Shit."

"Yeah, shit," I say back.

Cars start arriving to pick up kids ending our conversation. Once everyone's picked up, Kara, the boys and I head to our vehicles. Before I close the hatch, Kara gives me a hug and I hold tight, feeling her love and support in the embrace. She pulls back and whispers, "Hang in there." Before getting into her car and leaving the lot.

I climb into my own car and pull out of the lot and head to the house. "Why did Aunt Kara give you a hug?" Hudson asks, looking at me.

I inhale a deep breath through my nose and hold it for a few beats before releasing it. Tapping my finger on the steering wheel, I mull my words over in my head, making a decision. "Hudson, there's something I have to talk to you about." I stop at the light and turn to look at him. "About your father."

Hudson's eyebrows shoot up and his mouth opens slightly. "My dad? But why? I, what?" he says, confusion in his face.

A horn honks behind me making us both jump. I hold my hand up in apology and drive through the light and head towards our house. Hudson's quiet the rest of the drive, playing with a loose thread on his shirt. I pull into the driveway and turn the car off, casting us in silence. I unbuckle my seatbelt and turn towards him. "Hudson, before I tell you what I need to tell you, I hope you know I would never do anything to intentionally hurt you. I love you and you have and always will be my whole world. Everything I've ever done since having you, has been for you and me. Ok?"

He looks at me, eyes wide, and nods his head. "Remember a few years ago, you asked why you didn't have a dad?"

He nods.

"And I told you he decided it was a lot of responsibility to have a kid and that was just something he wasn't ready for?"

He nods again, picking at the string again.

"Well that part is true, he wasn't ready for the responsibility. The part that wasn't completely true was that it was just someone I knew from college." My heart rate speeds up and my heart feels like it's trying to beat out of my throat. I take a steadying breath and swallow past the lump that's formed in my throat. "You actually met him, about a month ago, at Judd's game. I didn't know you had until the other morning when you said something to Kessler, when you saw him on TV," I end on a whisper.

Hudsons head snaps up, his blue green eyes, the only thing he got from his father, connecting with mine. "What? You mean, you mean, Jared Cox is my dad?"

I nod, not trusting my voice to say anything.

"But... how, what? I don't understand."

Sometimes I have to remind myself Hudson is only 11. He's always been so mature for his age. Side effects of being raised by a single mom I guess. So sitting here seeing his emotions cross his face, makes me wonder if I've done the right thing.

"We dated for a very short time in college, I got pregnant with you and he decided he wasn't ready for a kid, so I raised you on my own," I tell him, leaving out the details an 11-year-old doesn't need to know.

I can see the wheels turning in his head, trying to make sense of what I've just told him.

"So why are you telling me now?" he asks.

"Because with Kessler in our lives, it's going to come out eventually. The media likes to dig."

"So Kessler knows?"

I shake my head. "No, not yet, I'm-" I blow out a breath. "I'm telling him tonight, after his game. I wanted to tell you first." *Incase Kessler leaves me, us.* I think to myself.

Hudson nods. "So you think that's why Mr. Cox, uh my dad?" He stops trying to figure out what to call him.

"You can just call him Jared," I tell him

"Ok, so do you think that's why Jared acted weird when he met me?"

I raise a brow, my heart beat that was slowing back to normal, speeding up again. "What do you mean?"

"Well, when we met Jared after Judd's game, Kessler introduced us to Jared. When he saw me, he got a weird look on his face and left." He shrugs his shoulders. "He told Judd he didn't feel good, but do you think it was because he knew who I was?"

I release my bottom lip I was biting and shake my head. "I'm not sure," I tell him.

I'm pretty fucking sure thats exactly what happened. He probably took one look at Hudson and saw his own eyes staring back at him. But I don't say that.

All I care about right now is two things; One: How Hudson is feeling after telling him all of this & Two: How Kessler is going to react when I tell him tonight.

There's nothing I can do about the second thing right now, so I focus on the first.

I lay my hand on Hudson's arm, getting his attention. "How are you feeling about all of this? I know it's a lot to take in, and I want you to know you can talk to me. Even if you're mad or want to yell."

Hudson sits quietly, the wheels turning in his head. I sit there letting him mull everything over. It's killing me not knowing what's going through that brain of his. When he finally looks up at me, I know we're going to be ok. "I think I'm ok? I mean, he's never been in my life, so I guess it's not going to be any different, right?"

I shake my head. "Not really no, unless you want it to be? I-" I close my eyes not believing I'm going to say the words that are coming out of my mouth. "I can always reach out to him to see if he wants to formally meet you...if that's something you want?" I suck in a breath.

*Please don't let it be something you want.*

I know it's absolutely awful to wish something like that, but I don't want Hudson near Jared and his destructive behavior.

He shakes his head slowly. "I don't think I want that, Mom."

I blow out my breath I'd been holding. "Ok, if that ever changes, just let me know. Ok?"

Hudson nods. "Can we go in now? I'm hungry, and I want to catch the rest of Kessler's game."

"Yeah Hud, we can go in."

He reaches for the door handle, then pauses, looking back at me. "Is it going to be weird?"

I scrunch my eyebrows. "Is what going to be weird?"

"Watching the game and seeing my... dad? On the TV?" He scrunches his nose at the word 'dad'.

I think about it for a minute then shrug my shoulders. "I don't know, but if it is, we can just turn it off. Ok?"

He nods and gets out of the car. I feel a small weight lift off my shoulders.

We head into the house and Hudson makes a beeline for the TV to turn on the game.

I kick off my shoes and go to the kitchen, pulling stuff out for tacos. I still don't have much of an appetite, but Hudson needs to eat. I hear the sound of the announcers in the background as I dump the hamburger into the pan. I'm chopping up the cilantro when I hear the announcer's voice rise in shock, I look up in time to see Kessler's fist land straight into Jared's nose. My stomach drops and the knife clatters to the counter. Hudson looks at me with wide eyes before turning back to the TV as we watch all hell break loose on the field.

# CHAPTER 21

## Kessler

"You're suspended," Coach Dixon says to me from across his desk. "And there will be a fine, but that figure hasn't come down from the home office yet."

I knew that was coming. You don't get into a fight during a game and not expect the organization to dish out punishment.

"Six games."

"Six games!" I shout, sitting up in my chair. "That mother-fucker provoked me!" I take the ice pack that was sitting on my hand and chuck it across the room. The bag breaks open, sending ice cubes scattering everywhere.

Coach Dixon doesn't bat an eye at my outburst. Working with athletes for as many years as he has, he's seen it all. "That may be true, but you took the first swing, and then kept swinging."

Fuck yeah I did. Cox was talking shit the minute he walked up to the plate.

*"Davis, how's your cleat chaser?" Cox asked with a twisted smirk.*

*I stood up and ripped my mask off. "What the fuck did you just say to me?"*

*I vaguely remember hearing the umpire say something to us. I really couldn't hear him over the rush of blood pumping through my ears.*

*Cox lowers his bat and levels his gaze to mine. A snap of realization hits me in the chest. I've seen those eyes before. I know those eyes and claim them like my own.*

*He must realize it too because a disgusted chuckle leaves his mouth. "Oh, she didn't tell you huh? Yeah, that little bastard is mine."*

*The minute those words leave his mouth all I can see is red. My breathing becomes erratic and before I realize what I'm doing, my fist clenches and is flying at his face. His eyes widen as I make contact with his nose. A sickening crunch echoing through my ears. Blood immediately pours from his face. Jared grabs his nose with a yelp of pain. Before he can even think about hitting me back, I'm on him with another punch to the face, sending him to the ground. I follow him down with a third blow before I feel hands grabbing at me, trying to pull me off.*

*It took three of my guys to finally pull me off and keep me off of him. When Reese finally got my attention, I looked around and saw both teams on the field, dugouts completely bare. The Devils are always looking for an excuse to fight, and I just gave them a big one.*

Coach Dixon clears his throat, snapping my attention back to him. "Take the suspension time, and get things right. Figure your shit out and come back 100%. Anything less and you might as well hang up your mitt." He levels me with a stare I'm not stupid enough to argue with.

I nod my head and decide to keep quiet. Rapping on his

desk with his knuckles, he leans back in his chair and nods to the door. "Get out of here, go start figuring it out."

I leave his office and go to my locker. Checking my phone, I see numerous missed calls and texts from Lucy, my mom, even Judd. My phone starts ringing and Dale's name appears across the screen. I hit the answer button, more to delay dealing with everyone else than my desire to talk to him.

"Dale," I say, grabbing my gym bag and heading out of the locker room.

"Kessler, what the fuck is going on kid?" His normally calm, and collected tone sounds a little rattled.

"A lot, Dale. A lot," I say, exiting the side door and making a beeline to my truck before the press realizes I've left. Once securely inside, I put my phone on speaker and lean my head back against the headrest, taking a breath I haven't been able to take since Jared opened his mouth.

"But a fight kid? You don't fight, ever." He's right, I don't fight. I've never once thrown a punch in my 14 years as a professional baseball player. I've always been the one to talk guys down or pull them off.

"I know," I sigh, digging my thumb and forefinger into my tired eyes.

"So, what happened?"

"Jared fucking Cox happened." I pause, still in shock over the words that are about to come out of my mouth. "He's Hudson's biological father. Lucy's ex."

Silence greets me on the other end. I pull the phone back to see if my call is still connected. "Dale? Are you still there?"

He clears his throat. "Yeah, son. I'm still here. I'm just. Shit, I didn't see that coming."

I laugh a humorless laugh. "Yeah, neither did I."

"Lucy didn't tell you?" Shock evident in his tone.

"Nope. I had the privilege of learning it first hand from

Jared himself." Anger burns through my gut recalling Jared's words. How could I have not seen it? The way he acted seeing Hudson after Judd's game, Hudson has his eyes for God's sake. Although I can't say I've spent my time gazing into other men's eyes. And Lucy. How could she not have told me? She said she trusted me with everything.

"Shit."

"Yeah, shit."

"I hate to pour salt in the wound, but we need to get ahead of the shit storm and make a statement." I hear the regret of bringing it up in his voice.

This time I won't even fight it. "I agree, Dale. Word it how you want, but my statement is, 'No one fucks with my family.'" Because at the end of the day, no matter how fucked up this situation is, that's what Lucy and Hudson are. My family. And I'll be damned if I let anyone talk about them the way Jared did.

"That's it?" Dale asks. Sounding shocked I'm not fighting this, but also pained that's all I'm giving him.

I start my truck and pull out of the parking lot. "That's it. You're good with words. I'm sure you'll put a good spin on it." Turning my truck in the direction of my apartment I head there. I want to see Lucy, more than anything, but I need time to wrap my head around this.

"Ok, call me if you need anything. You know I'm here for you."

"I know, Dale. I appreciate it." I end the call and make the quick drive to my apartment. I park my truck and make the lonely elevator ride up to my empty apartment.

When I open the door, I enter the quiet dark room. Air stale from lack of use or open windows. I sit down on the couch and notice a film of dust on the sleek, cold coffee table. A far cry from the warm wood toned one at Lucy's. Even in my apartment, where Lucy's never been, I find myself thinking about her and how much her home has become a sanctuary for me.

Which is probably why this hurts so much, and I don't mean the pain in my hand. Which fucking hurts but I can deal with the physical pain. What I'm having a hard time dealing with is the pain in my heart. Why would she not trust me with this? Needing answers I dial her number. My heart beats a thousand miles an hour as the line rings. She picks up on the third ring.

"Kessler?" Relief and worry mixed in her tone. "Are you ok? How's your shoulder? You didn't injure it did you?" She peppers me with questions.

Her concern does nothing to ease my irritation, instead it just amplifies it. "Stop, Lucy," I command, my tone is harsher than I intended, but I don't apologize for it.

I hear her suck in a breath, but remain quiet.

The silence stretches into several seconds, until I finally break it with the question burning in my brain. "Why didn't you tell me?"

Her breath shutters over the line and my heart squeezes, knowing she's crying. I close my eyes against my own pain, waiting for her answer. "I was going to tonight," she whispers.

I bite out a laugh. "Were you really? Or are you just saying that because Jared exposed your little secret?" I know what I'm saying is cruel, but I can't seem to stop myself.

"Kessler, I, it's not like that. I wanted to tell you." She protests.

"So why didn't you Lucy? You told me the night you told me about your parents that you trusted me with everything. Yet, you didn't trust me to tell me about this!" I rake a hand through my hair and get up to pace the short length of my living room. "Answer me!" I demand when she doesn't say anything.

"I think we should talk about this in person. Where are you? I'll come to you."

"No. I don't want to see you right now." The words are out of my mouth before I've realized what I've said.

I hear Lucy suck in a shocked breath.

The words hang between us and instead of taking them back, I pour more salt in the wound I've torn open. "I need some time and space to think. I think it's best if we just hit pause for a second and think about things."

I hear a muffled sob on the other end and I feel my heart crack. My brain screams at me to take it all back, but my hurt won't let me.

"Ok," I hear her whisper through sniffles.

My heart cracks a little more at the resignation and hurt in her tone. I open my mouth to tell her bye when my phone beeps at me and dead air greets me. I look at my phone and see that she's disconnected the call. I sit there for I don't know how long, staring at the phone, wondering if I just made a huge mistake. A surge of anger burns through my veins and I toss the phone at the wall, shattering it. I get up and go to my cabinet where I keep my whiskey. This night calls for some strong drinks.

I'M TWO, ok three, whiskeys in when a knock sounds at my door.

"Who the fuck is that?" I stare at my almost empty glass, like it's going to answer me.

The knock sounds again. Louder this time. With a groan I get up from my, not as comfy as Lucy's, couch and look through the peephole. My brother's face stares back at me. I contemplate just acting like I'm not home, but he beats on the door again, adding a "Open up Kessler, I know you're in there. Mom called Lucy and we know you're not there."

*Fuck.*

I unlock my door and hang my head, stepping aside to let my annoying little brother in.

He breezes in like he owns the place. "Dude, way to go radio silent on everyone."

I silently shut the door, and head back to the living room. I pick up my drink, draining the rest of it. I walk into the kitchen and pour myself another generous glass, taking it back to my couch. I plop down on the cushion, taking two generous gulps before I turn to my brother. "What do you want, Judd?"

He nods to the glass in my hand. "How many have you had?"

I snort. "That's none of your business."

Judd raises his eyebrows at me. "It's gonna be like that huh?"

I take another drink and suck my teeth. "Yup."

Judd nods his head, but doesn't say anything. Instead he pulls his phone out of his pocket and taps on the screen. A few seconds later he joins me in the living room, taking a seat in one of the arm chairs. Judd props his feet up on my stupid coffee table. Seriously, why do I have this table? It's awful, and cold, and ugly. It reminds me of my life before Lucy, not that my life was awful. Just... empty, like I feel now. A burst of anger shoots through me thinking about all that's happened in the last few hours.

"Why are you staring at the table like it stole your girlfriend?"

Not answering him, I get up and head to my spare room where I keep all my random shit. Looking around, I grab what I was looking for and charge back out to the living room. Judd looks up from his phone, eyes widening when he sees me coming out of the bedroom with a sledgehammer. He lets out a yelp and pulls his feet back just before I slam the hammer into the table. The glass top shatters into a million pieces, scattering across the floor, but the frame remains intact. I pick the hammer back up and swing it again. Denting the metal frame. Not satisfied with the destruction in front of me, I raise the hammer again and again until the heap of metal in front of me is unrecognizable as a table and my chest is heaving, sweat dripping down my face.

Judd's staring at me from behind a throw pillow he grabbed to protect himself, his legs tucked up to his chest. He slowly lowers the pillow and stares at me. I toss the hammer onto the floor and plop back onto the couch. Grabbing my drink from the side table I take a sip. Judd sits forward and puts his feet on the floor. "What did that table do to you?" he asks, staring at me like I've grown another head.

"It's not Lucy's," I say simply.

"Oookay," Judd says getting up and coming over to me, grabbing my glass out of my hand. "That's enough for you tonight."

I don't even protest when he takes my glass from me. It's not making me feel better like I want it to. The only thing that could make any of this better is something I can't have right now.

"Have you talked to her?" Judd asks, returning from the kitchen where he put my glass.

"Yep," I say, popping the 'P' like Lucy does.

"I take it, it didn't go well?" he asks, nodding at the coffee table.

I shake my head still staring at the remains of what used to be my coffee table.

A knock sounds at my door again. *What is this? Grand central station?* Moving to answer it, Judd stops me. "I got it."

"It's my apartment," I grumble, but sit back down.

Reese and Brent's faces appear from behind the door Judd opened.

*Fucking great.*

They walk in both emitting a long low whistle as they take in the damage. Brent sets two plastic bags down on my kitchen counter. Whatever's in them smells fucking amazing. My stomach grumbles in agreement and I try to remember when I ate last.

"What happened here?" Reese asks, walking the rest of the way into the living room. He has his hands on his hips as he surveys the damage.

"I haven't seen your apartment this trashed since our last offseason poker night when we finished those two bottles of whiskey," Brent comments.

"Apparently someone was mad it wasn't Lucy's coffee table," Judd explains.

"Riiiight," Reese says, giving me a concerned look.

My stomach grumbles again, louder this time, making me get up from my spot and wander into the kitchen where Brent is taking white take out containers out of the bags.

*Chinese food.*

He hands me a container and chopsticks without a word. Opening the top, I inhale the delicious aroma of my favorite lo mein, my mouth immediately waters.

Taking a seat at the breakfast bar, I dig in, not stopping until half the container is gone. When I look up, three sets of eyes are staring at me from various places in the room. Brent, beside me in the kitchen, Reese and Judd in the living room.

"What?" I ask, shoving another helping of food into my mouth.

Reese raises his eyebrows and gives Judd a look before turning back to me. "You're seriously going to ask us 'what' like you didn't just destroy a perfectly good coffee table for no reason?"

I shrug my shoulders. "I had a reason."

Judd snorts. "Not a good one."

"Fuck off," I spit out, feeling my temper rise again. "No one asked you. Actually-" I swivel in my chair to face the two assholes judging me from the living room. "No one invited any of you here. How did you two know where I was anyway?"

Judd holds up his phone and shakes it back and forth in his hand indicating that he told them.

I tip my head towards Brent who's silently munching away on an eggroll. "He can stay, he brought food and is actually silent for once. You two can fuck off right out of here."

"Chill out, no one's fucking off anywhere," Reese says, holding out his hands. "We want to help, we just want to know where your head's at."

Lucy's face flashes in my head. "With Lucy, it's always with Lucy."

"Have you talked to her?" Reese asks the question my brother asked earlier.

I turn back to the counter and stare into my lo mein. With food in my stomach I'm starting to sober up, which means my rational side is making its appearance.

I nod.

"And?" Resse asks, "Did she explain what happened?"

Not answering right away, I get out of my chair and grab a glass from the cabinet. Turning on the sink, I fill the glass and drain it. I fill the glass again before turning back to them and leaning against the counter. "I really didn't give her a chance. She wanted to talk about it in person and being the asshole that I am, I told her I didn't want to see her."

"Shit," Brent says, grabbing another eggroll, half of it disappears into his mouth.

I blow a breath out between my lips and grab the back of my neck. "I might have told her we should press pause too."

Groans erupt and Brent throws the remainder of his egg roll at me. It hits me in the chest and falls to the floor. I just stare at it, not making a move to pick it up.

"What the actual fuck, broski?" Judd asks. "I'm not the relationship type and even I know that was stupid."

I tip my head back and groan. "I know, ok? I know, I was just so mad, and she was asking if I hurt my shoulder and if I was ok, and I just snapped." I sigh. "It wasn't my finest moment ok? Nothing about today has been normal for me. I just want to go to bed and wake up tomorrow and everything be back to normal."

"I think it's a little late for that bro." He holds up his phone. "Mom just texted me, she said she tried calling you but your phone goes straight to voicemail."

"I uh, might have smashed it." I nod to the wall opposite of the couch where my phone still lays.

He nods, taping on his phone some more. His fingers freeze and he looks up at me, giving me a wide eyed look.

"What?"

Brent and Reese's phones go off and they both pull their phones out, giving me the same look as Judd.

"What?" I ask louder, the hairs on the back of my neck standing up.

Judd tosses me his phone. I look at the screen and ice runs through my veins. An article is already up about the fight. It looks like someones been busy digging for information because the truth about what the fight was about is there in black and white.

**_Trouble in Paradise?_**

**_An uncharacteristic fight on the diamond from Kessler_**

*Davis today is the talk of the baseball world tonight. Davis, who has been in the big leagues for 14 years, has never once thrown a punch. Tonight is the night, it seems, for that stretch to end. Davis and Jared Cox, Short Stop for the Denver Devils, came to blows tonight, resulting in Cox sustaining a broken nose and several lacerations to the face.*

*What caused this usually mild mannered, leader of the Salem Silverbacks to become violent? Sources say Cox said some unsavory things about Davis' girlfriend at the plate, resulting in Davis losing his cool.*

*Sticks and stones, Davis, sticks and stones.*

*Upon some research by our team, it has come to our attention that Cox shares a connection with Davis' girlfriend Lucy Carver, who he recently announced he was dating. It seems Carver and Cox went to the same college and dated for a short period of time before Cox was drafted. Shortly after,*

*Lucy gave birth to her son, Hudson. Is it a coincidence or did Davis find out who Hudson's real daddy is?*

*We reached out to Davis' agent, who would only tell us it's a personal matter and that Davis' was protecting his family.*

My grip tightens around Judd's phone, turning my knuckles white. He reaches forward and grabs the phone out of my hand. "I'll just take that back, I don't need you breaking my phone."

I let out a frustrated growl and grab the whiskey glass Judd took from me earlier, draining the rest of its contents. I let the smooth brown liquid slide down my throat, a trail of fire following its path. Taking a deep breath through my nose, I set the glass down before I smash that against the wall too. "I need to see Lucy," I tell them

Reese shakes his head. "You just told her you didn't want to see her."

"That was before I knew about the article. I need to see if she's ok. I may be mad, but I still love her."

Judd steps in front of me, blocking me from going to the front door. "I don't think that's a great idea right now."

"Why not? She wanted to talk in person." I move to go around him, but he puts his arm out stopping me.

"Mom texted me, she talked to Lucy." He stops scratching the back of his head. "Lucy told Mom you were right and that pressing pause on your relationship was probably best. You guys went from zero to sixty so fast." He gives me an apologetic look. "She said it was only a matter of time until you guys crashed."

I stagger back like someone just punched me in the stomach, gripping the counter for balance. The food I ate turns sour in my stomach, and I just stare at Judd, not wanting to believe the words he just said.

I asked for this, and she was giving me what I didn't want.

# CHAPTER 22

## Lucy

It's been three days since the fight and the dreaded article that came out. I never thought I'd be thankful for my sleep walking, but apparently when I was sleepwalking one night, I put my phone in the dishwasher and turned it on, needless to say, I don't have to worry about any reporters contacting me, since my phone is toast. I used Kara's phone to call into work, telling them I'd be out for the week. Thank God my boss was understanding, telling me to take the time I needed. I also had Kara run practices for the week. There's no way I could focus on baseball when all it did was remind me of Kessler and what I've possibly lost.

Besides getting up to get Hudson off to school, I've stayed in my bed, not having the energy or desire to do much of anything else. Kara has been bringing food over for us that her mom has cooked, so we don't starve. She offered to have Hudson stay with them for a few days, but I didn't want to disrupt his schedule because of my crisis. I let him stay home from school the first day and we just laid around and watched movies. He asked me if Kessler was coming back and I was honest with him and told him I didn't know.

I roll over and face the picture I took from the living room. The one that was taken when we weren't looking. I haven't heard a single word from Kessler, which is probably for the best, but doesn't make it hurt any less. We're not even going to mention that I'm wearing his T-shirt he left on the floor the morning before all hell broke loose.

A knock on the front door pulls me from my thoughts of Kessler. I'm not expecting Marie until later today, so I ignore the knock and bury myself back under the covers, hoping whoever it is just goes away. They knock again, louder this time. I sigh and throw the covers back. I pull on my leggings that have seen better days and march down the hall, ready to tell off whoever is on the other side.

I yank the door open and whatever I was going to say dies on my lips. Marlene is standing on the other side. Tears spring to my eyes at the sight of her warm welcoming face. Not saying a word she opens her arms to me and I go to her, sobbing into her chest. Marlene wraps me tight in her embrace and runs a soothing hand over my head, letting me get out all the hurt and anger I've bottled up.

Once my sobs have subsided a bit I pull back, using the bottom of Kessler's shirt to wipe my face. "I'm so sorry, Marlene. I don't know what came over me," I say, embarrassed by my outburst of emotion. "Please, come in." I step back letting her into the entryway.

Marlene waves a hand at me, dismissing my apology. "Honey, don't ever apologize for your emotions. You have every right to be emotional right now."

I close the door and wave a hand at the living room. "Please, have a seat. Do you want something to drink?"

Marlene shakes her head. "Don't worry about me dear. I'm here to check on you. Why don't we go for a walk?" She raises a brow and looks over my clothes. "After you shower."

I feel my cheeks heat and I run a hand over my unwashed hair and look down at my clothes. "I'm a mess."

Marlene turns me around and points me in the direction of the hallway, patting my shoulder. "Don't worry, a nice shower and change of clothes will help. And don't be embarrassed, we've all been there."

She gently pushes me forward and I start down the hall. Before entering I look over my shoulder. "Thank you, Marlene."

""Don't mention it dear. " She gives me a warm smile and I head into my room, stripping off my clothes and stepping into a welcoming hot shower.

ONE LONG, hot shower later and I'm feeling a little better. I pull my favorite pair of mint green leggings and matching sports bra out of my drawer and put them on. Tossing a matching sweater on over the top. Deciding to let my hair air dry, I walk out into the living room and am greeted by the smell of fresh brewed coffee.

"I hope you don't mind dear," Marlene says, turning from my picture wall, holding up a coffee mug. "I figured you could use some caffeine."

"Not at all." I grab my favorite mug from the cabinet and pour myself a cup. Grabbing the creamer out of the fridge I doctor up my coffee and take a seat at the island, watching Marlene. She's smiling at the picture of Kessler, Hudson, and I. "Why are you here?" She turns and gives me a questioning look. I realize my question sounded rude so I add, "Not that I'm not appreciative that you are. I just-" I pause and shrug my shoulders. "I figured you would be mad at me too."

Marlene comes over and sets her mug down on the island next to mine. She puts both her hands on my shoulders, causing me to look up at her. "No one is mad at you," she tells me, her gray-blue eyes staring back at me.

I let out a snort. "Pretty sure your son is, and he has every right to be."

Marlene shakes her head. "He's hurt, which unfortunately came out as anger. But he's not mad at you." She takes another drink of her coffee, then pats my hand. "Come on, let's go for that walk. You'll feel better getting some fresh air."

Taking one last sip of my coffee, I slide off the stool and slip on my shoes. After locking the door, we head off down the road at a leisurely pace. We walk two blocks in silence before Marlene speaks. "We missed you and Hudson at Sunday dinner."

Truth be told, we missed them too. Hudson asked about it but didn't push the issue when I told him that it probably wouldn't be a good idea for us to go this week. This 'pause' has been hard on him too, and the guilt I feel for him having to go through any of this is immense.

"I didn't think we would be welcomed," I admit, biting down on my bottom lip.

Marlene scoffs. "You're always welcome. You and Hudson are a part of this family." She stops and smells a rose that's growing between the slats of a fence. She gives me a smile and continues on, "You're going to go through rough patches, lord knows Henry and I have been through our fair share." She links her arm through mine. "What matters is that you learn from them and move on. Grow together. Life isn't going to be perfect and peaceful all the time." She pauses, and gives me a look.

"Kessler told me about your parents. You know first hand how hard life can be"

I nod, kicking at a rock in our path. We watch it skip down the sidewalk and drop off into the road. "I'm just so scared I've messed things up and he'll never forgive me," I whisper.

Marlene stops walking and turns to face me, putting her hands on my shoulders. "No," she says in a stern voice I've never heard from her. "There's nothing to forgive if you ask me. You had every right to choose when to tell Kessler about your past, if at all. The way he found out was terrible, but that is not your fault." Her sharp eyes give me a look that says 'don't argue with me I'm right'. "The way my son reacted towards you about the whole thing is not something I'm happy with him about, and I told him just as much on Sunday."

My eyebrows shoot up in surprise. Marlene defended me to her own son. My mother would have never done that. Tears well up in my eyes and I swipe at them with the back of my hand. "No more of that dear," Marlene tells me. She links our arms back together, and we continue on our walk.

"Jared wasn't always like the way he is now," I say softly.

Marlene pats my hand in the crook of my arm. "You don't have to tell me anything, dear."

I nod. "I know, I just–I feel like I owe you an explanation."

Marlene shakes her head. "You don't owe anyone anything. But if you need an understanding ear to listen. I'll gladly be that for you."

I nod, continuing with my story. "He wasn't always a dick. Did he have an ego? Absolutely, I don't know a baseball player who doesn't." I smirk. "Even Kessler."

She throws her head back and laughs, making me chuckle. My heart feeling a little bit lighter, I continue on, "He started to change the closer the draft got. He became distant, ignoring me."

I shake my head at the memories. "I broke it off with him the summer of our junior year. He didn't really seem to care much that I broke up with him, just that I did it in front of his friends."

I leave out the part where he told me in front of said friends that I was a horrible lay. That he just stayed with me because he felt sorry for me because my own parents didn't love me. Something I regret confiding in him to this day.

"Of course, about a month after I broke things off, I found out I was pregnant. At first he denied it, saying Hudson wasn't his and that I just wanted money from him because he was going to be high in the draft." Marlene lets out a disgusted noise and I nod in agreement. "When I told him I'd gladly take a paternity test, he said it didn't matter because he wanted nothing to do with either of us anyway."

I feel Marlene squeeze my arm and I let out a deep breath. "I dropped it after that. I didn't want him in Hudson's life if he was just going to make him feel unwanted. I grew up like that and I wasn't about to have my son go through it too."

"Good for you, standing up for your son and yourself," Marlene chimes in.

I give her a weak smile. "I didn't feel proud of myself at the time, but looking back, I should have been. Anyways, you know what happened with my parents. So I won't bore you with that again."

She makes a tsking sound and shakes her head. "They should be ashamed of themselves."

I shrug, and leave it at that.

We're almost back to my house, when I look up and see Kessler's truck in the driveway, he's perched on the tailgate, waiting. I come to a sudden stop and a gasp escapes me. Marlene follows my gaze, and she lets out a little huff.

Kessler must feel eyes on him, because he picks his head up and looks around. When his gaze lands on where we are a half block away, our eyes lock and the air grows heavy with uncertainty. Even from here, I can see the dark circles under his eyes. His T-shirt is rumpled and his beard looks thick and unkept. We stare at each other, neither one moving towards the other.

Marlene clears her throat, and I jump, forgetting that she was there. She gives me a smile and tugs me forward. "Come on dear, let's go see what my son has to say for himself."

# CHAPTER 23

## Kessler

MY EYES TAKE LUCY IN LIKE THEY'RE ON A DESERT island and she's the water they're craving. Her hair is down and flowing around her shoulders making her look like the goddess she is. The mint color she's wearing brings the green out in her eyes. I can't take my eyes off her as her and my mom make their way to me.

Hopping down from my tailgate, I put my phone, which I replaced the day after I broke it, in my pocket and wait for them to reach me. I tried calling and texting her, but was met with silence. So I reached out to Kara, who was less than happy with me. Not about punching Jared out though. No, she applauded me for that. The way I treated Lucy however, that she chewed my ass for. She informed me after my ass chewing that Lucy had an unfortunate incident with her phone. She suggested I give Lucy some space, even though that was the last thing I wanted, no matter what I said when I was angry.

So here I am, three long, excruciating days later hoping I

can make this right. When Lucy finally reaches me, it takes everything in me not to reach out and pull her into my arms. She stops a few feet away from me, arms around her middle, not looking at me but past me. It reminds me of the way she looked at me when I unexpectedly showed up at that first practice. My stomach sinks knowing she's rebuilt some of her walls that I worked hard to tear down.

I risk a glance at my mom and I'm met with that motherly stare. You know the one that says you've really done it now? My mom turns to Lucy and wraps her in a hug. For a moment I feel a twinge of jealousy that my mom can so easily embrace her when that's all I want to do.

"Thank you for everything, Marlene," Lucy says, pulling back.

My mom reaches up and pushes a lock of Lucy's hair out of her face. "Anything for you, my girl." Lucy's face lights up with a small smile and I wish more than anything it was me making her smile. Mom turns and walks the couple steps to me. Stopping beside me she pats me on the chest. "You better fix this, Kessler," she whispers to me. She gets on her tiptoes and gives me a kiss on the cheek, then gets in her car. Backing out of the driveway she gives us a wave and drives off, leaving us alone.

I put my hands in the pockets of my cargo shorts to keep from reaching for Lucy. She stands there with her arms wrapped around her middle looking like she'd rather be anywhere than here, talking to me. After a few minutes of uncomfortable silence, I clear my throat. "Lucy, can we talk? Please?"

She looks around, and nods. "Let's talk in the house, in case someone with a camera decides to take pictures." I hate that she has to think about that. I nod my head and follow her to the front door. She unlocks the door and steps inside, tossing her keys on the table and taking her shoes off. I follow her in but stay in the entryway. This is the first time I've walked in here and felt out of place. I don't like it.

Lucy goes to the kitchen and gets herself a glass of water. "Do you want something to drink?" she asks, filling her glass.

I shake my head. "No, thank you. I'm, I'm good." I stuff my hands back in my pockets and look around, feeling awkward for the first time ever in this house. My gaze lands on her picture wall and I notice the picture of the two of us is missing. I snap my eyes back to her and she's watching me from behind her glass as she takes a drink. I nod my head to the empty spot on the wall. "Where's our picture?" I ask, not knowing if I really want to know the answer.

"I took it down," she says, no emotion in her voice. She drops her gaze to the counter in front of her, like she can't look at me.

"Lucy I," I start, striding into the kitchen .

"You were right," she says at the same time, stopping me in my tracks.

I raise a brow. "Right about what?" I ask, not liking the resigned tone in her voice.

She takes a breath and pulls her shoulders back, looking me directly in the eyes. "We should press pause, take a break, whatever you want to call it."

I stumble back, shock hitting me square in the chest. "Is that really what you want?" I ask, praying she says no.

Closing her eyes, she wraps her arms around her stomach. "No," she whispers, and I exhale an audible breath. She continues, "But, it's what we need."

I shake my head against her words, not wanting to believe them. "No," I tell her, taking a step forward.

She holds up a hand, stopping me. "Please don't make this any harder than it already is." Her voice wavers and her eyes plead with mine. "I love you, and I'm not saying any of this to hurt you. You shutting me out, on one of the worst days we've both ever experienced, instead of coming to me and talking to me, brought up a lot of pain from my past. It was like I was back at my parents, being told I was a disappointment. Or Jared tossing me and Hudson aside like garbage." She pauses when my hand curls into a fist at the mention of his name. "I'm not comparing you to him, I'm just telling you how the way you handled things made me feel."

I relax a fraction, and nod. "I know, I just-" I rake a hand through my hair, tugging at the ends. "I never wanted this to happen. I'm so sorry for making you feel like you aren't enough." I chance a step forward. When she doesn't move, I take another step, and another, until I'm in front of her. I reach out and cup her cheek. She closes her eyes, taking a shuddering breath. "You are my everything," I whisper, leaning forward until my forehead touches hers. We just stand there breathing each other in.

After a few seconds of bliss, I feel her hand on my wrist and she pulls her head back and my arm away from her face. Taking my hand in hers, she looks at me, giving me a sad smile. My heart stutters and dread fills my veins. "I'll call you in a couple of days, when I get a new phone, and we can talk."

Remembering one of the reasons I'm here in the first place, I reach into the side pocket of my shorts and pull out a phone. "I uh, I bought us new phones with new numbers. Kara might have mentioned an unfortunate incident yours had with the dishwasher." I hand it to her and she takes it. Her hand covers her mouth when she sees the cover I had made and overnighted. It's the picture of us that's missing from her wall. She looks up at me, tears glistening in her eyes. "You didn't have to do this." Her voice broken.

"It's the least I could do." I step back, needing to leave before I go against her wishes and wrap her in my arms and never let her go. I turn on my heel and walk to the door. I hear Lucy softly crying behind me and it takes more will power then I wish I had to keep myself from going back to her. I open the door and turn to her one last time. Tears are streaming down her beautiful face and I want more than anything to be able to kiss them away. "My number is already in there. Call me when you feel like you're ready to talk."

She closes her eyes and nods, clutching the phone to her chest.

"I love you, Lucy."

"I love you too, Kessler."

I walk out the door, praying that's not the last time.

THERE'S one more game left of my suspension, and for the first time in my career, I'm not looking forward to getting back on the diamond.

I haven't heard from Lucy yet, and the longer she's silent the more I worry I won't get her back. I know it's just a pause, one I stupidly suggested in a moment of anger, but it feels like I've lost my future, and I'm desperate to get it back.

I send a text to the one person I know can help me. Hoping they will. Setting my phone down beside me I turn on my TV and flip through the channels before landing on ESPN. The show is recapping events that have happened in the last week, and surprisingly enough, my fight with Jared is still ranked at the top, even though it was more than a week ago.

Dale released another statement shortly after my visit to Lucy's, asking people to respect our privacy. I had him add that I'm not proud of the way I handled things on the field and that I'm truly sorry for exhibiting the behaviors I did that day. I also asked him to say how disappointed we are in the magazine that released the article about Lucy being a cleat chaser. Fans ate it up, saying that they were behind Lucy and I 100%. I heard sales of that particular magazine have plummeted dramatically.

My phone buzzes and I snatch it off the couch, hoping it's my saving grace.

KARA

Why should I help you?

ME

Because Lucy and I belong together and you know I'm right.

KARA

Maybe... Are you done being a dick?

ME

*sigh* Yes, Kara, I'm done being a dick.

KARA

😊 I don't know...

ME

Remember you said you owed me one for taking Kade to the baseball game last month?

KARA

... yes...

ME

I'm cashing in.

KARA

Fine, let's hear it.

# CHAPTER 24

## Lucy

"GET UP!" AN ANNOYING VOICE YELLS, JARRING ME OUT of my amazing dream. I let out a groan turning over, which I soon realize is a mistake. The person that annoying voice belongs to pulls my curtains open, blinding me with sunlight.

"Gah! Kara! What the actual fuck!" I yell at her, pulling the covers over my assaulted eyes. There's no way I'm going back to my dream now. Echoes of the dream where Kessler and I weren't on a break, fading fast.

I hear drawers to my dresser open and close. "Here put these on." I feel her toss something onto the covers, where my face is currently hiding.

Pulling the covers back, I squint up at the ceiling, letting my eyes adjust to the brightness. Once I'm convinced I'm not going to be blinded by the light, I sit up and see a pair of black leggings lying on the bed next to me. I raise an eyebrow at Kara, who is now rifling through my closet. "Why do I need these?" I ask, "and what are you doing in my closet?"

She ignores me and dives deeper into the back of my closet, muttering something about needing to take me shopping for more than T-shirts and jeans. Rolling my eyes, I raise my arms over my head and stretch. Last night was the first night since Kessler's fight that I've slept more than a couple hours at a time. Needing to use the bathroom, I leave Kara to whatever it is that she's doing and head into my bathroom.

When I come out Kara is out of my closet and a shirt I don't recall buying is laying on my bed next to the leggings she pulled out for me. A pair of strappy silver sandals are on the floor. "Are you going to pick out my bra and underwear too?" I grumble.

Kara sets her hands on her hips and gives me a smirk. "I probably should, since you'll just pick a sports bra and your granny panties."

"I do not wear granny panties," I retort. "And what's wrong with sports bras? They're comfortable and I'm all about comfort." I pull open my drawer and grab exactly what Kara told me not to.

"Oh no you don't," she says, marching over to me and grabbing them out of my hands. "That shirt does not pair well with a sports bra." She rummages around in my drawer, while I throw up my hands in defeat and flop back onto my bed.

"Why do I have to get dressed again?" I ask, propping myself up on my elbows, watching her.

She holds a lacy black matching bra and panty set up like a trophy and tosses them to me. "Because, Marlene invited us over for brunch, and we're going."

I pinch the bra between my thumb and forefinger, holding it up. "I don't think Marlene would mind if I'm wearing a T-shirt and jeans."

"You're dressing up. You've been moping around for days, not that I blame you. You have every right to take this time and figure shit out, but getting out of the house will do you some good." She gives me another smirk. "The dressing up is just for fun."

I deadpan her. "We have different ideas of fun."

Kara clasps her hands together. "Please, dress up. If not for yourself, for me?" She finishes her plea with puppy dog eyes.

I bark out a laugh. "Fine, fine I'll dress up. Do I have time to shower and do my hair?" If I'm going to dress up, I might as well go all out.

"Yes, if you hurry," Kara replies, clapping happily.

Rolling my eyes again, I gather my clothes and head into the bathroom. I stop and peek out from the door frame. "Thanks Kar, I don't know what I would have done without you this week."

She flutters her hand in front of her. "Stop, you'll make me cry and I'm not ruining my makeup. But anything for you, babe," she says, giving me a wink.

I laugh and shut the door behind me, turning on the shower. Feeling lighter than I have all week.

SHOWERED, dressed and feeling fresh, we're on the road and heading to Marlenes. Hudson and Kade stayed with Kara's mom at Kara's, so we could just have some girl time. I offered to drive, since I've been there before and know the way, but Kara insisted on driving and said that's what GPS was for. She's being a little weird, but I just chalk it up to her trying to cheer me up.

Kara turns on the radio and I sit back in my seat, humming along to a song and enjoying the view. It's one of my favorite drives and I missed making it last week. My heart squeezes, that's not the only thing I miss. Kara nudges my arm and I look over at her. She gives me a reassuring smile. "It'll get better babe, you'll see. You just need to talk to him."

I sigh.

I know she's right. I've been putting off talking to Kessler, letting my fear overcome me. The fact that he so easily shut me out still bothers me and I don't know if I can trust him not to do it again. Marie encouraged me to talk it out with him when she came over last night. She even suggested we go to counseling, not only to help us get past the hurdle we face now, but to help us communicate better in the future. It's something I'm going to bring up when I talk to Kessler, whenever I get the courage to do that.

Lost in thought I look out the window, the scenery around me is unfamiliar. Grabbing Kara's phone, I look at the address she typed in. It's not Marlene's, but it's close, just up the road. "Kar, you typed in the wrong address." I tell her, holding up her phone.

"Oh did I? Darn it. Where's that one taking us?"

Darn it? Kara never says darn it. It's damn, or shit, or any other four letter word, never *darn it.* I narrow my eyes at her, my warning bells going off in my head. "Kara Cahill, what are you up to?"

She doesn't get a chance to answer because the phone in my hand tells us in 500-feet our destination is on the left. I give her a pointed look as she turns into the unfamiliar driveway. Old maple trees line both sides of the driveway, stealing my breath with their size. Their branches wave hello to us in the breeze. At the end of the driveway sits a beautiful one-story farmhouse. It's painted in a soft mint green tone with white trim and wood-stained a porch that wraps around it.

"Wow," I whisper in awe. "That house looks like it's right out of one of my Pinterest boards." I may have a whole board dedicated to my dream home, and what exactly I would want it to look like.

Kara comes to a stop and puts the car in park. I whip my head to the side to look at her. "What are you doing? This isn't Marlene's."

She gives me a mischievous smile and I don't like it one bit. "Get out of the car, babe."

"Uh no, I don't know who lives here."

She nods her head toward the house and I turn to look where she is. There's a man standing on the porch now.

*Kessler*

He's leaning against the porch railing, hands tucked in the pockets of his dark-wash jeans. Wearing a black button-up shirt, that makes his moss-green eyes pop. The sleeves are rolled up to his elbows, showing off his muscular forearms. His beard has been trimmed since the last time I saw him, making his features sharper. My heart catches in my chest at the small, shy smile he gives me. I turn to Kara, my eyes wide.

"Get out of the car, Lucy," she says, giving me a reassuring smile.

I slowly shake my head back and forth. "I don't understand."

She pats my hand. "You will."

"What if it doesn't work out?" I whisper.

"You won't know until you try," she whispers back.

Kara leans across the console of the car and gives me a hug, squeezing me tight. I wrap her in my arms and squeeze back. When we pull back, our eyes are both wet. She reaches out and swipes her thumbs under my eyes. "No crying, you'll ruin your makeup."

I give her a small laugh and take a deep breath. "Ok, I'm doing this."

"You're doing this," she repeats back to me.

Before I can talk myself out of it, I unbuckle my seatbelt and get out of the car, closing the door behind me. Kara pulls away, leaving Kessler and I standing there, staring at each other. Butterflies take flight in my stomach as he moves slowly down the stairs, never breaking eye contact with me. My heart rate increases every inch he gets closer, until I think it's going to jump right out of my chest. He stops in front of me, the air between us crackling with built up energy begging to be released.

I inhale a sharp breath and his spice and leather scent hits my nose. I feel myself lean forward, taking another breath. Breathing him in.

He reaches out and gently brushes my cheek with his fingers, making my skin tingle in their path. Neither of us says a word. We just stand there, taking each other in.

A crow caws from one of the maple trees, causing me to jump, breaking our trance. I let out a little chuckle and look around.

"Who's house is this?" I ask, my eyes wandering around the space.

While the house looks brand new, the property around it is worn down, and in need of some love. Flower beds are over-grown with weeds and grass. A door to what looks like a small tools shed hangs crooked on its frame off to the side. After my small tour of the yard, I look back at Kessler, who's watching me intently.

"Do you like it?" he asks with a whisper.

"I love it," I tell him, his shoulders visibly dropping, like a weight has been lifted. "I told Kara when we drove in that it looks like one of the houses off my Pinterest boards." His face splits into a smile and I narrow my eyes at him. "Kessler... Why does this house look like my Pinterest board?" I ask, realization hitting me. I think I know what's going on, but I need him to say it.

His smile grows wider and he reaches into his pocket, pulling out a set of keys. Jingling them in the air he asks, "Want to take a look inside."

Shaking my head, I take a step back. "Answer my question first, Kessler."

With his free hand he reaches up and rubs the back of his neck, looking off to the side. "I uh, may have bought it," he mumbles. His gaze comes back to mine, gauging my reaction.

"You bought it? This house." I point to my dream house behind him. "It's yours?"

Kessler drops his hand from his neck and tips his head to the side. "Well, not just mine."

My mouth drops open, while my brain catches up with what's going on.

"You, you bought me a house?" I squeak out. The back of my eyes burn with the threat of tears.

Kessler comes forward, placing both of his hands on my arms. I tilt my head up to look into his eyes. "I bought *us* a house," he says, his voice soft.

"When? Why? How?" I ask in succession, needing answers and needing them now.

He takes a step back and jingles the key again. "Come look inside and I'll answer your questions." Kessler turns and jogs up the four steps that lead up the porch, going to the door he inserts the key and it turns with ease. He looks back at me over his shoulder. "Coming?" he asks before stepping through the threshold.

Needing answers, I follow his path up the steps and through the door. A gasp escapes me as I step through. The open floor plan of my dreams is in front of me. The kitchen and living area are separated by a huge island, big enough to fit half my baseball team. The counter top gleaming under rustic pennant lights. Rich hickory floors run throughout the house, giving it a warm feeling. My eyes bounce everywhere and I'm overwhelmed with all the perfect details.

"It's not done," Kessler says, pulling my attention from the house to where he's leaning up against the stone fireplace. Yes, a freaking *stone* fireplace. The picture above catches my attention. It's a blown up copy of Hudson, Kessler and I. "I left the other three bedrooms blank so Hudson can pick out which one he wants and decorate it the way he wants." He walks over to me and takes my hand, leading me to rich wooden barn doors to my left. "Open them," he whispers.

With a shaking hand, I push one side open. Beyond the doors is an office painted in a darker version of the house. A pristine white desk and chair sit off to the left facing a set of double doors that I assume lead to the porch. I turn around to look at Kessler, searching in his face for answers. He gives me a sheepish look. "I left it pretty bare so you can decorate it how you want. If you don't like the desk, we can get you a different one. I-"

I rush forward and silence him with a kiss. Sighing in relief that after too many days, I'm finally kissing his warm lips again. Kessler groans into my mouth. One hand grips the back of my neck, while the other grabs my hip. Running my hands up his chest, I circle my hand around his neck and link them at the back. I open my mouth wider and Kessler takes the silent invitation and deepens his kiss. I cling to him, like he's the breath I've been fighting to take and all my thoughts that have been running through my brain the last week, finally come to a halt.

Kessler pulls back, gazing into my eyes. "I want to show you one more room," he whispers, taking my hand and leading me across the entryway to a door beside the kitchen.

Turning the handle he pushes open the door and leads me

inside. A massive king sized bed with a gray tufted headboard sits on the far side of the room. Fluffy emerald green bedding decorates the bed, contrasting with the shiplap accent wall. It's straight out of a picture on my board.

"How?" I ask him.

He confirms my suspicion with one word, "Kara."

I breathe out a laugh. "Of course." Everything from the beginning of this has been thanks to Kara's gentle pushes. The sneaky bitch. I love her.

Kessler takes me in his arms, peering down at me with so much love, I think I might burst. "The house was my idea though, well technically it was yours, when you mentioned it the night you told me you loved me."

I gasp. "You bought the house that long ago?"

He nods, leaning down, running his nose along mine. "I came out here the next day and offered the Peterson's their full asking price. They were so happy to know it'd be going to another family who would love and cherish it like they did."

Tears are running freely down my face as I wrap my head around what Kessler just told me. He bought me a freaking house and made it into my dream home and all I did was mention *once*, early in our relationship, how nice it'd be to live close to his family.

Any doubts I had about Kessler walking away from me one day fly out the window. He wouldn't have bought a house for *us* to live in, if he wasn't truly in this forever.

"Are those happy tears?" he asks, a concerned look in his eyes.

I nod my head, unable to speak. My throat, thick with emotion.

Kessler wipes my tears away with his thumbs and takes my face in his hands. "I'm so sorry for everything, Lucy. I never wanted to hurt you the way that I did. I should have talked to you, instead of hiding behind my shock and lashing out. I promise for as long as you'll have me, I'll work on communicating every single day."

I sniff and wipe my eyes. "I'm sorry too, for not telling you about Jared." Kessler shakes his head to argue, but I stop him. "No, I need to apologize too. This whole thing isn't just on you. I let my fear keep me from trusting the one person who never gave me a reason not to trust them." I take a steadying breath. "Marie suggested we go to counseling to work on our communication skills. And I think it'd be beneficial." I raise my eyebrows in hopes that he'll agree.

"If that's what we need, then I'll do it. I'll do anything for you, Lucy." He lifts his hand and moves it across the room. "I think I've proven that."

Laughing I pull his face down to mine and give him a searing kiss. He pulls back, eyes dark with desire.

"What do you say we break in the mattress?" Before I can give him an answer, Kessler bends down and throws me over his shoulder, making me squeal.

He tosses me gently on the bed, then reaches back and pulls his shirt over his head. My eyes drink in his toned abs and chiseled chest. Biting down on my bottom lip, I drag my teeth over it. He reaches forward and pulls my lip out of my mouth, tracing his thumb over it. I bite down playfully, getting a growl in response.

Kessler surges forward and captures my lips with his. Our tongues tangle together, his hands tug at my clothes. We separate, panting like we just ran a marathon. Kessler tugs my shirt off, leaving me in my black lace bra. He licks his lips as he takes in the sight.

*Thank you, Kara.*

I lay back and raise my hips, pushing down my leggings. He helps me take them off and sits back on his heels, his eyes eating up my body. "You are the most gorgeous woman I have ever laid my eyes on, Lucy," he says in a strained voice. Like it pains him to even look at me.

Pushing up on my elbows, I give him a seductive look. "I think you need to show me."

His nostrils flare and his eyes dilate. He crawls over me, making me lay back on the bed. His lips tease a path down my neck to my breasts. Sliding my straps over my shoulders, he frees my tits and gives them the attention they crave. I gasp at the sensation his tongue and his beard create. My hand grips the back of his head encouraging him.

Once he's satisfied with the attention he's given my breasts he continues his descent towards the one place I crave him the most. Hooking a finger on either side, he pulls my underwear off and tosses them to the side. Tracing me with his tongue before plunging it into my wet center.

My back arches, and I grip the comforter, crying out with pleasure. "Yes, Kessler," I encourage. I rock my hips into him, quickly finding a rhythm to get me closer to my release. My breath becomes ragged and I feel a deep pressure building quickly. I make a strangled noise in the back of my throat, indicating I'm close.

I'm just about over the edge, when Kessler pulls back suddenly. "No!" I cry out in frustration.

Kessler stands up and pulls my body to the edge, fisting himself. "As much as I'd love to have you come all over my face, I need to feel your tight pussy come on my cock."

I nod, words escaping me. He lines himself up with my entrance. He looks up at me. "I want you bare, Lucy. I'm clean and haven't been with anyone besides you in over a year."

"I'm clean," I tell him, finding my voice. "I want to feel you, Kessler."

As if that's all he needed to hear, he pushes into me, both of us releasing a moan. He stretches me, filling me full, completing me. We lay there for a moment, him letting me adjust, before his hips start moving. "I'm not going to be able to go slow baby, I need you. A week is too long without you."

I pull his face to mine and kiss him hard and deep. Looking him in the eye I whisper to him, "I don't want slow."

Permission granted, his hips flex into me over and over, creating a delicious friction that quickly brings a pressure of an orgasm back. Our skin becomes hot and a layer of sweat coats us. Our moans and the sound of our bodies coming together are the only things we hear. Kessler adjusts his angle, hitting the perfect spot, sending me into a tailspin of pleasure. My walls clamp down around him and a few seconds later he lets out a deep groan, following me into bliss.

He braces himself on his forearms so as to not crush me, as our pleasure subsides. Rolling off of me, he gathers me into his arms. We lay there panting, catching our breath.

"This is my favorite room in the house," Kessler says a few minutes later, making me chuckle. He places a kiss on my temple. "I love you so much, Lucy."

I prop myself up on my elbow and caress his cheek with my other hand. " I love you too, Kessler."

LATER ON, after another round in the bedroom. We're sitting on the back porch, in the rockers Kessler had placed back there, taking in the sunset. I'm lost in my thoughts at how much my life has changed for the better over the last couple of months.

I roll my head to the side and smile looking at the man I never thought I wanted, but was everything I needed.

Kessler's phone buzzes and he grabs it off the table between us. His eyebrows raise and he turns his screen to me. I read the text Dale sent him. My eyes shoot back up to his. "That explains it," I tell him.

Turns out the magazine that kept publishing all the trash about Kessler and me is owned by none other than Tommy's father. The pictures that were taken at our practice, were taken by Linda. My number was given out to the press by her too. "That's why she was so mad when I declined dinner," I say more to myself than Kessler.

"Probably thought she was going to get an inside scoop for her husband to sell," he says.

I shake my head. What people will do for money. I feel sad for Tommy having to grow up with parents like that, but there's nothing I can do about it.

Gravel crunches in the front yard and I cock an eyebrow at Kessler. He gets up from his chair and holds his hand out to me. "Come on, let's welcome Hudson home."

Taking my hand in his, we walk around to the front of the porch where we welcome Hudson, Kessler's parents and Judd.

Hudson flys out of the passenger seat of Judd's car and races up the steps. "Kessler, is this your new house?" he says in greeting. "It's *huge!*" He spins in a circle on the porch, taking it all in.

Kessler laughs. "Actually, Hud, it's your new house too," Kessler says, hugging me tighter into his side.

Hudson's eyes widen in shock and he looks from Kessler to me. I tip my head towards the front door. "Go pick out your room."

With a whoop, Hudson rushes through the front door. We can hear him yell "Woah! So cool! I can't wait to show Kade" as he wanders deeper into the house.

Marlene and Henry come up the steps. I peel myself from Kessler and meet Marlene for a hug. "I'm so happy for you, dear," she whispers into my ear. I manage a nod, but don't trust myself to speak with the flood of emotion that has hit me. This woman has been an absolute godsend, and I am so grateful she's a part of Hudson and mine's life now.

She steps back and swipes at her eyes. "I know for a fact this is a big house. Lots of rooms to fill," she says, giving me a wink. I give Henry a quick hug before going back to Kessler.

Kessler's arms come around me again and I tuck myself back into his side, where I belong. "We haven't discussed that yet. But I'm not opposed to it," Kessler says, looking down at me hopefully.

I never really put much thought into having more kids, but it doesn't sound like such a bad idea now that I have someone who I know will be there with me through it all. I nod. "It's definitely open for discussion."

Judd clears his throat. "Well now that that's settled, can we have a tour? All I've seen are pictures Kess has sent us throughout the process. He didn't want anyone seeing the finished product before you."

We walk towards the door and Kessler opens it with his free hand.

"Welcome to our home."

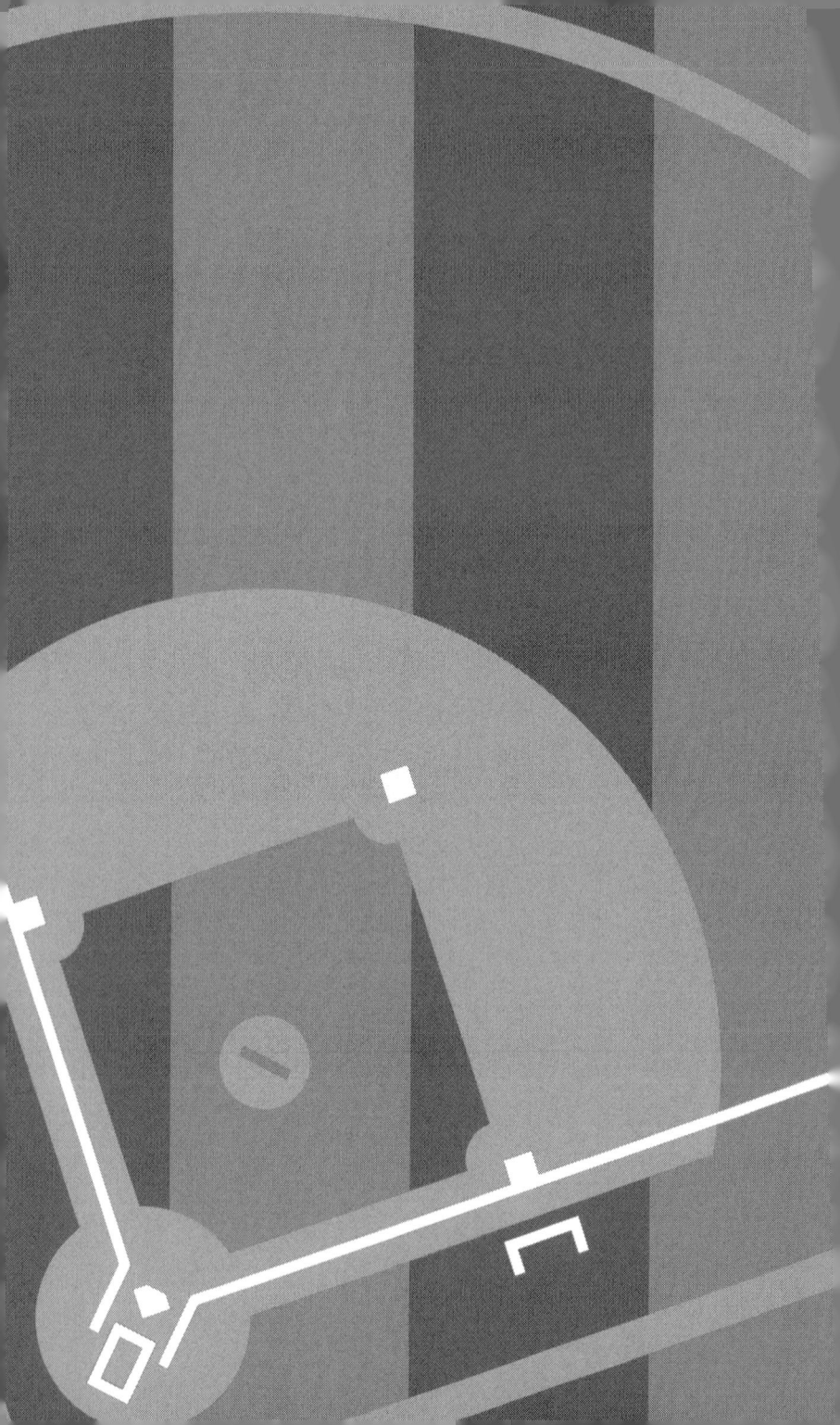

# EPILOGUE

## Kessler

I'm going to throw up. I close my eyes for a second and take a couple of deep breaths.

"I don't think I've ever seen him this pale," I hear a voice whisper to my right.

"Not even when we were all hungover as fuck after that bachelor party and had to play at that noon game in Philly," whispers another voice.

I open my eyes and look at the three goons staring back at me with shit eating grins.

"You good, brotato?" Judd asks, slapping me on the shoulder before taking a seat.

Judd is a Silverback now. I did as Coach asked and talked to him about making the switch when he became a free agent. It's been fun playing on the same team as my brother again, and I like to believe our team work is a big reason we've made it as far as we have this season.

"Does it look like I'm good?" I ask. I'm not good. "I'm

freaking out. What if she says no? Why did I think it would be a good idea to do this in front of a stadium full of people? What if she hates the ring?" My breath comes faster, making me a little light headed.

"Chill dude," Brent tells me, slapping my other shoulder and sitting down at his cubby on my right. I lean forward and scrub my face with both hands. "This shit is romantic as fuck. Of course she's going to say yes. You guys fell in love on the diamond, what better way to ask her?"

"She's not going to hate the ring," Reese says. "You agonized over that design for weeks, I thought the jeweler was going to fire you." He laughs, pulling on his socks.

I finally picked up the rings yesterday and he's right. The delicate band has an engraving of the seam of a baseball and one perfect half carat diamond sits on top. I would have gone much bigger, but Lucy isn't a flashy jewelry person. The matching wedding band has the same seam pattern but inlaid with tiny rubies. My band is a gunmetal gray with a red seam. They're perfect. It's us.

"You bought her a house numb nuts, do you really think she's not going to want to marry you?" Judd asks.

I blow out a breath. "You're right, it'll be fine... Right?"

"Plus, she won't say no and bring us bad luck on our first game of the championship series. So, you picked a great time to ask," Brent says, digging around in his locker.

There's a knock at the door and cracks open slightly. "Everyone decent?" a female voice asks.

"In terms of if we're naked? You're good, we're all dressed. If you're asking if we're decent people, two of the four are," Reese tells the voice.

Charlie chuckles, pushing through the rest of the way. She helped set this whole thing up for me, so she's probably here to go over everything one last time.

"Hey, who are you insinuating isn't decent?" Brent asks, throwing a towel at Reese.

"You, nut sack," Reese says, throwing it back.

"Guys! We have a lady in our presence," Judd says

Charlie waves him off. "Please, I grew up in this clubhouse, remember? This doesn't phase me a bit." She shrugs. "Side effects of being the coach's daughter." Charlie isn't only our PR rep, she's also Coach Dixon's only child. So naturally she was thrown into the world of baseball whether she liked it or not. Luckily for us, she loves everything baseball.

"Ok," she says, clapping her hands together. "Everything is set and ready to go. Lucy is with her team, down on the field. Once Hudson throws the ball, you'll run up to them. We'll take a quick picture of the whole team with you. I'll give you the thumbs up when we got it and then you can turn to her and do your thing."

I nod, taking another deep breath.

Charlie pats my arm. "Everything will be perfect Kessler." She looks at her watch and back at me. "It's time, we should get going."

I give her another nod and turn to my locker and grab my chest plate and catcher's mask, feeling robotic in my movements.

"Come on, let's get you engaged," Brent says, grabbing his mitt and following Charlie out the door.

Judd gives me a fist bump and takes off after Brent.

Reese grabs his mitt and sets a hand on my shoulder, looking me in the eyes. "You good?"

I take one last grounding breath and nod. "Good."

He slaps my shoulder and turns. "Let's do this!" he yells, walking out the door.

"Let's do this," I repeat, following them all through the door.

## LUCY

*I'm going to puke*, I think to myself, standing on the field with my team. We were invited to throw the first pitch to start the Championship series after winning the Little League State Championship this summer. The stadium is packed, there's not an empty seat to be found. I look over at Hudson to make sure he's good. He's laughing and joking around with his team, no nerves in sight.

I had the team vote on who got to throw the first pitch, they all chose Hudson. He sealed the deal for our win at state. He got the out at home plate and kept us ahead by one point. I rub my arms chasing away the goosebumps. It was a beautiful play. But that's not what I'm remembering that's giving me the chills. It's how Kessler and I celebrated later that night after Hudson went to bed.

Another wave of nausea rolls through me and I actually think I'm going to puke this time.

"Take a sip of your water," Kara whispers to me. I take a few tiny sips, letting the cold water ease my stomach. "Here, suck on this." She hands me a peppermint. I take it and pop it in my mouth.

"What would I do without you?" I say around the mint in my mouth.

She shrugs her shoulders. "You'll never have to find out."

I wrap an arm around her and give her a side hug. "Thank Jesus for that," I say grinning at her.

"You ready for this?" she asks, returning the squeeze.

"As ready as I'll ever be," I say. I pat my back pocket, checking it for the millionth time.

Kara turns and gives me a quick full body hug. "I'm so happy for you," she whispers.

I return the hug and clear my throat. "Ok ok, enough of this." I blink my eyes multiple times to keep myself from crying. "I can't redo my makeup again. Kessler will be out any minute."

As if saying his name summons him. I see Kessler appear out of the dugout and jog over to the plate. I shiver as he gives me a wink and places his mask over his face. Charlie is directing Hudson over to his place and the team cheers from behind him. He looks over his shoulder and meets my eye. I give him a thumbs up and cheer with the rest of the team. The announcer introduces Hudson and the team and we all give the stadium a wave.

The announcer gives Hudson the go-ahead and he throws the pitch at Kessler easily sending it over the plate and into Kessler's glove. Kessler jogs over to Hudson and gives him a fist bump before walking the rest of the way to the team for a picture.

Kessler gives me one of his panty melting smiles, making my stomach flip like always, and I wonder if he'll always make me feel that way.

"Coach," he says, finally reaching me.

"Davis," I respond back, my grin growing bigger.

"Ok, everyone get in for a picture quickly so we can get the game started," Charlie yells over all the noise. Kessler takes his place beside me and puts his hand on my lower back sending a new round of goosebumps through my body.

"Cold?" he whispers into my ear, humor in his voice.

"I'm good," I say back, looking over my shoulder and giving him a smirk. A sense of déjà vu sweeps over me as I think back to our first meeting.

"Ok, everyone look forward. 1-2-3," Charlie counts and the photographer takes pictures.

Charlie gives a thumbs up and I take that as we're done. I look at Hudson who's grinning up at me, but not unbuttoning his jersey like we planned. I'm about to remind him when I feel a hand on my shoulder. I turn and Kessler is smiling down at me. The team has moved away from the mound but is still on the field. I look over at Kara who's holding her phone up and swiping at her face. I try to turn back to Hudson but Kessler grabs my hand stopping me.

"Lucy," he says looking into my eyes. He moves his hand from mine and brings it to my face, cupping my cheek. I see his Adam's apple bob a few times before continuing.

"You and Hudson have been unexpected lights in my life, when I needed them the most." He pauses and takes his hand from my face.

I stare up at him. My brain frozen. *What is going on? He has a game to win.*

Kessler takes a step back and reaches into his pocket pulling out a mini baseball.

I let out a gasp and my hand flies to my mouth. *No. He's not. He's going to...* Then my mind goes blank as he gets down on one knee.

The full stadium collectively gasps and I look up to see us on the Jumbotron.

"Lucy," he starts grinning up at me. "Coach, I don't want to spend another day without knowing you are mine, forever." He looks to my left, making me turn my head. Hudson has come to stand besides me and is grinning up at me. "You and Hudson. You guys complete what has been missing in my life."

I can feel the tears streaming down my face now and I don't even try to hold them back.

"Lucy," Kessler says again, grabbing my left hand and

placing a kiss on the knuckles. "Will you please do me the honor of becoming my wife?"

*Words* my brain says, *use words.*

I can't seem to make my mouth work so I just nod *yes* vigorously. Hudson whoops beside me and Kessler launches from the ground and picks me up, spinning me around.

The crowd erupts and cheers sound from all over.

I place both my hands on his face and he leans forward and gives me a kiss once we've stopped spinning. He puts me down and opens the box. A beautiful ring shines back at me. I let out a gasp. "Kessler, it's beautiful," I whisper as he takes the ring out of the box and slips it into my finger.

"Just like you," he says, stealing another kiss.

"We better get this show off the field so we can get the game started," he says, turning Hudson and I towards the dugout.

"Wait!" I call out, remembering I have a surprise for him too.

He stops and looks at me, eyebrows raised. "I have something for you too."

I nod at Hudson who opens his jersey revealing a shirt underneath that says *best big brother.*

While Kessler reads the shirt I pull a sonogram out of my back pocket and hold it up. Kessler's head whips back to me and he spots the sonogram. He looks from the sonogram, to me, back to the sonogram, then back to Hudson.

The crowd gets even louder realizing there's something else happening on the field.

He turns back to me with tears in his eyes. "Really?" he asks, grabbing the sonogram and looking at it again

"Really," I say looping my arm over Hudson's shoulders and pulling him closer.

"How do you feel about going from a family of three to a

family of five?" I ask, grinning so big my face feels like it's going to split in half.

Kessler's eyes grow big and he slowly looks up at me. "Five?" he croaks out.

I nod and grab his hand placing it over my stomach. "We're having twins."

# Acknowledgments

First off, Holy Shit! I can't believe I wrote a dang book! The fact that I'm even writing this completely blows my mind!

Now for the acknowledgement of all the amazing people who made this possible.

To my lifelong friends Ustina and Ladisa. You two were the very first people I told I was doing the damn thing this year. Your never-ending encouragement and support has fueled me for the entire journey. I am forever grateful. I love you both so much and couldn't ask for better childhood friends and sisters.

To my T-ball team. Without you guys, this book would have NEVER happened. Brittinee, you and I made an awesome team and I am so happy to have found a new best friend in you. Thank you for believing in me.

To my Husband, Travis. There is no way I could have gotten this done without you giving me multiple kid-free weekends to work on my writing. Thank you for always reassuring me people will like my book when my imposter syndrome made an appearance. Your support and encouragement mean the world to me.

To Taylor, my amazing PA. There is absolutely NO WAY my Social Media stuff would be nearly as good without you. Thank you for the words of encouragement and always checking in on me to see if there is anything you could do to help me in my writing journey and for being one of my BETA readers. I hit the jackpot when I found you.

To Amber and Jess. Thank you for being my very first BETA readers. The love you had for Kessler and Lucy's story was everything to me. Your feedback helped me tremendously. I am forever grateful you took a chance on my story.

To Savannah, my forever hype girl. Your excitement over my book is the much needed ego boost I needed. I'm forever grateful to be able to bounce future book ideas off of you. I'm so happy and thankful I found a friend in you.

To Kate and Erica. Thank you so much for working with me and taking me on as a client. My book wouldn't be what it is without you two!

Finally, to my readers. Thank you a million times over for taking a chance on this book and on me. I hope you enjoy Kessler and Lucy's story as much as I do. I hope you continue to follow my journey and watch my growth in future stories.

# About the Author

D.B. Axtell has loved to read since her Great-Grandmother taught her how at the age of three. Although the type of stories she likes to read has changed dramatically throughout the years, one thing that has stayed the same is her love of getting lost in others stories. In 2023 she finally decided to take a chance and write a story of her own, with hopes of providing a story other readers will love getting lost in.

When she's not arguing with her characters on whose story is next or encouraging them to speak to her, she's living her best life in the northernmost part of Oregon as a wife and stay at home mom of two very active boys. Her favorite pastime is drinking Starbucks and spending time at the barn with her four legged baby, Phoenix.

Keep a lookout for her future books because there is plenty more to come.